"I could fire you right now."

"Do it, then," Heath dared Lora. "But let me tell you something else so you can make an informed decision. If you do that, you're going to have a storm on your hands that not even you will be able to handle. I've been running Larimar for the past year but beyond that, I own the gift shop downstairs, and Larimar doesn't have enough money to pay me off."

Lora stared, shock in her eyes. "What are you talking about?"

He shook his head. "Why don't you take a moment to really look at Larimar and see all the changes that have been made since you've been gone? Someone had to do something to start making some money, because the one with the marketing degree…well, she was unavailable."

With that, he stalked past her. He was done with her for the day. If he stood another minute in her presence, he'd choke on his own frustration—or choke her.

Dear Reader,

I love difficult people. There is something so subtle and nuanced beneath the surface of bad behavior that has always fascinated me. When you pick at the behavior, eventually you see the motivation beneath, and it gives you additional insight to that person. In my experience, most often the prickliest people have the softest hearts. What a fascinating contradiction, yes? I think so. And difficult people make for very interesting characters!

With this book you're about to meet the Bell family, starting with Lora Bell. She's the epitome of difficult. Known as a hard-nosed businesswoman, Lora is merciless in the boardroom, but she struggles to relate to her sisters as they try to save Larimar, the family resort in St. John. Add to the mix a special man from Lora's past whom she can't bully or forget, and you have a love story just waiting to happen.

This newest cast of characters has already stolen my heart. They feel as real to me as my own family. I had the privilege of traveling with my family to St. John in the Virgin Islands to research the location and I'm happy to share my experience through the Family in Paradise trilogy. Look for the next book later in 2012.

Hearing from readers is a special joy. Please feel free to drop me a line via email through my website, www.kimberlyvanmeter.com, or through snail mail at Kimberly Van Meter, P.O. BOX 2210, Oakdale, CA 95361.

Kimberly Van Meter

Like One of the Family

Kimberly Van Meter

TORONTO NEW YORK LONDON
AMSTERDAM PARIS SYDNEY HAMBURG
STOCKHOLM ATHENS TOKYO MILAN MADRID
PRAGUE WARSAW BUDAPEST AUCKLAND

Recycling programs
for this product may
not exist in your area.

ISBN-13: 978-0-373-60702-0

LIKE ONE OF THE FAMILY

Copyright © 2012 by Kimberly Sheetz

ABOUT THE AUTHOR

Kimberly Van Meter wrote her first book at sixteen and finally achieved publication in December 2006. She writes for the Harlequin Superromance and Harlequin Romantic Suspense lines. She and her husband of seventeen years have three children, three cats and always a houseful of friends, family and fun.

Books by Kimberly Van Meter

HARLEQUIN SUPERROMANCE

1391—THE TRUTH ABOUT FAMILY
1433—FATHER MATERIAL
1469—RETURN TO EMMETT'S MILL
1485—A KISS TO REMEMBER
1513—AN IMPERFECT MATCH
1577—KIDS ON THE DOORSTEP*
1600—A MAN WORTH LOVING*
1627—TRUSTING THE BODYGUARD*
1694—THE PAST BETWEEN US**
1700—A CHANCE IN THE NIGHT**
1706—SECRETS IN A SMALL TOWN**

HARLEQUIN ROMANTIC SUSPENSE

1622—TO CATCH A KILLER
1638—GUARDING THE SOCIALITE
1666—SWORN TO PROTECT‡
1669—COLD CASE REUNION‡
1696—A DAUGHTER'S PERFECT SECRET

*Home in Emmett's Mill
**Mama Jo's Boys
†Native Country

Other titles by this author available in ebook format.

The biggest thanks must unreservedly go to my good childhood friend, Dulcey Rood, who helped us "live like locals" while we were in St. John. She went out of her way to be an excellent ambassador for St. John by sharing books on local customs, the Crucian language and common etiquette, as well as letting us borrow her Jeep so we could do our own island exploring. She found an apartment for us to stay in—rent free!—and treated us to dinner. She gave us the lowdown on what to do, where to eat, and where to find the best beaches. Dulcey was in a word: invaluable! We love you, Dulc! Simply put, you rock and I miss you already.

Also big thanks to Acacia for being the lovely young woman she blossomed into. She was a big help getting us to the grocery store so we could stock the apartment, as well as always being so accommodating whenever we needed her help.

Big thanks to Richie 16, our taxi driver, who educated us on the "island ways" and got us safely from St. Thomas to the ferry all the while sharing local color about the wondrous place known as St. Thomas.

To the woman whose apartment we borrowed for a week—thank you for availing to us your cool pad. Sitting on the porch during a tropical storm was the best.

And to the real Maho…coolest cat ever. If it'd been possible we might've tried to smuggle him home with us.

CHAPTER ONE

THE WARM, SALTY BREEZE lifted Lora Bell's hair from her damp neck as she stepped from the ferry platform after docking in Cruz Bay, St. John. She knew the fierce humidity would wreak havoc on her carefully maintained cut and color so that by the time she reached Larimar, which was only a short drive out of town, the curl she fought to tame would spring to life with a vengeance.

Home sweet home, she thought sourly, pausing to quickly wrap her shoulder-length hair into a messy knot at the back of her head. Everywhere she looked paradise stared back—calm, azure water lapping at spun-sugar beaches, vibrant green foliage rimming the shorelines—but Lora really saw something different. She saw obligation, poverty, decaying infrastructure, greed and corruption leaking through the cracks in the cement and stinking up the air like the open-air Dumpsters that everyone used to dispose of their trash. And she was angry as hell that situations beyond her control had dragged her home against her will.

Although quieter and more low-key than St. Thomas, St. John still saw its share of tourists and Lora was reminded of this fact as she navigated the throng of people walking by with their coconut-rum concoctions, clutching at wide, floppy straw hats in an attempt to shield their skin from the tropical sun. Unlike them, Lora wasn't here on a pleasure cruise.

She jerked her Louis Vuitton rolling luggage over the worn plank dock and continued, her steps quick and purposeful, toward the man awaiting her by the Jeep Wrangler her family had purchased many years ago and that had begun to wear its age like an embattled war veteran. She didn't bother hiding her frown when she saw the Jeep but Lora knew it was pointless to complain. Island cars were a special breed. The more banged up, the more street cred they acquired. But it'd been quite a while since she'd lived on the island and she much preferred a smoother ride nowadays, such as her company's sleek Lincoln Town Car, which had always been at her disposal when she'd been the company darling.

How the mighty have fallen. She gritted her teeth against the unexpected sting of moisture in her eyes and focused again on the problems facing her in the here and now. The long flight had been excruciating enough with nothing but her rapidly deteriorating sense of self to keep her company; who was she without her punishing work schedule to keep her busy? Who was she if she wasn't out there making mincemeat of anyone who stood in her way? Just as she discovered that the answer was not to be found at the bottom of a Chardonnay bottle, it was not here, either. All that awaited her in St. John was more problems. She could only hope her problems in Chicago would wait—the ones greeting her in St. John would not.

Her gaze searched and settled on the one man she'd hoped she wouldn't see. Given that her luck had been somewhere in the toilet region, she shouldn't have been surprised that Heath Cannon would be the one to pick her up from the ferry.

Coincidentally, he wore the same expression of put-upon pique as she felt. Great. So they were both pissed. This ought to make for an uncomfortable ride to the resort. She met his hard stare with one of her own—

intimidation was a tactic she had perfected. "I still don't understand why you couldn't take care of this situation until I could get here when my schedule allowed," she said to Heath who neither offered to take her bag nor cracked a welcoming smile in spite of being her ride. Not that she'd expected or needed such niceties, of course. "I can't imagine that Lilah couldn't handle whatever is going on."

Lilah, the younger of her fraternal twin sisters, had moved back home three months ago with the intent to help their grandfather with the resort, but apparently the job was too much for her flighty little sis and all hell was breaking loose with some sort of calamity. She swore under her breath when the wheel of her luggage snagged again. When Heath still hadn't said a word, she gave him an irritated look. "Are you even listening to me? Why'd you come, anyway? Why couldn't Lilah pick me up?" she grumbled, mostly to herself. She hated feeling as if she were to blame for this mess simply because she'd failed to jump at the slightest mention of a shadow on the horizon. But Heath was making it quite clear that he blamed her. The knowledge pinched and in turn, angered her further. She wasn't to blame and she certainly wouldn't accept the burden just because others were incompetent. "Well?"

"Lilah had things to do," came his curt reply as he rounded the Jeep to the driver's side. "So that left me holding the short straw."

As in, neither had wanted to pick her up. Nice. They were in an all-fired hurry to get her here but now that they'd succeeded they wanted to avoid her like the plague? Real mature. And just like Lilah. The spoiled brat. Everyone made allowances for the twins but when it came to Lora, she was expected to be the iron maiden, impervious to every slung arrow. She bit back a sarcastic reply and instead ignored his statement. She wasn't going to waste her energy sniping at Heath. She had precious little of it after the exhausting travel day. It was too hot and humid and she wanted nothing more than to stand under a very cold shower for at least five minutes.

Heath, fit as a surfer with nothing better to do than ride the waves and pick up bikini-clad chicks, remained silent, which suited her perfectly. The less they interacted, the better. He looked as she remembered from her childhood and subsequent sporadic visits home, though she didn't quite recall the muscle cording his shoulders and the way his broad chest tapered to slim hips. She yanked her carry-on, lifting it onto the backseat of the Jeep before climbing in, still angry over the entire situation and the wretchedly bad timing in regards to her career.

Oh, wait, what career? She winced inwardly at the recollection of what had gone down only a handful of days ago when her boss had not-so-gently fired her after losing a major, multimillion-dollar account to a competitor. The memory, fresh and humiliatingly devastating, caused a sick roiling in her stomach that completely soured the airline-issue ham sandwich she'd choked down during her flight. And now this? Family issues were the last thing she wanted to deal with, but Lilah and her grandfather had made a right mess of the family business and she had to clean it up or else lose everything.

Reversing her decision to remain quiet for the drive, she said, "I know it's difficult for you to comprehend but this is the absolute worst timing for me." She needed to be doing damage control to find another job before news of her untimely and *involuntary* exit rippled through the grapevine. Marketing was such an incestuous little circle with everyone knowing everyone else's business because oftentimes, the person sharing the hotel bed was the same person you were trying to seduce information from about the competitor. Once word spread about her firing, one of two things would happen: either her former company's competitors would start sniffing around, making offers because—prior to her unfortunate lapse in judgment—she'd been the best in town; or they'd treat her like the plague because, in this economy, no one could afford to hire someone who lost accounts. Period. Thus the need for damage control. Closing her eyes for the briefest of moments to recollect herself, she opened them when she realized Heath was talking.

"He's your grandfather and he needs you," Heath said, his voice a strong yet low timbre that hinted at the temper he was holding back.

She glared even as a slight shudder, undetectable to anyone aside from herself, danced along her backbone. *Since when was it okay for Heath Cannon to reprimand her like an errant child?* Damn him for being so self-righteous. He had no idea what she'd been through in the past week. She was tempted to tell him to zip it but she held the impulse in check by the smallest grace.

"I've been trying to get you to come for

months and you've ignored every call, every email, every letter. Until now."

"Well, excuse me for misplacing a little faith in my sister to handle what was happening here," she shot back, reaching up to hold on while Heath took the Jeep out of town and up the winding road to the resort. "How was I supposed to know that little Miss Butterfly Brain would flake when it mattered most?"

"Don't call her that."

"Why not? It seems to fit. You forget I've known her her entire life," she said drily.

"Oh, then should we start calling you by what you've been known for?"

She cast a sharp glance his way, knowing full well how she was perceived both on the island and elsewhere. For lack of a better word: the Bitch. She wasn't naive and she wasn't sensitive about it, either. She firmly believed that strong women were often labeled out of insecurity. She lifted her chin. "Yes, well, I'm here now."

"Yes, finally."

"There you go being dramatic again," she muttered, adjusting the thin band of her watch against her skin, hating that every square inch of her skin was damp. She could already feel sand in all sorts of places it didn't belong.

"You said Pops was about to lose the resort. Something about back taxes and a lien against the property, which honestly isn't something I'm going to freak out about until I've had my lawyers take a look." Oh, damn. *She* no longer had lawyers. The *company* had a vast stable of lawyers at its disposal, something she'd learned to take for granted, which is why the statement had rolled so blithely from her tongue. But why admit that to Heath, she thought churlishly, the heat and the situation leaching away the last vestige of grace available to her. "I'm sure it's not as bad as you're making it sound," she snapped, wiping at the sweat dotting her hairline. She'd forgotten how awful the island humidity was. It felt as if a big, wet elephant were sitting on her chest. Just the act of breathing was a chore. How had she ever lived here without keeling over in a drippy, soggy mess?

"If it were just the taxes, I wouldn't have taken your precious time," Heath said, the caustic note in his voice hard to miss and stinging just a bit. "You knew that Lilah wasn't up to the job," he said, not even trying to hide the accusation in his tone. "She was in way over her head and now..."

"So what is it then? What weren't you willing to tell me about Pops unless I came? Lilah wouldn't say, either." Well, Lilah wasn't exactly speaking to her at the moment, not after Lora berated her within an inch of her life for not handling things herself, which may have been a little harsh but she'd deal with *that* later.

Heath's mouth firmed and he seemed to falter under her direct query. His obvious hesitation gave her an odd, apprehensive tremor in the pit of her stomach. What could be so bad that Heath didn't just spit it out? Oh, God, not cancer... Her fear conjured images of her mother and grandmother dying and she felt sick. "Just tell me," she said, the words tight in her mouth but it was becoming hard to breathe.

He shook his head, waving away her fear. "On the outside, Pops is healthy as a horse," he said, confusing her. He shot a quick assessing gaze her way, then finished with a sigh. "It's not his body that's failing. It's his mind. Pops has early onset dementia. He's losing it and I don't mean in the general sense that he's becoming forgetful at times. He... Well, you need to see for yourself."

A chill washed over Lora. Pops? Dementia? Her grandfather was the only father figure she and her sisters had since their biological father decided he couldn't handle being a daddy any longer and split, which was followed with impeccable timing by the death of their mother from cancer. It'd been a double tap of anguish with a nice sledgehammer slam just for fun. There were parts of her childhood she'd purposefully blocked out. Her parents splitting, both voluntarily and involuntarily, was a particularly painful topic that she rarely visited.

Lora didn't dare risk a glance at Heath. She didn't want to see his condemnation. She heard it in his voice plain as day. If it was true that her grandfather was slowly losing his mind and she'd left Lilah and Heath to deal with it, she could understand why they were so pissed at her. Wouldn't she feel the same? Yes. A small part of her wanted to rail at fate for being so cruel to her family. Wasn't it enough that cancer had struck twice? Now they had dementia to deal with, too?

She swallowed the lump that rose in her throat but she refused to let Heath know he'd struck a nerve. She made a living by concealing the tiniest flicker of unease or distress and she'd found a certain usefulness for the ability in her personal life. She focused on the road.

"Last time I checked you were a handyman, not a doctor. Let's not jump to conclusions."

"You're a piece of work," he muttered, throwing the car into the next gear without finesse, causing her to jerk against the seat belt. "Chicago is the perfect place for someone like you."

"Is that so? And why is that?" she asked without a trace of humor to soften the sarcasm in her tone.

"Because all the snow and ice is perfect for the frigid bitch you've become. I can't believe you and Jack are related and, frankly, if anyone else's name had been on the legal documents I would've gladly given them the information. As it is, you're the one listed as the next of kin in the event something were to happen to Jack, and obviously Lilah isn't cut out for this kind of stuff. I didn't have much of a choice," he added with a dark scowl.

Lora stared out at the passing scenery, ignoring the sharp stab of hurt his words caused. As the oldest sister, she had assumed the responsibility of the family estate, such that it was, if one resort could be considered an estate, but Pops had never made it a secret that he wanted his little "sugar birds" to inherit the resort when he passed. With her other sister Lindsey, Lilah's twin, in Southern California doing the actress thing, it seemed appropriate for Lilah to come and help out since she was the only one of the three who was still searching for a career—and failing miserably—but Lora hadn't imagined that things could implode so badly with Lilah at the helm. "Just drive, please. I didn't fly all the way here from Chicago to listen to you lecture me."

She longed to pinch the bridge of her nose to stem the sudden pounding in her sinuses caused by too much flora and fauna all at once, but she'd allow nothing that would betray her discomfort or the nagging sense of guilt that she'd shrugged off her responsibility and dumped it on her baby sister when deep down she'd known it wasn't a good idea. But honestly, the woman had to grow up some-time and now had seemed as good a time as any, particularly when Lora had been too busy to attend to the issues herself.

"Yes, ma'am," Heath replied, the flip tone smacking in the face of his obvious anger. He kept his attention on the road, for which Lora was inordinately glad; it kept them from suf-fering through too much eye contact.

It hadn't always been like this between

them, though the time when they'd actually been friends seemed far away now. She supposed she might've been to blame for the change, but it was so long ago she saw no point in picking apart history to reminisce.

In an effort to ease the silence filling the car like a throat-clogging perfume, Lora asked, "So…how are things on the island? Everything seems pretty much the same as when I left."

"Small talk, huh? You sure you want to try something out of your field? I know your penchant for success in all things. I'd hate to witness your attempt at niceties crash and burn so badly."

"I'm just trying to be civil."

"Don't bother. I lost any respect I had for you four months ago when my last email went unanswered and I had to sit in the urgent care with Pops after he'd wandered out and fell and hit his head. He needed twenty stitches, by the way."

Pops had fallen? Lilah hadn't told her. "I don't recall that message," she said stiffly, shifting against the uncomfortable squeeze her conscience gave her for losing Heath's message—not intentionally, she'd been buried under deadlines, meetings, dinner appointments and whatnot of her hectic life, she was tempted to point out—but she held her ground. "Neither you nor Lilah must have tried very hard. I'm always accessible as you discovered when you sent me the certified letter demanding I come home over this situation with the resort."

He cut her a short look and snorted. "Yeah, I'll keep that in mind. If I want to get your attention, a certified letter is necessary." Heath scrubbed at his head, irritation hardening his features. "I always wondered why Pops put you in charge of his affairs. Something tells me you must hide that predatory nature of yours behind pretty smiles for the old man because if he saw what I see...he'd likely change his mind, right quick."

Pops adored them all. Their mother, his only daughter, had given him three little sugar birds that he'd delighted in spoiling. And it was true, she did soften her natural inclination to go for the jugular when she was around Pops. She narrowed her stare at Heath for his spot-on observation.

"My relationship with *my* grandfather is none of your business," she said sharply. "I fail to see why you're so up in arms over a problem that doesn't truly concern you. It's not as if anyone asked you to take on my family's problems. If you're so bothered by the way I am, then by all means, find some other family to attach yourself to."

At her rebuke, he stiffened and she felt the overwhelming urge to apologize. It seemed her mouth didn't know when to rein it in or offer mercy. She struggled not to grimace. That was similar to what her former boss had said to her when he fired her. According to Stan Brothers, CEO of The Pershing Group, Lora *lacked tact,* and was *unnecessarily abrasive.* Of course, Stan hadn't cared when she'd been bringing in the big accounts, only when she'd lost one account. Okay…if she were being honest, the biggest account The Pershing Group had ever managed but was that truly enough to warrant termination? Realizing her mind was traveling off topic, she returned to Heath with a barely restrained sigh.

"I thought everyone on the island was supposed to be easygoing and *nice.* What happened to you?"

Heath's mouth tipped in a slow smirk that didn't quite reach the storm of his hazel eyes. "You happened, Lora Bell. Plain and simple… you happened."

Heath nearly bit his tongue in half as he let the words fly, wishing he'd just held to his earlier decision to keep his mouth shut for the duration of the car ride and then move on after he'd deposited her in the driveway. But the minute he'd seen her, looking stiff as steel, poured into the tailored business suit that was ridiculously overdressed for the humid tropical climate, he'd been unable to listen to his own good advice.

Seeing the woman made it difficult to remember the girl.

She hadn't always been chipped from granite like she was now. Hell, he didn't think she remembered that fact or if she did, she didn't much like to be reminded. Maybe that's why they'd always rubbed each other wrong. He knew a few of her secrets, even if she pretended otherwise. He remembered a girl with tears on her face, struggling to hold it together for her sisters' sake on the day of her mother's funeral. Lindsey and Lilah had been looking to her for strength and she was determined to give it to them, even if she'd had nothing left for herself.

He remembered laughter between two kids, running along the surf, and eating fresh coconut when they were hungry. He also re-

membered the way she'd looked at him, as
if he were the funniest, brightest, most awesome boy alive. He remembered a basket of
food when he'd been most certainly about to
starve.

That's how he remembered Lora Bell. And
damn it, that might've been the moment he
lost a tiny piece of his heart to her, too.

Sometimes he wondered if he'd imagined
all of it.

The woman she'd become wasn't even a
shadow of the girl she'd been.

Everything changed when he'd returned to
the island after a year of being gone.

Suddenly, he'd become just the boy who did
odd jobs for Pops, the unwelcome presence at
the dinner table on some nights, or the lanky
teen who'd burned with humiliation as Lora
dismissed him as any kind of romantic possibility.

He was ashamed to admit there was some
small part of him that hoped he'd see a remnant of the girl she'd been so long ago even
though it'd been years since she'd put in an
appearance. He was an idiot for hoping—he
knew—but buried deep, that hope still flick-
ered, even if it was a very dim ember.

"You know if you weren't so damn difficult

all the time, people might have an easier time liking you," he bit out in spite of himself.

"You suffer under the mistaken assumption the opinions of others matter to me," she replied simply. "I couldn't care less what other people think of me. You've known me long enough, surely you remember that about me."

He gritted his teeth. "I also remember you being a bit nicer at one time."

She seemed momentarily shaken by his admission, as if they'd both quietly agreed to never talk about the times before he left for St. Thomas for a year, and within a heartbeat she'd stuffed away any hint of discomfort or raw feeling.

"Your memory is flawed."

"Maybe," he acknowledged with a shrug. "But doubtful. However, why you would take pride in being so difficult, I don't understand. You know, you catch more bees with honey than vinegar and spreading a little goodwill might be helpful considering you haven't been on the island for some time. You never know where you might need help."

She leveled a short look his way. "Thanks for the advice I didn't ask for. I take pride in being *efficient*. If you consider that being difficult, then so be it. As far as needing goodwill…I don't see how that applies. I'm here to solve a problem, not run for mayor."

Ah, hell. Why did he even try? She was a lost cause. "Fine. Whatever. Just trying to help."

"Your help would've been useful before I was required to hop a plane and put my life on hold," she said evenly, staring straight ahead, though her grip tightened ever so slightly on the roof handle, betraying something. Heath couldn't be sure if his comment had struck a nerve or she just really had to pee and she wished he would drive faster.

"Yeah, well, I guess if you were more *efficient* about getting your messages, we might not be in this mess now."

He expected a cutting retort but she remained silent. Whether she secretly agreed with him or she simply had run out of steam to argue, he didn't know.

One thing was for sure, he was pretty certain whatever had been lodged in his heart for all those years was dead and gone. Now he was just here for Pops. He loved the old man and would do whatever was necessary to help him—including putting up with Lora.

Lilah had tried to mop up the mess but she'd been out of her element and completely clueless as to how to keep a resort running while her beloved Pops held imaginary conversations with her long-dead Grams. Actually, he felt kinda bad for the kid. Lora had put her in a bad spot and now was ready to crucify Lilah for failing.

Time for damage control. If there was a way he could reel back the words he'd carelessly uttered, he'd do it. Barring that, he needed to focus attention on what mattered.

"Listen, here's the deal. Pops loses time. One minute he's totally fine and acting like the Pops I've known since I was a kid but then he slips and he's not in the here and now."

"What does that mean?" she asked.

"It means sometimes he thinks Grams is still alive," he answered grimly.

Lora exhaled softly, shocked by his admission. He knew how close Lora and Grams had been. Losing her had been nearly as tough as when she'd lost her mother. When she spoke again, her voice was strong, betraying nothing of whatever she was feeling inside, leaving him to wonder if she had a shred of humanity left in her. "Well, we'll just have to remind him of reality. Grams died ten years ago. We can't let him marinate in fantasy. That can't be healthy."

"Yeah, well, sometimes it's better than watching him lose her over and over again. When you tell him that Grams is gone, it's as if she's just died."

"Oh," she breathed, and this time her voice softened and real distress was etched on her face. He found that a good sign. Maybe there was hope for her yet. "What can we do for him? Is there medication he can take? What does the doctor say?"

"Well, if you'd come when I first started calling...you'd know."

She pressed a delicate finger to her temple and waved him off. "Yes, yes, I'm the big bad bitch and my sisters are irresponsible twits. We've already sufficiently covered that topic. Time to move on before my head explodes. Something in the air is making my sinuses riot. Do you have any allergy medication at the resort?"

He was tempted to say no, but he wasn't that big of a jerk. "Yeah," he said.

"Oh, good," she said, relieved, closing her eyes. "I propose we postpone this episode of the *I Hate Lora Bell Show* until I've had a chance to stop this pounding in my head. I have enough to deal with as it is, I don't need sparring with you added to the list just yet. I'll keep quiet, if you will. Deal?"

"Fine by me," he muttered, pissed that she was ending what he hadn't planned on starting in the first place. "Welcome home."

Good as her word, she buttoned her lip, content to finish the drive in silence, although his mind stubbornly continued to hit him with what was to come.

No doubt she thought she'd make whatever fixes she figured were necessary and then jump on the next ferry out of here. She was going to discover, quite quickly, it wouldn't be that simple.

If only she'd shown up sooner...maybe things might've been put right more easily.

Now? It'd be a miracle if Larimar wasn't sold out from underneath their feet.

And if that happened? It would surely send Pops toppling over the ledge of sanity and into the land of no return.

He hoped Lora couldn't live with that on her conscience.

But risking a glance at the woman seeming to drowse in the island heat, he couldn't help but fear that a conscience was the first thing Lora had sacrificed for that high-pow-

ered career of hers, and if that was the case...
likely Larimar was screwed.

And by proxy...so was he.

CHAPTER TWO

HEATH PARKED IN THE SMALL spot designated for the resort vehicle, and Lora sprang from her seat, eager to get away from Heath and his condemning scowl.

She went to grab her bag but Heath was already jerking it free from the Jeep, being none too gentle with the expensive luggage. Lora reached for the handle, exasperated. "A little care, please? This probably cost more than what you make in a month." He shot her a quelling look and she immediately felt bad for the comment, but her temper was in full control of her mouth, and frustration had dissolved whatever portion of empathy and common courtesy she'd possessed before she'd even landed at Charlotte Amalie Airport in St. Thomas.

"Sorry about that," she muttered, in an attempt to soften the insult but Heath had already turned his back on her. She could almost see the disgust he felt for her emanating from him in waves with each step that carried him farther away. *Fine, be that way,* she wanted to shout even knowing she'd been the one to snap first. What was it about Heath Cannon that made her act like a ten-year-old? She'd fired people for less.

All right, so let's get this over with. Maybe with any luck she'd have this crisis figured out before the week was out and she could hop another plane back to Chicago before her hair permanently frizzed into an iguana's nest of knots. As far as Pops went, she couldn't believe that his mind was deteriorating. He was the smartest man she knew. Likely, his memory gaps were simply a product of the natural aging process. For crying out loud, if she didn't have her BlackBerry to keep her on track she'd forget plenty of important things, but that didn't mean she had dementia. Everyone seemed to be pulling a Chicken Little. Chances were that the sky was not actually falling.

Larimar—named after the agate stone found only in the Caribbean that locals claimed had magical qualities—came into view with its swaying tropical foliage flanking the entrance with bay rum and giant kapok trees creating a green canopy of various shades. Bright wild flowers dotted the underbrush and lizards of all kinds darted away from the approach of human feet.

She'd thought her pique would insulate her from nostalgia but the minute she crossed the threshold into the airy lobby of Larimar, her high heels clicking sharply on the travertine tile floor, memories drifted from hidden corners like the smell of coconut suntan lotion on the ocean breeze. Lora halted, her eyes closing for just a moment as her Grams floated into her mind's eye and her beloved voice echoed in Lora's mind.

"Little Miss Bell, have you had at least one hour of fun at the beach today?" Grams had asked one day when she found Lora studying instead of doing what every other kid was doing during summer vacation. Grams had gently closed the book, her eyes smiling but faintly serious as she instructed Lora to go act like a teenager for once. "Go get into some trouble, but not too much trouble, mind you. Just enough to make interesting memories to giggle over when you're an adult. And for land's sake, get your nose out of those books."

Lora had been focused on her grades, not goofing off or finding boyfriends like most of her friends, or twin sisters for that matter.

Lindy was a shameless flirt who basked in the adoration of every pair of male eyes that crossed at the sight of her bouncing around in her tiny bikini; Lilah, the younger twin by one minute, had also enjoyed her share of boys clustered around her, though she'd been more carefree about her love life, choosing to float through relationships until the wind took her elsewhere.

Oh, Grams... Lora took a quiet moment to collect herself, shaking off the memory of her beloved grandmother with effort. Of all things, she missed Grams the most.

Grams had been the calm in the storm that had become Lora's life when they were forced to move to Larimar after her father abandoned them. Lora's mother had been so heartbroken, so lost after her husband split. And then, shortly after they'd arrived in St. John, the cancer diagnosis had followed. It had seemed a colossally bad cosmic joke but it'd been no joke. Her mother had died with little fight. In fact, it had seemed to Lora that her mother had simply given up. For that, Lora found memories of her mother difficult. More so than memories of Grams. At least with Grams, Lora had plenty of great memories to temper the sad ones. Intellectually, Lora knew it wasn't fair to judge her mother based on the memories of a ten-year-old girl, but she did anyway. Just one more reason Lora was known as the Bitch, she supposed.

But Grams was gone—the problems facing Larimar were in the here and now and that's why she'd come.

Her lids flipped open and she purposefully walked toward the front counter where a dark-skinned woman she didn't recognize sat in reception.

"Welcome to—"

"Not necessary." She cut the woman's spiel in half with a wave of her hand, ignoring the startled look at her abruptness. Glancing around, she looked for someone she knew. "My name is Lora Bell. Can you tell me where my grandfather or my sister Lilah is? I need to see them at once."

"I know who you are," the woman said, her voice thick with the local Crucian accent common to the island. Her stare narrowed and the judgment in her expression caused Lora to pause. "You finally come to help Mistah Bell? 'Bout time."

"Excuse me?"

"You heard me. Mistah Bell needed ya and ya too busy to make time for him."

She was being schooled by the receptionist? What next? Lora made a mental note to start looking for a replacement right away. "You seem to know a lot about me, but I know very little about you," Lora said coolly. "What is your name?"

"Celly," the woman answered, her chin rising. Her dark brown stare neither flinched or shifted away, and Lora knew this woman felt fairly confident in her position and wouldn't scare easily. Fabulous. With the luck Lora was having, her grandfather had probably written this Celly into the will. *Good gravy.* She felt a cloud at her back and her pessimistic attitude certainly wasn't helping.

She forced a brief smile. "Can you tell me where to find my grandfather?"

"Mistah Bell in de back," the woman answered with a small sniff. "You know your way?"

Lora ground her teeth, irritated. "Of course. I did grow up here, you know," she muttered, gripping her luggage handle, then said over her shoulder, "We'll be talking again soon, I'm sure."

"I look forward to it, missy," Celly called back.

Oh, I bet you will, she thought blackly. She had a feeling if she didn't put finding a new receptionist on top of her list, Celly was going to give her an earful that Lora definitely wasn't in the mood to hear.

The back terrace was attached to the part of the resort that was reserved for the Bells and afforded a breathtaking view of the ocean. Larimar was a spacious four-plex with access to a secluded private beach via a short walk but the Bells' section of the resort opened to beachfront property right off the terrace. It'd been Grams's and Pops's favorite part about Larimar; they'd often eaten their breakfast of papaya and coconut right there, followed by a quick dip in the water. Grams had been a water dog. Pops had often joked that he'd married a mermaid without her tail.

There, sitting at his wicker breakfast table, sat Pops, the empty chair opposite him pricking unexpected tears from Lora's eyes as the loss of Grams hit her hard all over again. Maybe it was because her life was a mess and Grams had always known how to settle her "Little Miss Type A" as she'd lovingly called Lora, or maybe it was because her cycle was near and she was prone to bursts of emotion at the oddest moments, but sadness swamped Lora before she could guard against it. Thankfully, Pops was oblivious and simply grinned his jack-o'-lantern smile and exclaimed with pure pleasure at the sight of her, "There she is! Come here, my sugar bird." He rose and gathered her into his embrace as if she were still a child and not a grown woman of thirty-two. But God bless him, her grandfather was her lifeline to sanity and she clung to him as if she was afraid to let go. He drew away, his blue eyes brimming with pride and not the least bit unclear—maybe they were all wrong about Pops and his supposed dementia—and she felt a bit of the tension ebb from her shoulders. "So good to see you, Lorie," he said, his use of her nickname causing her to smile. No one but Pops was allowed to call her Lorie. She purposefully eschewed nicknames in her business life for fear that it might weaken the lines she drew to keep business and personal separate. Not that she had much of a personal life to keep separate but it was a good policy. Of course, all that went out the window the minute she saw Pops. He could call her whatever he liked.

"You look the same, Pops," she said, somewhat relieved. When Heath had told her Pops was beginning to suffer mentally, she'd imagined a diminished shell of the robust man she'd known her entire life. But the man standing before her looked the same as he always did, like someone who still rose with the sun and worked as hard as he played. Lora smiled, straightening her tight skirt before taking a seat opposite her Pops. "You don't age. Must be the clean island air. Or the rum," she teased.

Pops winked and whispered conspiratorially, "Well, I have a secret but don't tell your Grams…" Lora's breath caught painfully in her chest and her smile froze but Pops didn't seem to notice. He leaned forward, saying, "I slather on a bit of that pricey lotion your Grams buys from her catalogs. That stuff really works. Keeps my skin looking smooth as a baby's behind. And smells good, too. But let's keep that between me and you. If your Grams found out she'd never let me live it down."

Tears filled her eyes before she could stop them. She swallowed and forced a smile, gentling her voice as she said, "Pops, remember…Grams died ten years ago." Lora placed a hand on his, squeezing in a show of support, hoping he'd snap into reality with the reminder.

But Pops didn't snap or bounce or any such thing. He broke.

His expression faltered, confused, and Lora tried to mend things with more logic. "Pops, she's in a happy place now. And she wouldn't want us to waste tears when she's no longer in pain and—"

"I just saw her this morning," Pops said, his voice shaking, his eyes darting as if trying to find the truth in the memory. Turning accusatory, he looked disappointed in Lora and that nearly crushed her. "Lorie, why would you say that? Your Grams is fine. She's doing just fine. Clean bill of health."

"No, Pops," Lora said, her own voice clogging with tears. "She died of breast cancer ten years ago. She found a lump and it had already moved to her lymph nodes. Grams died—"

"Stop saying that!" he demanded, his voice roughening as he rose from his chair to get away from her. Lora's heart hammered hard in her chest and she didn't know what to do. Her Pops had never been short with her in her entire life. She didn't recognize this man and it broke her heart. "Lana," he called out, going in search of Lora's grandmother and leaving Lora to stare in horror and dissolve into tears.

And that's how Heath found her.

THE WORDS DANCED ON HIS tongue, *I told you so,* but he wasn't that big of an ass. He ought to walk away and leave Lora to soak in her own misery. Although his brain told him to go, he couldn't quite get his feet to obey. He sighed, knowing he was about to try and console a wolverine of a woman and was likely to get his hand bit off, but he couldn't just walk away when she was clearly heartbroken.

"As long as we play along that Lana is still alive…he's the same old Jack. It's when reality is forced on him that he balks and freaks out. Lilah makes sure to keep Grams's things clean, even going so far as to put a load of folded laundry on the bed for Pops to put away like she used to. Lilah also started replacing some of the lotions and stuff that Grams used so that Pops wouldn't get thrown off."

Lora wiped at her face. "You're continuing an elaborate farce? Doesn't that seem the slightest bit inappropriate?"

He flung his arm in the direction Pops had gone, growing angry all over. Damn the woman. Didn't she see that Pops needed that illusion? "It's a small price to pay for his happiness. The man means everything to me. I'm willing to play along for his sake."

"This is awful," she said, shaking her head in horror. "You can't keep pretending Grams is going to walk through the front door because she's not going to! She's gone. He needs to come to grips with that."

"He doesn't have the mental agility to do that any longer. The harder we push, the worse his dementia becomes. Lilah and I agreed, it was best to let him have his fantasy. Besides, who's it really hurting?"

She stared. "Who's it hurting?" she repeated incredulously, but even as she said the words, she stalled, and he knew the truth of it. It hurt *her* to pretend Grams was alive. Lora had never truly dealt with the pain of losing Grams. She just stuffed it down in that locked box where she put everything that was painful in her life and then never opened it again. "It's not right," she finished lamely.

He softened in the face of her subtle vulnerability. He knew that Grams had always been Lora's safe haven, her voice of reason. Losing her had been a blow to her emotional foundation. "The good news is, it doesn't last long," he said, trying to reassure her. "By dinner, he'll go back to thinking Lana is here and she's just out shopping or taking care of Larimar business."

Lora's head shot up and her look of open distress at being caught in such a vulnerable position robbed her of words for a moment. But that moment didn't last long. Soon enough her mouth tightened as her stare narrowed. "That's the good news?" she said, grinding any residual moisture from her eyes and smoothing the tiny skirt as if the motion alone could release the wrinkles that a long plane ride and the humidity had created. "This is a nightmare. There is nothing good about it. How long has he been like this?"

He shrugged. "A year, give or take a few months."

"A year?" She stared. "Why didn't someone call me?"

"We did. Remember?"

Her blank stare may have fooled someone else but he knew right at this moment she was searching her memory, looking for some way to refute his blunt statement. Heath knew as much as she did that she was wrong. She'd flat out ignored every bit of correspondence that'd come her way when it'd come from her sisters or himself. He knew it—and better yet—so did she. Still, he was curious how she planned to wiggle her way out of that knowledge.

He waited, one brow lifting in question and she had the grace to flush. Unable to hold his stare, she looked away. "Fine," she conceded grudgingly, eager to move on. "What's being done about it? This pretense isn't a long-term solution." She pressed her fingers to her temple, and he remembered her mentioning a headache earlier. For a second, she seemed to waver on her feet and Heath started forward but she shooed him away with a murmur of annoyance at her own reaction. "Damn humidity is getting to me. I need to change and get something to drink before I can think straight."

"Your room is in the same place," Heath said, his mouth firming. Still the same hard-nosed woman she ever was. He held back the irritation that swelled when he remembered how he'd once thought the sun rose and set in her eyes. What a fool he was then. Things had certainly changed. "I assume you remember how to find it?"

She shot him a look that said his sarcasm wasn't appreciated, then gripped her luggage handle and trudged past him, her back ramrod straight.

He didn't know why Lora had been the one that'd always caught his eye. Even though her sisters were pretty in their own way, there'd been no one prettier than Lora in his opinion. When he thought of all the ways he'd tried to catch her attention, to get her to see him as more than the poor island boy who did odd jobs for her Pops…ugh, it twisted his gut in disgust.

The first thing he remembered about Lora Bell was that impossibly dark hair streaming down her back like a waterfall at midnight. Lora, her sisters and their mother had arrived by ferry to St. John wearing sadness as plainly as their summer tanks. Except Lora—no, in her little face, he saw a cold knot of anger that twisted beneath the layer of grief. Whereas her younger sisters were wide-eyed with apprehension at their new surroundings, Lora had taken it in with the air of a soldier grimly going to battle. Looking back, he suspected Lora had been a different child before her father skipped out on them and her mother had died of cancer a year later. As they'd grown closer during those first few months, he'd known a different side of her, a softer side, so he'd been doubly shocked and broken-hearted when she'd given him the cold shoulder on his return. It hadn't been his choice to leave the island; his parents had abandoned him and he'd gone looking for them. It wasn't exactly a typical situation but Lora knew none of that. He'd never told her and she'd never been interested enough to ask.

That's not true, a voice whispered, reminding him of *that* day…

Stop! Resurrecting a childhood memory wasn't going to help him deal with the Lora Bell of today, he growled to himself. Annoyance at his own useless mental sojourn down Useless Memory Lane, made him want to do something reckless, like give Lora a piece of his mind for neglecting her family when they needed her the most. But as much as it would feel good to abrade her for her actions, he knew the satisfaction would only last a moment. The Bells would stand by Lora—as they should—and he'd lose out on the only family he'd ever known.

He drew a deep breath but his chest remained tight. Lora had only been back for less than an hour and already she was turning his life upside down. The smart thing would be to keep his distance. If they weren't around each other, they couldn't rub each other the wrong way. Sounded like a plan—even if Heath knew following through was going to be damn near impossible. What Lora didn't know was that Heath had been running the resort in a shadow capacity since Pops had started to show signs of dementia creeping on. He knew more about the day-to-day operations of Larimar than any of the Bell girls. And as soon as Lora found out, he was willing to bet his firstborn, she wasn't going to like it.

THE FOG IN JACK'S MIND scared him. Why would Loric say that her Grams was dead? Why would his sugar bird say something so mean-spirited? He'd known Lorie to be a little on the no-nonsense side, unlike her sisters who were happy-go-lucky most times. "Lana?" he called out again, the silence bouncing back at him scared him more. "Lana? Where are you?" he said, rounding the corner to her favorite sunning spot. Maybe she went to town to get supplies, or even Lorie's favorite beef pâté from Simon, the guy who made them from scratch in his kitchen and sold them out of his cooler. A smile found him as the explanation for Lana's absence made sense. Lana always went out of her way for her sugar birds. Of course, that's where she was. Relieved, he let his fear and confusion melt away and detoured to the shop where he could hear Heath tinkering on something. Jack had known Heath since he was a skinny, starving boy hanging around the resort looking for work.

He entered the shop, smiling as he saw Heath pounding out some nails from a board he was going to repurpose for something else needed for the resort. Heath was no skinny boy now. The boy had morphed into a strong, able man whom Jack and Lana considered family even though they didn't share a drop of blood. If only Lorie saw what they saw in the man. "Whatcha working on, son?" he asked, forgetting his earlier moment and eagerly looking to Heath. The man was a whiz with his hands. If it could be built, Heath could build it. If it needed fixing, Heath found a way to fix it. Larimar was lucky to have him and Jack knew it.

"Just a new mailbox. I found this in a stack of wood being tossed out. Thought I'd fix the mailbox out front," Heath answered, his focus on pulling the nails from the wood. But Jack knew the man pretty well and could sense something was eating at him.

"Lorie's home," Jack said, brightening. "You ought to see her. She's pretty as the day is long. You remember, Lorie, don't you?"

Heath jerked a short nod and continued to work but Jack wanted to chat. The boy worked too hard. "Let's take a break," he suggested, smiling. "What's the drink of the day today? Is it that vanilla rum and banana drink that tastes like a banana smoothie with kick? I love that drink. Very refreshing, *yah?*"

"You go on ahead, Jack. I've got to finish this and then get on home."

"Stay for dinner at least," he said, liking the idea of Heath seeing more of Lorie. He and Lana thought the two would make a great couple. Although Lana said Lorie was too focused on her career to ever consider the slow, laid-back life on the island but Jack held out hope. His sugar bird had island in her blood. She just needed to be reminded what made it special.

Heath gave the offer some consideration before shaking his head. "Sorry, Jack. Another time, maybe."

"I'll hold you to that," Jack said with mock seriousness. "All right, I'm off to find out if

Lana brought home an extra pâté, or two. I'm starved."

Heath gave him a tight smile and short nod, then went back to pounding nails.

CHAPTER THREE

LORA CLOSED THE DOOR behind her, leaning against the wood. Pops was losing his mind. There was no getting around that fact when the evidence had just slapped her in the face. Her breath hitched in her chest as the pain spiked in her heart. How could she pretend for Pops's sake that Grams was still alive when she'd worked hard to put that grief behind her so that she could cope with the loss?

No, Grams, no...I can't pretend you're still here...it'll kill me... Lora sank to the floor and clutched her knees to her chest, hating how lost she felt. Losing Grams had been far more painful than losing her own mother, if that was possible.

She remembered her mother's funeral as if watching a scene from someone else's life. The memories she had of Lisa Bell were fogged and distorted, snatches of a life she barely recognized. At one time, her mother had laughed with joy but the Lisa Bell Lora remembered had tears in her eyes from her husband's abandonment. Lora hated her father for that. Cancer had taken her mother, but Lora always believed that a broken heart had been the true killer.

Lora shuddered, gulping against the tightness in her chest. She was stronger than this, she told herself fiercely. *Get up! Get off this floor and stand tall.* There were people depending on her to figure things out. Wiping the tears from her face, she struggled to her feet with the fragile resolve of someone pulling themselves together with little more than grit and determination. This, too, felt familiar.

Snatches of her earlier conversations with Heath came back to taunt her without mercy. Why did he bring out the worst in her? Granted, she wasn't a girl who was known for her niceties but there was something about Heath that had always made her snarl.

But even as the thought ran through her head, something nagged at her. No, she hadn't always disliked Heath. In fact, once... She shrugged off where her mind was going. It was so long ago, she could hardly remember how she'd felt *then* about Heath Cannon. All she knew was that *today* he rubbed her the wrong way. And he seemed stuck to her family like a pervasive mold.

Lora dragged her luggage to the bed and swung it on the bed. She popped the lock, slid the zipper open and threw open the top. Everything was packed with military precision, making it easy to find what she was looking for—her bikini and cover-up. Grateful to get out of the constricting and smothering business attire she wore for the plane, she made quick work of slipping into her island clothes, then put away her packed clothing into her dresser. She didn't plan to stay long but she never kept her clothes tucked in her luggage. She liked everything to be where it belonged, if even for a short visit. After she'd hung her blouses and put away her luggage, she took a quick survey of her room. Nostalgia tugged at the corners of her mind but she pushed it away. She'd spent half her childhood here, in this room. Her mouth softened as a small smile threatened. She closed her eyes and drew in the soft scent of coconut suntan lotion that seemed a part of the wicker furniture and let the peace that followed permeate her soul, if even for just the barest of moments. She would allow herself that small comfort.

The sound of her youngest sister's voice echoed below in the terrace. Lora's eyes opened. She needed to speak with Lilah immediately and seeing as Lilah had failed to meet her at the ferry, that told Lora her baby sis had deliberately avoided her to circumvent a confrontation. Well, time to get this out of the way....

Lora headed downstairs to have a chat with the youngest of the sugar bird Bells.

LILAH BELL HAD WATCHED her sister disembark from the ferry from her perch at the Rush Tide Bar and Grill. She'd pleaded with Heath to go and pick up Lora for fear of what her older sister might say to her in light of her failure. Lilah chewed the side of her cheek, her stomach gurgling in distress at the turmoil causing havoc in her intestines. She'd always had a persnickety tummy, as Grams used to call it, which had resulted in Lilah being the pickiest eater. Lilah knew she gave off the impression of being frail, so most people continued to baby her, except Lora.

And while Lilah sometimes chafed at the way people coddled her, Lora had made her realize that people babied her because she was incapable of handling a true crisis. Her failure at being able to navigate the obstacles facing Larimar and necessitating the SOS call to Lora only served to deepen her own disappointment in herself. And frankly, her oldest sister was the last person she wanted to see right now. She certainly didn't need to hear Lora berate her for letting things get this bad.

So, she'd begged Heath—who had his own issues with Lora—to get her from the ferry. Yes, it'd been cowardly, but Lilah hadn't cared.

She could only imagine the fireworks that'd accompanied that car ride.

But Lilah knew she could avoid Lora for only so long because the island was a mere nine miles wide and eventually, the odds were that they'd bump into each other.

And that moment had come, she realized as Lora descended from the private section of the resort to meet Lilah's wary gaze. If it'd been Lindy, Lilah's twin, there'd at least be hugs and exclamations of affection before the shouting. At twenty-eight, Lilah shouldn't be afraid of her oldest sister, but her stomach was roiling even as she forced a smile.

Of course, Lora looked stunning as she always did, if it weren't for the grim set of her jaw. Lora had changed from the plane into island clothes, though she didn't look local. Too much time in the corporate world had sharpened Lora's gaze as if she were constantly looking for the angle people were trying to use to their advantage. It saddened Lilah to see how much her sister had changed—and not for the better. In that moment, she deeply missed Lindy, but her twin was off in Hollywood, well on her way to becoming famous.

"How was your flight?" she asked, trying for some sort of civility before the fight began. Lora's lips pressed together before she cocked her head to the side with an expression of exasperation. Lilah sighed. "So no small talk first? Okay. I missed you, too. We should probably go into Pops's office to do this."

Lora nodded and turned to pad barefoot into Pops's tiki-themed office. Lilah had always loved Pops's laid-back style to business, but now that she'd been thrust into the management department, she'd realized a more orthodox style would've been easier to step into. As Lora would discover, Pops had left a nightmare to untangle when it came to the books. But as they entered, they found Heath sitting in Pops's chair. This wasn't an uncommon sight for Lilah, but it certainly was an unwelcome shock to Lora, as evidenced by her hard stare.

"What are you doing?" she queried sharply to Heath, and Lilah sent him a silent apology for her sister's rudeness. Lora looked to Lilah for an answer, crossing her arms and looking sorely *vexed,* as the islanders would say. "Last time I checked you were a handyman... now you're sitting in my grandfather's chair? I want an explanation and I want it now."

"God, Lora, stop treating Heath like he's a criminal or something," Lilah muttered, knowing Lora wasn't going to like the explanation. Heath had been stepping in for some time to help and Lilah had been terribly grateful. He'd always been like the older brother she never had and she cared deeply for him. The fact that Lora had treated him as if he were beneath her notice had pissed off Lilah. "He's sitting at Pops's desk because he's been helping me keep Larimar afloat. You know I don't have a head for business and Heath does."

"Oh, really? Since when? I hardly consider doing odd jobs as having the business acumen necessary to run a high-end resort," Lora answered back, focusing her laser stare on Heath who only stared back, the heat between the two enough to fry an egg. "You can bet that I'm going to have a chat with Pops about this but something tells me you probably convinced him—in his current confused state—to let you take over as you saw fit. Well, I can tell you right now, that ends now."

"Lora!" Lilah exclaimed, horrified that her sister would imply such a thing. If she only knew… "You haven't been here. You haven't seen what Heath has done for Larimar. Maybe if you took a phone call every once in a while I wouldn't have had to ask for Heath's help. Unlike you, he found the time to take an interest in what's been going on." Tears stung Lilah's eyes and she couldn't hold them back. She'd never been good at yelling at someone, least of all one of her sisters, but she couldn't sit there and allow Lora to believe the worst of Heath when he'd been nothing but kind to this family. Lora looked unmoved by the sudden show of tears, as if she'd expected some sort of reaction from Lilah, and the knowledge that her older sister knew her that well only served to pour salt in the wound. Seaming her mouth shut, Lilah spun on her heel, only too eager to get away from the ugliness in the room. If her sister wanted to be a coldhearted bitch, then she could deal with the fact that no one liked her or could stand her company for more than five minutes—including her sisters. "I'm sorry, Heath," she muttered as she ran from the room. Whether she was apologizing for abandoning him in the moment or because Lora was such a she-beast, Lilah wasn't sure. She just knew she was sorry.

HEATH WATCHED LILAH FLEE the room and he felt compelled to follow, if only to see if she was okay. Lilah was like his little sister and the fact that he felt more protective over her than her own flesh and blood only served to stoke the banked anger.

"You sure know how to alienate every single person you come into contact with. Tell me, is this how you conduct yourself in Chicago at your big fancy corporate job?" he asked with a calm he certainly didn't feel. He wanted to put his hands around her slim neck and shake some sense into her, but he willed that white hot anger into an icy calm, using a tactic he'd seen Lora use more than once.

At the mention of her career, he almost thought he saw a bit of an inward wince, but that was impossible. Lora Bell was a shark who ate guppies that had the misfortune of wandering into her pool. A show of vulnerability wasn't in her nature. "Nice try at deflection. Now that the hysterics are over, can you tell me what the hell is going on here?"

"Simple. As I told you earlier, your grandfather started to lose time about a year ago and when that happened, he forgot to pay bills. Of course, no one knew this until the water and power was shut off one day. I discovered months' worth of bills that had been stuffed into your Grams's in-box, which at first I thought your Pops was simply using as an easy place to remember where to put the bills, but then I realized, he was following what he used to do when your Grams was alive."

"She always paid the bills," Lora finished in a murmur, her fingers massaging her temple. "So how many bills were behind?"

"Everything," he answered, sugarcoating nothing. "And that prompted me to look a little more deeply into the finances and the taxes. He hasn't paid in years. The government started sending letters six months ago. That's when I started calling you. When we received this—" he picked up a letter from the desktop and tossed it to her "that's when I sent the certified letter to get your damn attention." He paused a minute to let her read the letter. "Because I'm not family and I don't have power of attorney on the estate I couldn't negotiate on Pops's behalf. Unfortunately, we needed you for that."

He knew the letter word for word. It said that if the back taxes weren't paid in full by the end of the quarter, the government would seize the property for payment against the debt.

"Oh, God," Lora breathed, true distress on her features. He wished he could feel some sort of satisfaction for her finally admitting that the situation was serious, but he was too worried to feel anything but anxiety. For him, there was more at stake than his loyalty to the Bells. Two years ago he and Jack had went into business together and Pops had invested a fair amount of capital—money that Pops didn't have to give, which Heath didn't discover until it was too late. Pops had taken money socked away for the estate taxes and given it to Heath instead. Once Heath had discovered the source of the money, he'd felt sick inside. In essence Jack had banked Larimar's future on the belief that Heath's business would thrive. At least, that's what Heath wanted to believe. But there was a dark shadow of doubt that lurked, that Jack had already been slipping in his mental abilities when they'd struck the deal, and if that were the case, it would appear to Lora that Heath had taken advantage of her grandfather. The very idea made him ill—but he knew he'd have a helluva time trying to convince Lora otherwise. He braced his knuckles against the desktop and stared at Lora. "Listen, we can stand here and snipe at each other all day but it's not going to solve anything. We both want the same thing—to save Larimar. I say we work together to that end and put the personal stuff aside."

Her stare narrowed at his suggestion and he felt filleted. "Why do you care so much? This is my family's problem. Not yours. I can't imagine that you're so attached to being a handyman. Surely there are other handyman jobs out there that you could get."

His temper rose but he choked it back until he could talk without shouting. "Why does it matter? I care. Whether you like it or not, I love this family. And if that doesn't jive with how you think I should behave just because I don't share DNA, then too damn bad. I don't care. I love them. Deal with it."

She stared as if shocked by his admission but when she could find no fault with his statement, she backed down—if only incrementally. "Thank you for your help," she managed to offer with a stiff show of gratitude and he knew it must've cost her soul to utter. She straightened and crossed her arms across her ample chest, which only drew his attention to the full swells barely contained in her bikini top hidden beneath the gauzy white cover-up. He jerked his gaze away as if what he saw had the ability to turn him to salt, and he mentally berated himself for looking at all. Lora held up the letter. "If I'd known it was this bad...I would've come sooner."

It was as much of an apology as she was going to offer but frankly, it wasn't enough. Her self-absorbed act needed to go. "You need to talk to Lilah. You're too hard on her."

"I'll thank you to keep your nose out of my business with my sister," she said, but he wasn't afraid of her and continued.

"You knew when you put her in this position that she wasn't up to the challenge. Hell, Lindy would've been a better choice and you and I both know that Lindy is as flighty as a butterfly on the breeze, but at least she wouldn't have cracked under the pressure."

"Lilah is a grown adult. I wish everyone

would stop treating her with kid gloves," Lora snapped, but he saw guilt in her eyes. "Besides, she'll get over it. Nothing bothers Lilah for long."

"That's where you're wrong. It's really sad that you don't know your own sister."

"Oh, and suddenly you're an authority?" she mocked.

"More so than you," he said bluntly.

"Watch it, Heath," Lora murmured. "You're treading on dangerous ground. My Pops may have a soft spot for you but I don't suffer from the same feeling. In essence you're my employee. I could fire you right now."

"Do it, then," he dared her in a silkily dark tone. "But let me tell you something else, so you can make an informed decision. If you do that you're going to have a shit-storm on your hands that not even you will be able to handle. I've been running Larimar for the past year but beyond that, I own the gift shop downstairs and Larimar doesn't have enough money to pay me off."

She stared, shock in her eyes. "What are you talking about?"

He shook his head. "Why don't you take a moment to really look at Larimar and see all the changes that have been made since you've been gone. Someone had to do something to start making some money because the one with the marketing degree…well, she was unavailable."

With that, he stalked past her. He was done with her for the day. If he stood another minute in her presence he'd choke on his own frustration—or choke her.

CHAPTER FOUR

LORA DIDN'T KNOW WHY but the weight of Heath's judgment sat heavily on her shoulders. Why should she care what Heath thought of her relationship with her sister? Clearly, Lilah had Heath believing she was helpless, just like everyone else. Lora refused to feel guilty over her decision to make Lilah take on more responsibility for once. So what if Lilah had no real business sense, was it so hard to write a check and pay some bills? Lora silenced the ongoing argument in her head, annoyed that Heath had managed to make her feel culpable and wrong in the same breath.

She sat in Pops's chair with a huff and started shuffling papers, looking for some semblance of order. She didn't know where to start. She looked in the files and found folders with marked headings written in a clearly masculine hand. She knew Lilah's handwriting was flowery and her Pops's handwriting was an illegible scrawl that only her Grams could decipher, which meant Heath had sorted these papers and put them in order. She pushed away that acknowledgment, not ready to make amends with Heath just yet. It was childish and worse, she knew it, but she couldn't quite deal with the feelings that rose when she thought of Heath's honest admission.

He said he loved her family. Obviously, she was not lumped up in that admission. Lora sniffed. Who cared? She didn't need nor want to be included in Heath's affections. She had enough family, she didn't need more. She paused. And what did he mean that he owned the gift shop? She put aside the tax file for the moment and started sifting through the other files. She found the gift shop and pulled it.

After she finished reading the paperwork pertaining to the business arrangement between Pops and Heath, she leaned back in the chair and stared at the ceiling. She'd found the reason Heath had been so involved in her family's affairs and it wasn't so much altruistic as it was self-serving.

It shouldn't surprise her. In the corporate environment, no one did anything without a reason—and it was usually because they served to benefit from the action. Why was she surprised Heath was no different?

Maybe because a part of her—locked away deep inside—hoped the man Heath had become had remained that trustworthy island boy who had watched her with furtive glances and rare smiles.

This paperwork showed that he was just a man—like any other—looking out for himself.

And for reasons she wasn't interested in pursuing—it hurt.

HEATH CAUGHT LILAH AS SHE was leaving, her eyes red but otherwise dry. She stopped and gave Heath a look of apology but shrugged. "I guess I knew that wasn't going to go well," she said, her voice scratchy yet soft. "I let her down. I knew it was coming."

"You didn't let anyone down," he disagreed, still hot. "She put you in a position where you were doomed to fail. Don't let her off the hook so easily. She has to shoulder some of the responsibility, too. It's not right for her to make you assume the role you were never groomed to take. Pops always made it pretty clear that he thought Lora would take over the running of Larimar, which is why she's on the estate paperwork."

Lilah nodded, but she was plainly still miserable. His heart broke for the young woman and even though she was an adult and clearly not a little girl anymore, he gathered her in his arms and hugged her tight. "Don't let her get to you. She's all bark and no bite," he assured Lilah, and she shuddered against him, clinging to him like a spider monkey. "She has a tendency to lash out when she's backed into a corner. She'll come to her senses and realize what a royal—well, for lack of a better word—bitch she's been and maybe if an apology isn't in her vocabulary she'll at least show with her actions that she's sorry."

At that Lilah lifted her head and gave him a wry look. "My sister? Show that she's sorry? I don't think she knows how."

"Well, one can hope there's some shred of humanity left in her, right?" he joked, coaxing a smile from Lilah. "It's going to be okay. I promise."

He could tell she wanted to believe him but Lilah knew the score. She knew Larimar was in trouble and she knew he was doing everything he could to fix it but if Lora worked against him instead of with him—they might lose Larimar all together. And if that happened, Pops would lose whatever bit of sanity he had left.

And that would kill them all.

"Thanks, Heath," Lilah said, pulling away. "Maybe you're right. She'll come around."

As soon as she said it, they both realized how ludicrous the statement was and burst into rueful laughter just in time for Lora to round the corner.

Lora took in the two of them sharing an easy familiarity with one another and stiffened. A warning tingle went up his back and he realized a moment too late that she'd taken the situation and spun it in a completely different direction in her head. And to prove his fear, she observed in an icy tone, "I see you're not only preying on an old man but a naive young woman, too. Tell me, Heath, are there no boundaries you won't cross?"

Lilah looked shocked and simultaneously grossed out at Lora's implication but before Lilah could defend his actions, he simply waved away her attempt with a snort of disgust Lora's way, saying, "Don't waste your breath, Lilah. Your sister is not only blind... she's an idiot."

And he stalked from the room.

LILAH FELT CAUGHT BETWEEN two opposing forces and while her loyalty ought to be with her sister, she had to admit Lora seemed to be acting deliberately difficult.

"Why are you doing this?" she cried, angry. "Can't you see that he's been nothing but helpful through this whole ordeal? When you weren't here, he stepped up and did everything he could to save Larimar."

"Do you know about the deal he struck with Pops on the gift shop?" Lora asked.

Lilah winced, knowing how her sister would interpret the deal. "Yes. But you have to know that he would never do anything that would hurt Pops or the resort. This place and our family has been his family since he was a kid. You know this better than anyone and yet, you're so willing to throw him under the bus. For what? So you can feel justified in your anger, or so you don't have to deal with the fact that when we needed you the most, you didn't come?"

Lora appeared shocked at Lilah's impassioned speech, but no one was more surprised than Lilah. She wasn't the one who took stands and got involved beyond the superficial. She hated confrontation and always sought to avoid it, but she'd reached her limit with Lora's cold and cruel attitude and since Lindy wasn't here to back her, she had to stand alone and tell her oldest sister the plain truth. What was the worst she could do? It wasn't like Lora would ground her—or worse slap her—for her opinion. And it was high time she stood up to her, anyway.

"You don't think it's coincidental that he struck that deal when Pops's mental acuity started to fail?"

"No one knew Pops's mind was slipping. He hid it from all of us for a long time. When Heath discovered what Pops had done…he felt terrible. But don't take my word for it, just ask him. He'll tell you," Lilah said, hoping she was right and that Heath would indeed, swallow his pride and tell Lora the straight truth about his guilt. But even as she knew that Heath never seemed to shy away from sharing personal information with her, there seemed to be some block between Lora and him. At one time, Lilah had wondered if Heath had had a crush on her sister but given the tension between them as they grew to adulthood, she discarded that idea. Instead, she settled on the notion that they simply didn't get along, which was a shame because Heath was probably the only person on this planet that Lora couldn't bully.

"Lilah...I know you have a soft spot for Heath but—"

"Stop. I won't listen to you pile more bricks on Heath when you have no proof that he did something to swindle Pops. It's ludicrous to begin with but I won't listen to another word so don't waste your breath. You can spend all the time you want trying to nail Heath to the wall or you can spend that energy helping us."

"I am trying to help. Don't you find it the least bit suspicious that Pops handed over all the money in the reserve account to Heath for his business when we needed that for repairs, taxes and other resort expenses?"

"No." Lilah refused to budge. Lora wanted to vilify Heath, needed to, perhaps, for her own sake but Lilah wouldn't take part. No, Lora would have to shoulder that burden on her own. "You need to take a good look at your motivation. As much as you say that you're just looking out for Pops's interests, you should look inside and see if that's true. For what it's worth, and I know you don't value my opinion because I'm just the *baby* of the family, Heath feels more like family to me than you right now. If you go after him, you're going after me, too, because I'll stand behind him." Lilah started to leave but decided to leave her sister with one final thought. "Oh, and before you start thinking something completely far afield like I've got the hots for Heath or vice versa, he's like a brother to me and I love him as such. For the record, the only Bell sister he *might've* ever had eyes for was you. A long time ago, that is. Now? I think you pretty much destroyed whatever he might've felt for you. But that should suit you just fine, right?"

And then Lilah, her heart thudding quickly and painfully in her chest, left her sister standing in the hallway with her mouth open.

Welcome home, Lora.

CHAPTER FIVE

LORA STARED AFTER HER SISTER, wondering what had just happened.

First, if she could manage to get over the shock of her baby sister bawling her out when she'd never said a cross word to her in all her life, then she could focus on the bombshell Lilah had dropped as if it'd been common knowledge and not some major revelation.

Heath? What? Of course, it mattered nothing to her if Heath had once had a crush on her, but surely she would've noticed, right?

Lora searched her memory for evidence of this so-called fondness and something sat like a forgotten relic in the recesses of her mind. A flash of laughter echoed and the image of Heath's twinkling eyes bounded back to her. Her heart warmed instantaneously until she remembered something else.

He'd left her when she'd needed him the most. She stiffened against the wave of pain that followed. It was the memory of her mother dying, a small girl's heartbreak and the search in vain for the island boy whose shoulder soothed her most. It was the pain of abandonment and loss, the humiliation of being easily left behind; Lora shied away from it as if afraid of being burned.

Stop it. Stop wallowing in stupid childish thoughts that can help no one or nothing, she berated herself even as she floundered momentarily. In Chicago, she'd been able to be exactly what she chose to show people. Here, there was too much history to hide from and too many memories that followed. She'd preferred the anonymity of her windy adopted city. She'd even come to appreciate the loneliness that dogged her when she'd found herself a moment without work to fill it. Now that she'd returned home to the island, she was surrounded by everything she'd tried to run away from.

She barked a mirthless laugh tinged with embarrassment at the idea of Heath feeling anything but animosity for her because of the way she'd treated him. Lora stared at her bare toes, squirming privately at the feeling that admission caused. She hadn't been friendly or nice to anyone, really. Lora had been hyperfocused on getting good grades so she could get into a top college and leave St. John. It wasn't that she hated the island, but her dreams were bigger than the island could hope to sustain. She returned to the memory of doing homework—a lot—and Grams teasing her about missing out on her childhood to keep her nose in a book.

She picked at a mental image, unraveling it from her cache of treasures and exhaled softly at the wince of pain from its bittersweet sting.

"You're such a lovely girl," Grams had said one day, frowning, her eyes sad. "Don't you want to go to the school dance with a nice boy?" she'd asked.

The high school had hosted a dance, something tiki-themed, of course, and Lora had been happy to miss it. The idea of mingling with the very people she sought to avoid during most days at school didn't appeal. But Grams had been truly distressed at her choosing to remain home, which Lora had found odd. "Aren't you glad I'm not running around giving you something to worry about?" Lora had said, hoping to coax a smile free from Grams's worried frown. "Enjoy the calm before the storm that will be the twins when they get to high school. Trust me, at the rate they're going through boys, they'll have to start dating from the British side of the islands just to meet someone new." She added with a shrug, "Besides, Grams, I don't have a date. No one asked me."

"How about Heath?" Grams had suggested, and now that she recalled the conversation she realized Grams had been a little quick to throw Heath's name out there. Had she known, too?

Heath, the boy who had appeared at her family's dinner table one night, obviously hungrier than she'd ever been in her life, the planes of his face sharp and angular from eating too little for too long, and she'd been shocked to see him after he'd virtually disappeared from her life overnight. After she'd recovered from the painful surprise, she'd pretended not to know him at all. It was easier than admitting that she'd been devastated when he'd disappeared. She'd had enough people abandon her in life; she didn't need another.

And if she'd noticed the furtive glances her way, she didn't acknowledge them. She supposed he had tried to make a few attempts at explaining his disappearing act but by that point, Lora had sealed her heart tight and wouldn't listen.

If she'd been nothing but cold and dismissive, the twins, on the other hand, had been delighted.

"Can we keep him?" Lindy had asked, passing the fresh papaya with a grin. When Lora had gasped that her sister had even suggested such a thing, Lilah had simply chimed in.

"I've always wanted a brother," Lilah had said in her soft, wistful voice that always managed to make it sound as if she were somewhere else in her head and not planted in the here and now like everyone else. "He seems like he'd be a very good brother."

Grams and Pops had been vastly amused by the conversation while Lora had plainly been the opposite. Now that she remembered that day, she wondered how Heath had felt about being inducted into a family without so much as a voice in the matter.

She supposed he hadn't minded—he was still hanging around.

Lora exhaled loudly and climbed to her feet, needing to clear her head. There was too much clanging around in her mind, too many variables to consider. The best course of action would require concise thinking.

Larimar was in serious trouble. And by

Lora's way of thinking, Heath was partially to blame. If he hadn't talked Pops into that business deal, at the very least the money would be there so she could straighten out this misunderstanding with the IRS. But the reserve was terribly low—barely enough to cover a plumbing issue if the need arose—and that made her alternately nervous and angry.

Well, anger was something she was familiar with and even if she wasn't proud that she'd been perpetually accused of shouldering a chip her entire life, at least she knew how to handle herself.

She didn't have enough in her own personal accounts to pay off the debt and if Heath had the money, she was fairly certain he would've paid the debt by now. At the very least, to her knowledge, he wasn't one to shirk his debts.

And, whether she liked it or not, Heath truly loved her family and they loved him.

So that left one option—an option she wasn't comfortable with, but when backed into a corner one could either spit and scratch or surrender quietly to fight another day.

Lora flopped on her childhood bed, the scent of summer and sun surrounding her, and stared at the ceiling.

"Damn it," she murmured, a well of frustration laced with something else. She'd have to put aside her grievances with Heath and work with him to fix this problem. However, as soon as Larimar was in the clear, she would be having a serious discussion with him about moving his business out of Larimar. If he wanted to be a businessman, he could peddle his goods elsewhere. She wasn't interested in his success or failure—only that of Larimar.

Tomorrow she'd call a meeting with Heath and try to work out a solution together. A small, reluctant grin found her lips as she chuckled without humor. Grams was probably watching from her beach in heaven—giggling.

The mad woman had always enjoyed stirring things up.

HEATH DOVE ONE LAST TIME under the dusky waves as the sun crested the horizon, bathing the beach in soft amber-yellow light. He always swam with the morning light, enjoying the way the water muted the early chorus of bugs and birds welcoming the day with a cacophony of noise. The brief moment of stillness soothed his turbulent thoughts and he welcomed the respite.

He was a ways from the shore. Flipping on his back, he floated, gazing at the breaking dawn sky, loving his slice of heaven no matter how difficult it seemed to make a living. If it weren't for tourists and the internet…he'd be screwed.

Sighing, he turned and made a slow, almost reluctant return to the beach, only to find Lora walking the shore, her white gauzy sarong swaying with the movement of her hips. She walked head down, gazing at her feet in the soft sugar-white sand as the water reached for her with each tidal surge. Her hair drifted down her back, rippling in lazy waves, the humidity curling her hair with wild abandon. Something in him clenched, twisting him in knots, a remnant from the time when he was a poor, neglected island boy with nothing to his name and even less to aspire to as both his parents had run off, leaving him to fend for himself at the age of ten.

What was it about Lora that made him want what she'd never offered? He'd been a fool then, but he wasn't the same love-struck boy now. Today he saw her for what she was, a beautiful woman with ice in her veins.

"I brought this for you," a voice whispered from his past, the hushed voice of a young

Lora as she handed him a basket of fresh fruit and beef pâté. "The pâté is fresh. Pops bought it from Simon today."

The sharp hunger cramping his belly roared like an angry beast at the sight of the basket and the knowledge that food was inside. He took the basket, not sure why she was being so nice. He'd seen her around the island in the square; she was hard to miss with that dark hair and exotic features, and he'd followed her home, curious to see where such a beautiful girl lived. Lora must've seen him creeping along the fringe of the private beach, but worse, she must've guessed the hollows in his cheeks weren't natural. He'd like to say he accepted the basket with some sort of grace, but as he flushed with the memory, he remembered how it'd happened.

He'd torn into the basket and eaten the entire pâté before Lora's astonished eyes with great gobbling bites, stuffing his mouth until he thought he might choke but he hadn't eaten anything aside from what he could scrounge from the restaurant scraps for the past month. He might've been two steps away from death, if it hadn't been for Lora's basket.

And then, clutching the basket to his chest, he'd run away.

He'd come back the following day, seeing her at the marketplace buying fresh fruit. She'd caught sight of him and waved him over. He'd shyly thanked her for the food, but stopped short of telling her just how bad things were for him. She seemed to understand that he was holding something back and must've known what it was like to need to keep some things private, because she didn't mention it again. In no time, they'd become fast friends. He'd meet her in the plaza and they'd spend the day romping around, swimming, fishing, sharing smoothies.

Until the day came when he'd come home and discovered his parents had truly taken off for good this time. He'd been terrified. So he'd tried to follow. With disastrous results.

It would be a year before he saw her again when Pops brought him to the resort on the guise of needing a young strapping boy to do the heavy lifting for him in the form of odd jobs.

That'd been the year Pops had unofficially adopted him.

Lora hadn't been happy. In fact, she was so cold and closed off, he almost wondered if she remembered that he was the same boy that she'd saved from starving only a year prior. She'd rebuffed any attempt he'd made to explain, sending the message quite clearly that whatever they'd had before he left, hadn't survived the absence. Which, honestly, if he hadn't developed feelings for her, would've been fine. But that's not how it had turned out. He'd been doomed to fall for Lora Bell because fate had decided his life hadn't been filled with enough turmoil.

Man, when he thought of how many nights he'd stayed awake thinking about Lora…good God. It made him sick to think of all that wasted time.

Shaking off the memory with effort, he exhaled and walked from the water, startling Lora with his appearance, as he headed for the towel he'd hung on a tree. Her eyes widened and her mouth dropped open as an involuntary, gasped squeak gave away her distress.

Probably because he was nude.

"WHAT ARE YOU DOING?" Lora managed to blurt out, squeezing her eyes shut and wishing she could scrub her brain but it was no use, nothing would erase what she'd seen—Heath in all his morning glory—and she was fairly certain she was scarred for life. A growing heat in the center of her belly caused her to squirm as disquiet at her own reaction made her want to run away. But she couldn't very well turn tail and run like a scared little rabbit just because she'd happened to catch Heath in his birthday suit. His wasn't the first penis she'd ever seen, for crying out loud. *But...* she thought miserably, clenching her fists at her sides, she'd be a liar if she'd said she'd seen a larger one. Admitting such a thing made her want to grind her eyes out—and her brain—for even allowing the unfortunate observation. "This is a private beach...with guests. Please put some clothes on!"

Heath's chuckle caused her to turn and glare. Thankfully, he'd wrapped the towel around his middle, covering his offending nudity, but oddly he looked twice as attractive as before—did she say attractive? No, she meant...distracting—and her breath caught unnecessarily in her chest. "What if a guest had stumbled across your early-morning swim? Did you think of that? Need I remind you we're trying to save Larimar, not scare away the income source."

"Calm down," he said, that damnable half smirk on his face. "I do this all the time. No one is up when I go out and because it is private, no one bothers me. Besides, you can't tell me you never went skinny-dipping in your life?"

"That wasn't my thing," she replied stiffly, hating how prudish she sounded. Sexually, she was as adventurous as the next person, perhaps even more so, but she had no wish to prove herself on that score with Heath. Just the idea made her intensely uncomfortable.

"Ah, that's right. That was Lindy who was always looking for an excuse to run around naked," he said, with the hint of a tease in his voice. She looked at him sharply, hating the idea of Heath looking at her sister with anything more than friendly attention and he shook his head at her narrowed stare of accusation. "No, Lora," he said, sighing as he did a quick shake of his head to clear the water from his ear. "I never thought of Lindy or Lilah that way. To me, they're like my sisters. If anything I was always chasing the boys away from the twins. You don't remember?"

Lora did a surreptitious search of her memory for something that supported that statement and when she came up with nothing, she gave a small shrug as if it didn't matter one way or another. "Whatever, Heath. Let's start over," she suggested, simply happy to return the conversation to business, which was more in line with her comfort level. "I've been thinking about everything that was said yesterday and—" she drew a deep breath "—it would seem that working together to solve this problem is the best course of action given your business arrangement with Pops is so tightly bound to Larimar's operations." She couldn't help the tiny strain of reproach that coated her words—she was still angry with him—but he appeared to let it slide and simply nodded. She continued, grudgingly giving him silent props for not taking the bait. "So, if your schedule allows, I'd like to set up a meeting sometime today so we can go over some plans to fix this mess."

"I'll check my calendar," he said.

She frowned. "Well, I assume it is your top priority as well as mine to get this figured out."

"Of course."

"Oh. Okay," she said, not quite sure what to make of Heath's answers. He was saying the right thing but she sensed something else beneath the words. "I was thinking early afternoon, say, two o'clock?" she suggested. He surprised her with a counter offer.

"How about lunch?"

"Lunch?"

"Yeah, you do eat, right?"

"Of course I do. I just don't know why we can't meet in the office…"

"Because I think better when I have food in front of me," he said, his answer immediately causing a memory of that undernourished, starving boy to crowd her mind. She ruthlessly pushed it away but offered a terse "Fine. Lunch. Rush Tide Bar and Grill?"

"The Wild Donkey," he countered.

"That's where the locals hang out," she said, not happy about his suggestion.

He stared at her with a faintly sardonic expression. "Aren't you local?"

Not for a long time. She swallowed, hating the fact that he was pointing out how apart she'd made herself over the years. But to admit that was to admit a weakness, that she'd allowed something to have power over her. She lifted her chin with a shrug. "Fine. But if it ends up being too loud and we can't hear ourselves think, you're buying."

He lifted two fingers to his forehead in a mock salute and said, "See you at lunch, then. Bring your appetite. Boiled bananas are on the special today."

He walked away, his calf muscles straining as he climbed the short hill in the soft shifting sand. She couldn't help but stare and not because his body was worth staring at—even though it was—but because she loved boiled bananas.

And somehow, she had the sinking suspicion he had remembered.

CHAPTER SIX

LILAH DUG HER TOES IN the warm sand and used a tiny stick to idly doodle while her thoughts did an excellent job of preventing any peace.

Having her sister home should be a joyous time of reunions, laughter and reminiscing, right?

Instead the arrival of her sister caused turmoil and a twisted stomach. As if on cue, her gut gurgled and she sighed. She tossed the stick and gazed out at the calm, azure ocean, watching the sailboats in the distance rounding St. Thomas or heading off to St. Croix. She'd never understood her sisters' need to escape the island. Here she knew peace and the island pace suited her perfectly. She ate papaya and fresh coconut for breakfast, swam in the afternoon and sunned like a lizard on a rock until she felt a tad overheated and then jumped back in the water. What wasn't to love? She particularly enjoyed the secluded nature of the island. It was only a twenty-minute ferry ride from St. Thomas and everyone knew everyone in the tight-knit community.

But Lora had always felt apart from the islanders, even though they'd lived there since they were little kids. She and Lindy had easily adapted whereas Lora had been uncomfortably distant with anyone who'd tried to make a connection.

Lilah loved her sister but there was a gap between them that as time had gone on had only widened. Now with the pressure of Lora's disappointment between them as well, that gap was nearly as wide as the ocean. Lilah rose and dusted the sand from her behind and walked straight into the surf before diving cleanly into the still tepid water. She swam with languid strokes, in no hurry or rush, the movement of her arms and legs through the water soothing her like a mother's caress.

She didn't know how to mend the situation with Lora.

She didn't know how to help save Larimar.

She didn't know how she'd ever manage to measure up to her superstar sisters.

But for the moment—she didn't care.

THE ONE THING ABOUT BEING on a Caribbean island that was sorely different from living in the Windy City was that getting ready to go out was shockingly simple. There was no need for makeup or complicated and fussy hairdos because within minutes the wicked humidity would have all your attention to vanity sliding down your face. And that same humidity made you so hot and sticky that wearing anything more than the barest of clothing was terribly ill-advised.

So dressing for her so-called business meeting with Heath was easy—a tank top and a light gauzy skirt, but she'd be a liar if she didn't admit to hesitating before the mirror wondering if she ought to put some effort into taming her wild hair. It was too hot to care, a voice said and she plainly agreed, but without her usual power accessories—the tailored business suit that clung to her curves like it was drawn on her body, the perfectly coiffed hairstyle, and the designer heels that cost more than any shoe ever should—she felt woefully vulnerable.

Added to that, the memory of Heath's naked body continued to badger her, popping into her mind at the most inopportune moments. Such as when she was in the shower, sliding the loofah soaped with lavender shower gel, inadvertently touching herself with more than a perfunctory scrub.

Her cheeks heated. Yes, that was a problem, she noted with a flush of irritation. She wasn't accustomed to discussing business across the table from someone whom she'd seen naked only hours before.

Had her gaze lingered? She'd thought that she'd jerked her stare away as if scalded but her mind was recalling every detail with the accuracy of a high resolution graphic.

Oh, gracious. It was readily apparent she'd gone too long without a lover. Her hormones were playing tricks on her brain. With that thought in mind, she raked her hair up to twist into a messy bun. It was too hot to have it down, she realized, and if she hadn't spent so much time considering the possibilities of her hairstyle, she would've come to that conclusion easily.

Except a tiny, infinitesimal part of her had noted how Heath's attention had been drawn to her hair—the look in his eyes betraying him as easily as if he'd admitted he was mesmerized by the dark mass and longed to bury his nose against her scalp. She gave a little involuntary shudder and it wasn't entirely one of disapproval. No…unfortunately, it smacked of something more akin to desire, arousal and need.

And that didn't bode well at all.

HEATH ARRIVED AT THE WILD Donkey a few minutes late, which by island time was actually considered early. Although judging by the stiff set of shoulders and tight jaw, clearly Lora didn't remember that fact about island life. He could've been on time, truth be told, he enjoyed messing with her just a bit. The woman needed to loosen up and, for God's sake, take that stick out of her ass.

"You order yet?" he asked, waving and smiling to some familiar faces before sitting across from Lora. Damn her, she was gorgeous. Her glorious hair was twisted into a messy knot at the back of her head but the balmy air had taken hold of the tendrils and curled them against her jawline, softening the angular lines of that classically beautiful face. Everyone had always thought Lindy was the hot sister, followed closely by Lilah because they both had that certain something about them that drew people, but he'd always thought people were clearly blind. Lora was simply stunning.

"No, I was waiting for you," she answered, clearly uncomfortable in the surroundings. Her gaze darted from one person to another, unsure of herself and the situation. He found her discomfort faintly amusing. A casual observer might think she was a tourist who'd inadvertently wandered onto local turf where the natives were hostile. But at one time, Heath knew for a fact that The Wild Donkey had been one of her favorite haunts for the boiled bananas alone. "The place looks the same, right?" he asked.

"It seems to," she answered, glancing around before quickly adding, "from what I can remember. It's not like I spent a lot of time here."

"That's not true," he refuted easily, curious as to why she was adamant about smothering any memory of her childhood. Was admitting she'd enjoyed the local fare some kind of weakness? "You and I used to hang out here a lot. Before I left."

Her gaze shot to his, faltering as if she wasn't prepared to talk about that. She swallowed then shrugged. "I'd forgotten."

"You know, I've always wanted to tell you where I went that year I went away..."

"Heath, please. I didn't come to talk about

our childhood. It doesn't matter to me where you went when you disappeared," she said with false laughter, the vulnerability in her gaze calling into question her flip tone. "Besides, I don't recall asking you for details then, and I certainly don't need details now. What's most important is putting together a solid plan for Larimar. I have some ideas that I'd like to go over—"

"Always business," Heath interrupted, sighing with disappointment. He'd hoped that bringing her to a local place would've softened her up a bit but she'd moved right past any nostalgia she may have felt and jumped headlong into the problems at hand. "Can the business wait until we've ordered, at least?" he asked, and she reluctantly nodded in answer. He stood and walked to the counter to give their orders, then returned with two beers.

"Oh," she started, when he put her drink in front of her. "I don't drink beer."

"Since when?" he asked, taking a healthy swig. Ah, nothing like cold beer on a hot day. He watched her, trying to see her as nothing more than a pain-in-the-ass business associate but it was a struggle. The island had already started to put a faint rose in her cheeks, pinking them prettily and those long dusky lashes were almost criminal. He ignored the pang in his chest and drained his beer.

She stiffened. "Since I prefer wine."

"Suit yourself. Right to business, then?"

"Yes," she said, seeming relieved. "I haven't had a chance to go into the gift shop yet to check the inventory but I assume it's the same stuff we used to sell years ago, right?"

"Wrong," he said, wiping the condensation away from his empty mug with his thumb. Her puzzled frown said it all. The islanders weren't the only ones who resisted change. "We stopped selling that stuff because it wasn't any different from any other place on the island. T-shirts, mugs, typical airport tourist stuff that was priced higher than the Captain's Corner in the square was just sitting on the shelves. So we scrapped that inventory and started fresh."

She narrowed her stare. "There was a significant dollar amount attached to that inventory. What did you do with it?"

"We put a deep discount on the merchandise that still had value and then we tossed the rest to make room for the new inventory."

Her eyes bulged. "You tossed it? On whose authority?"

"Pops." He held up his hand to calm the storm that was building behind her eyes. "And before you lose your cool, Pops agreed that the old stuff was a drain and it needed to go. Besides, that junk had been sitting on the shelves for so long it had long lost its value."

"What's done is done, I suppose," she said, though it looked as though she was conceding the point under duress. "So what's this new inventory?"

He drew a deep breath, feeling unaccountably nervous. It wasn't as if he needed her approval but somewhere deep inside, he wanted to show her what he truly did for a living and it had nothing to do with being a handyman.

IN SPITE OF WHAT SHE'D declared earlier, Lora grabbed her beer and took a sip. It was hot in the bar, she was parched and well, she might've fibbed a little. She did drink an occasional beer but only in private. It wouldn't do for clients to see her guzzling a brewsky like some blue-collar laborer when discussing million-dollar deals. She'd since learned to appreciate fine wine but she wouldn't say she loved it. In fact, as the beer hit her tongue, she realized with a soft noise of appreciation, there were times when she really wanted nothing more than a simple beer.

When Heath lifted a brow, she said in defense, "I'm thirsty," and gestured for him to continue with his explanation of why he thought it would be wise to levy the resort's revenue stream with something new and untried.

"We replaced the old inventory with items handcrafted by locals."

"Such as?"

"Jewelry and fused-glass creations mostly."

"Jewelry? Fused glass? Those aren't exactly impulse buys," she protested, frowning. "Tourists want T-shirts that say I Drank Rum at Larimar or Set Your Watch to Island Time at St. John for $19.99, they don't want expensive trinkets."

"They're not trinkets," he said, a scowl deepening on his face. "They're handcrafted works of art. And for your information, they're selling better than any of that other crap ever did."

"If that's the case, where's the proof? We're still in the hole and Larimar is being harassed by the IRS."

He looked away. "It's taking a little longer than I anticipated to recoup the investment but the return is there. We just started a new website and we're going to start selling through the site."

"Larimar isn't a port for internet commerce," she said in distaste. "My grandparents worked to create a brand for the resort as a high-end place with a bohemian style. It flies in the face of everything they've worked for to start hawking merchandise on the web. I don't like it," she said firmly.

"You haven't even seen what we're doing yet."

"What is this 'we' business?" she retorted, fresh annoyance washing over her for being so out of the loop. She hated that all this had gone down without her knowledge, particularly since now she knew that her grandfather had made all these decisions when he clearly hadn't been in his right mind to do so. She shifted her gaze Heath's way, hating that she was in this position with him and forced to work together. "To me, it seems all these decisions were made essentially by you. I haven't seen a business plan, you've avoided a real sit-down to talk this out, and all I see is my family's resort drowning because you made a bad call for selfish reasons. Come on, now. Seriously? Put yourself in my shoes for just a second and then tell me to relax. There's a lot at stake, Heath."

His mouth tightened and she knew she'd hit a nerve. Good. Surely he didn't think she'd just roll over and let him do whatever he pleased with her family's legacy just because he'd managed to talk her Pops into an ill-advised business arrangement? No, he was smarter than that but the way he was sending her hard stares told her he wasn't happy with her questions.

"I didn't agree to go to lunch with you so that we could argue," he said finally, leaning back in the chair as if he needed to put distance between them. "How about this…just look at the inventory and then decide if you hate it. Okay?"

She supposed that was fair but she doubted there was anything that would sway her opinion. She knew marketing, it was what she did back in Chicago and she did it well. Or at least she used to think so. She shook off that depressing thought.

She did know that a resort outside on the fringe of town wasn't likely to move a lot of ritzy inventory in their little gift shop—no matter how much Heath believed it would.

Lora withheld the sharp dressing-down that

she would've let fly if he were simply another business associate seeking her involvement with a cockamamy idea that was likely to cost a lot and return little, but she held her tongue. He was asking a small thing, and she supposed in deference to the care he'd shown with Pops and Lilah, she could give it to him.

"All right, I'll withhold my final judgment until I see what kind of inventory and marketing plan you've put together for the new gift shop, but—"

"No *buts*," Heath interjected with a short grin that was oddly endearing even though she hated being interrupted. "You said you'd give it a chance. I'd call that a successful business meeting. So let's call it a day on the business lunch and actually take time to eat and enjoy."

She opened her mouth to clarify but their order had arrived and with the first bite of that boiled banana, the distinctive flavor bursting on her tastebuds, she realized she hadn't eaten this particular island dish since Grams had died.

"As good as you remember?" he asked around a hot bite.

Tears stung her eyes and she ducked her head so he wouldn't see the moisture welling.

"Pretty good," she managed to answer. "But then how hard is it to boil a banana?" she said, trying for flip but even to her own ears it sounded woefully obvious that she was struggling to maintain her composure. *Oh, damn,* she thought, wiping away the tears that had begun to fall. She shrugged, suddenly without words. She missed Grams so much it hurt. This was why she avoided the island, her sisters, Pops, even boiled bananas.

And right about now, as the pain of her grief rolled over her, avoidance had seemed like a pretty good method of dealing.

CHAPTER SEVEN

SHE LOOKED UP AND SAW Heath watching her with knowing, something she wasn't used to seeing reflected at her on someone else's face. Mostly because she never allowed anyone to get that close. "I wish you wouldn't do that," she said.

"Do what?"

"Look at me like you know me." She lifted her chin. "Because you don't know me. Not really. I'm not the same person I was when I lived here and even when I was here I wouldn't say we were close."

Heath held her stare for a long moment and she was overwhelmed by the irrational and childish urge to jump up and run away but she held her ground. Then Heath lifted his shoulder in a shrug and took another bite, any warmth that may have been there before had fled. "Remembering that you liked boiled bananas doesn't mean anything. Don't read more into it than what it is."

"Good," she said, stiffly satisfied, yet she couldn't help the feeling that she'd just cut her nose to spite her face. "Good," she repeated, taking another bite. "Glad we're on the same page."

Same page, same book…so why did she feel a lingering sense of disappointment?

Lora knew how people felt about her—that surely she couldn't share DNA with the twins, who were both in their own way charismatic and engaging, or Grams and Pops who had never met a person they didn't like—and honestly, she hadn't cared what other people thought, which had come in handy when it'd been time to be ruthless in her career. But, right now, seeing the cool, open dislike shining in Heath's eyes, she felt more than disappointment, she felt the pinch of regret. It wasn't Heath's fault that she had difficulty letting people get close to her, and thus far he'd been fairly civil when she had not. But even knowing an apology was due on her part, she couldn't get the words free from her mouth.

It'd always been this way with her. For some reason, apologizing had been her biggest struggle. Something Grams had clucked her teeth in disapproval over each time she'd found herself in such a position.

But Grams wasn't here any longer and there was no one to remind her when she needed to swallow a bit of humble pie. Oddly, she missed Grams for that, too, even though when it'd happened, she'd wanted to howl at the moon with frustration.

"What's your job like in Chicago?" Heath asked, presumably to move the conversation to more neutral territory. Of course, he didn't know that her job was another subject she wanted to steer clear of. She avoided looking at him and tossed her banana peel onto her plate along with her other trash. "Pops says you're pretty important with your company. He's real proud, you know."

She dusted her hands and then wiped the beads of sweat away. If only Pops knew what she did for a living, he might not be so quick to praise. She'd never felt a twinge of conscience for any of the underhanded, dirty tricks she'd pulled to win a client over a competitor, considering all things fair in love and war—and the kind of business she dealt in was certainly war. But now that she'd been cast adrift by the very people who'd praised her ruthlessness a year ago, it'd forced her to take a hard look at what she did for a living. And she wasn't comfortable with what she saw. Why the attack of conscience she didn't know, but as of late she'd felt as though she'd been beaten with a sharp stick. It was a hard pill to swallow, realizing that perhaps at her core, no one liked her for good reason. "It's a job, like any other and I'm good at it," she said, hoping to put an end to the conversation. "It pays the bills. How about you?" Was she really making small talk? She almost grimaced at her own dialogue, wondering how normal people have meandering conversations about nothing in particular. When Lora went to dinner or lunch with someone, she had an agenda. She knew why she was going and had a strategy to put into play. Without that mental itinerary, she wasn't sure how to be social, especially with someone like Heath.

"Larimar keeps me busy, but I love it," he said simply. "Although I have bigger dreams than just Larimar."

She regarded him with mild surprise and faint embarrassment. Her expression must've been transparent because he said, "You didn't think I had dreams, too? That maybe all I ever aspired to be was a handyman for a resort I didn't own or ever have any hope of owning?"

If he was mocking her, she probably deserved it, since that's exactly what she'd thought of Heath. Well, that was giving herself too much credit. She'd never considered Heath's hopes or dreams. The conversation, she noted with an uncomfortable twinge, was making her appear terribly self-absorbed, yet another character flaw Grams had hoped to root out and failed.

Heath saved her from answering, saying, "It's okay. I get it. Why would the neglected kid of notorious drug addicts who *gahn een* have dreams bigger than he deserved to dream, right?"

Gahn een, Crucian for someone who'd lost their mind to drugs, she thought. Her knowledge of the language was rusty but coming back to her. She'd never asked about Heath's parents, but had gathered enough through the whisperings between Pops and Grams. Lora shook her head, murmuring, "No, of course not," she said, though her cheeks heated at the lie. It was one thing to admit she was self-involved to herself, yet another to admit it out loud. This conversation was becoming more awkward by the minute, she wanted to groan. She grabbed her purse, prepared to pay Heath back for the lunch, when he stayed her hand. She stared at him, perplexed. "I have to pay you back," she said.

He stood, flashing a brief subtle smile that made his hazel eyes look terribly alluring, and said, "Don't worry about it. I'm a businessman now. I need the deductions. You can catch the next one."

Lora nodded, her heart fluttering in an odd dance of impropriety, and rose, eager to get away from Heath, the painfully awkward conversation, and the disconcerting feelings that were suddenly making an appearance at the most inopportune moments.

"Right. Good. Yes, you want to keep all receipts," she said, searching for a way to lessen the discomfort she felt. "And make sure you have a date book or mile log that you can reference with appointments to prove business expenses. That way if you ever get audited you have backup of expenses. Well, at least that's what I do...I like to have all bases covered."

He gave her another mock salute as he said, "Thanks. Who'd have ever thought you'd be giving me business advice?" He grinned and she realized he was trying to lighten things between them. She attempted a small smile but felt completely out of her element so she stopped, instead clearing her throat and saying, "So, in light of your request that I check out the inventory before I judge the contents, would you like to meet back in about an hour or so? I have a few errands to run before then, otherwise, I'd say let's do it now. Every moment we don't put a plan into action, is another moment lost to fix things."

"Yeah, sure," he said, his eyes losing the faint amusement in their depths. "An hour sounds good."

"Great. See you then."

They parted ways and Lora exhaled the breath that had felt trapped in her chest.

Why was this happening to her now of all times? If she and Heath had been destined to suffer through some kind of relationship, it would've been more convenient to go through it in their teens when things had been far more simple. They could've gone through whatever angsty romance teens do and then walked away when it was time to end things. Now—and she wasn't saying she wanted to encourage whatever was happening at the moment—was terribly bad timing with the possibility of messy consequences.

Oh, who was she kidding? Lora wanted to snort. She wouldn't have been open to a relationship with Heath when they were teens. In spite of the fact that he'd always been around,

Lora had gone out of her way to make sure he knew she wasn't open to friendship, much less romance. She closed her eyes briefly before they snapped back open again. She'd been a royal pain, and even Grams, who'd loved her dearly, had been aggravated at times by Lora's rigid and disapproving attitude.

"Child, you've the soul of a grouchy old man whose shorts are too tight," Grams had scolded one day when Lora had sniped at Heath for something. She couldn't even remember what she'd been perturbed about but she surely remembered Grams reaction. "If you don't change your tune, you're going to end up singing alone."

She smiled in spite of the memory being a less than flattering one. Grams had always had her number. She missed Grams terribly—especially now when her world had been dumped upside down. Somehow Grams would've known what to say or do to get Lora to see things in a different light.

Of course, if Grams had lived, she likely would've had a few things to say about the way Lora lived her life. Grams would've said, "Didn't I raise you better than that?"

The short answer was yes. But nothing was as simple as that. She thought of Heath and somehow she knew that he would never compromise his values to get ahead.

That's half the problem, she grumbled to the idealistic voice in her head. Maybe if Heath had been less of a romantic, he might've seen that his business plan was flawed, which was why Larimar was in this pickle.

She didn't care what Heath said, pricey trinkets, homemade or otherwise, were not what people wanted to stuff in their carry-on bag when they left the resort. They wanted silly, fun, vacation mementos to put on their desk at work. They wanted a reminder of the fun and frivolous time they had in the Virgin Islands—and nothing said fun and frivolous better than a goofy magnet or coffee mug. In her experience, T-shirts were best because they rolled up easily in the luggage and after the cheap ink had faded after one or two washings, it could be used as a workout shirt or as a dust rag.

"Ohh, my…is that Lora Bell?" An incredulous and surprised voice cut into her thoughts and caused her to turn. She saw a woman, roughly Lora's age, walking toward her holding her straw hat on her head. It was a full, confusion-driven minute before Lora realized she was looking at one of her schoolmates. The woman approached and gave Lora a hug. "Look at you! You haven't aged a minute since we graduated! What are you up to?"

Lora forced a smile but for the life of her couldn't remember the woman's name. Talk about awkward. "Just working...visiting family right now. How about you?" she said, cleverly getting out of needing to use the woman's first name.

"Can't complain. I summer on the island and go stateside to make some cash. You know how it is. Times are hard. Even the locals can't seem to stay on the island all year-round unless they're rich." The woman grinned knowingly as she said, "But then you know that. Larimar is one of the nicest resorts on the island. I was real sorry to hear about your Pops, though. That must be a terrible burden."

"Oh? What did you hear?" she asked, not liking that a complete stranger seemed to know more about her grandfather than she did.

"Just that he was having a bit of a hard time nowadays. Happens to the best of us. My *nona* had the same problem. We ended up having to put her in a home because she wandered too much and we were afraid she was going to wander right into the ocean and drown. Have you considered a home yet? There's a nice one in St. Thomas that is real clean and whatnot. I should get you the name and phone number," she said, suddenly fishing in her purse. "Let me see if I can find a pen and paper."

Pops would hate being anywhere near St. Thomas. It wasn't his cup of tea, as Grams would often say. In fact, when the major shopping had to be done, Grams always did it because Pops did nothing but complain about the crazy drivers and the subsequent traffic. "Thanks but we're not to that point yet," Lora said. "He's doing just fine, actually. He's not wandering or anything like that."

The woman lifted her brow. "Really? I thought I heard someone say that he'd wandered about and fallen. Cracked his head open and needed stitches."

Damn small island. The grapevine was wicked quick with anything juicy. "Well, he's fine. Thanks for asking," Lora said with a smile, without actually addressing the woman's query. "It was great to see you again…" She trailed, hoping the woman would get the hint and move on as well, but she didn't.

"I can't even remember the last time I saw you. Last I heard you were leaving the island and never coming back." She laughed and Lora smiled wanly. Yes, she'd been a bit vocal in her disdain for island life. Her cheeks threatened to bloom with embarrassment but she managed to keep her reaction in check. Who was this woman, anyway? Before Lora had a chance to search her memory further, the woman eyed her speculatively, saying, "Well, you always had big dreams. How'd that work out for you?"

"Great. I was—*am*—the marketing director of a large firm in Chicago. I'm just here to help out the family with a few things then I'm back to Chicago," Lora lied with a bright smile as if everything in her life was just ducky and she had nothing but rainbows and butterflies in her rearview mirror. With a sudden flash of recognition, Lora realized who she was talking to and her gaze narrowed quickly. Natty George. They'd hated each other in high school. Natty had been one of those girls who had gone out of her way to make sure Lora had felt uncomfortable and awkward in social settings. And she was pretty sure Natty had had an insane crush on Heath.

As if zeroing in on Lora's train of thought, Natty said, "So how's it going with Heath? I always wondered how he managed to get in with your family resort when he's not even related. I figured he must've done something right with one of you girls," Natty said with a wink. "Not that I blame you one iota. That man could melt ice with that body."

Immediately incensed by the assumption that Heath must've been sleeping with her or her sisters to become a part of the resort had her snapping as she set Natty straight. "Heath has been a part of our family for years, since he was a kid. We might not share a drop of blood but my grandfather considers him family just the same and not because he's hooking up with any of us."

Natty seemed affronted by Lora's curt response and said, "Well, look who's all territorial all of a sudden. I certainly didn't mean to offend you. Of course, Heath's a great guy. No complaints in that department. I know firsthand what a generous and *loving* man he is."

"Oh?"

"Of course," Natty said, her gaze turning sly in a manner that made Lora inexplicably irritated. "Obviously, you've been off island for too long. There's a shortage of good men available and Heath Cannon is one of the top prizes here." She sighed, regretfully. "Unfortunately, none have managed to hold on to him for long. He's a confirmed bachelor. More's the pity. That man is a cool drink of water on a hot day, if you know what I mean. Oh, what am I saying, of course you know. You'd have to be blind not to."

Straightening, Lora didn't know what to say to that. It made her intensely uncomfortable to be standing there chatting about Heath's attributes to a woman she hadn't seen since high school and didn't have great memories of besides, and squirming privately at the thought of Heath knocking boots with this woman.

"Speak of the devil…"

Lora turned sharply to see Heath striding toward them. She groaned inwardly. She certainly didn't want him involved with this conversation.

"Natty, good to see you. What's shaking?" he asked, folding Natty into an easy hug. Lora couldn't help the way her body stiffened at the sight but her own reaction was troubling. She imagined quills poking out all over her body in response.

"She was just telling me how you two have

shared some quality time together," Lora said, turning to Heath and secretly taking pleasure in the way his cheeks pinked. Oh, so they *had* slept together. Natty wasn't embellishing for effect. Good to know.

"We went on a few dates," Heath answered carefully, shooting a look Natty's way that could almost be deemed quizzical. "But we figured out we were better as friends. Right, Natty?"

Natty shrugged. "I suppose that's how you remember it. But as I recall, I was ready to take it to the next level," she teased.

Lora had had enough of this particular conversation and tried to gracefully bow out. "So nice catching up with you but I have a ton of things to do so…"

"Actually, I was hoping to catch a ride with you back to Larimar. I just let Lilah take the other Jeep."

Natty momentarily forgotten, Lora frowned. "Where'd Lilah go? Who's watching Pops?"

Natty sighed and shook her head. "I can still get the number of that place in St. Thomas if you like—"

"Natty, please. I'm not putting my grandfather in a home. Now, if you don't mind, I have to go."

"There's no shame in admitting you've bitten off more than you can chew," Natty called after her as Lora and Heath walked to the Jeep. Lora resisted the urge to say something rude and kept walking. Put her Pops in a home? Yeah, right, like that was ever going to happen. And who said she'd bitten off more than she could chew? Lora was the queen of handling things others choked on.

"What was that all about?" Heath asked.

"I didn't know you dated Natty George," she said instead.

"Two dates...consisting of dinner and a movie in St. Thomas. Not exactly what I'd consider spending quality time."

"That's not what she said," Lora countered, wondering where she was going with the conversation. Was she fishing for information? Perhaps. She needed to know what kind of people Heath was associating with when he was supposed to be looking out for Larimar. "It's your business who you date—"

"Yes, it is," he said, amused.

She ignored that, continuing, "But I would advise you to be more choosy about your dating partners. Natty George, if she's anything like she was in high school, was not a very nice person."

"Neither were you," he pointed out, adding, "but I believe people can change."

She glared. He'd effectively boxed her in with that comment. "Well, I don't," she said. "People are who they are and other people just need to accept that."

"Why?"

His blunt question sucked the wind from her sails. Why did she believe that people couldn't change? Or was it that she believed *she* couldn't change? There were times when she wished she were more like her sisters, so easygoing and effervescently charming, but after she got over her little pity party she realized she had to stop wishing for the moon because no one was going to deliver. "They just do," she answered.

"Ah, excellent answer," he mocked, shaking his head. "Lora, of all people I have reason to believe that people don't change. My parents never gave me a reason to hope for anything different but I believe in my heart that if people have the will, they can change."

"That's naive," she retorted, climbing into the Jeep as Heath followed. "People cling to patterns because that's what life is all about, a series of repeating patterns. It's the same in marketing. Trends go in cycles. There are no new concepts, just the way we package them for consumption. If you're aware of this, you can stay ahead in the game."

"There is no game. Just people," Heath said. "And people can and do change if they want it bad enough."

Lora wanted to groan or worse, bop Heath over the head with something blunt. People didn't change. Plain and simple. Why'd he have to go all philosophical and Dalai Lama on her? It only made her look shallow and petty for being truthful. She switched subjects quickly. "So are there any more of our classmates you dated that I might know?" she asked, feigning some sort of conversational tone.

"Why the curiosity?"

"Why not answer the question?"

He chuckled and shook his head. "A few. Nothing really serious."

"No one?" She found that hard to believe. Maybe he was a truly confirmed bachelor. "No one caught your eye? What, are you difficult to get along with?"

He laughed. "I don't think so. What do you think?"

"I think you have a very annoying habit of answering a question with another question. That's definitely a character flaw. Shows that you have something to hide."

"Oh, really? I didn't realize you had a degree in that sort of thing."

"I might not have a degree but in my field I've had to become very good at reading people. Your evasive answers tell me you don't want to answer at all and are deflecting to take the attention away from you."

"Fascinating," he remarked drily. "And here I thought I was just being intellectually stimulating."

At that she actually laughed. "Well, I'd keep your day job."

They started up the winding road out of town and Heath suddenly said, "Let's go to Maho Bay for a bit. Go for a swim."

Lora startled, not sure what to say or how to react. "I'm not wearing my bathing suit," she started, suddenly wishing she'd worn hers under her tank top.

"No worries. Lilah always keeps a spare right here," he said, reaching toward the back of the Jeep and pulling what looked like a mass of string with tiny scraps of material attached. "You can wear hers."

"I can't fit into that," she protested. "Lilah is much smaller than me in the...chest region," she finished, blushing just a little before lifting her chin, daring him to comment on the difference. To his credit, he simply let it pass, more intent on convincing rather than teasing her.

"It'll be fine. I could use a dip. The humidity is wicked today. You look like you could use a little cooling off, too."

She glanced at herself in the rearview mirror and agreed. It was wretchedly hot. A dip sounded perfect. Besides, they wouldn't stay long. The gift shop inventory would wait for another half hour. "Okay," she reluctantly agreed and bypassed the entrance to Larimar.

CHAPTER EIGHT

LORA PARKED THE JEEP on the narrow shoulder and they climbed out. The skies were slightly overcast, reminding the islanders that it was hurricane season and anything could happen. The unpredictability was just a way of life for those who called this slice of paradise home—but it was something she'd forgotten.

"Is it supposed to rain?"

"Possibly...maybe later," Heath said, grabbing two snorkel sets stashed in the back.

"Where'd you get those?" Lora asked, surprised. "Next are you going to pull a Boogie board out?"

"Naw, just these. I always keep these in the Jeep. You never know when you need to decompress, *yah?*"

She fought the smile that threatened. Had he always had such a charming way about him? When he flashed that grin at her, her insides responded with a disconcerting little tingle that immediately put her on guard.

Usually, when she'd run across someone with whom she'd shared real chemistry, she had deliberately lost their number. Chemistry was a dangerous thing.

It caused people to act stupid, and she certainly couldn't afford that in her line of work. She couldn't count on her hands the number of people she knew who had tanked their careers because they'd let their heart rule their head. Well, not this girl.

That cocky, self-assured voice in her head was no match for the reality staring her in the face. She'd eschewed a personal life to protect her position within the company and she'd still been canned. Seemed her game plan had been flawed after all.

She swallowed a bitter lump in her throat. So maybe she should've gone out for drinks when asked instead of brusquely turning down every offer that hadn't represented some strategic advantage. One man in particular had been particularly insistent—arrogant yet charming in his pursuit—and she was fairly certain she could've bounced a quarter off his firm cheeks if she'd tried, but she'd given him the cold shoulder. So cold in fact, he'd never approached her again.

Looking back now, Lora was pretty sure

she should've given in. He'd looked as if he might have known his way around a woman's body and Lora could have used a good… Her cheeks colored as she realized her mind had wandered into places best avoided.

That was ages ago, she reminded herself, casting a furtive glance Heath's way. So long ago that she barely remembered the man's name. Heath, on the other hand, was a different story. Even when she'd tried to push him from her mind, he'd stubbornly remained. She'd always considered it an annoyance that Heath popped into her thoughts at the most inopportune moments, but being here with him, everything felt different, more visceral. And her awareness of him made her feel awkward and unsure.

"You got quiet all of a sudden," he said, breaking into her thoughts. She forced a small smile but didn't dare share what was going through her head. She didn't understand it herself, and until she did, she wasn't going to mention her feelings to anyone. The sand gave beneath her feet and a slight breeze carried the scent of dark, damp earth and growing green things. She inhaled deeply, filling her lungs and letting the calm she desperately needed follow.

The small knowing smile on Heath's mouth caused her to smile back. "I'd forgotten how much I love the smells here," she admitted. "It's so lush and heavy, but clean, too." She chuckled. "It doesn't smell like that in Chicago."

"What does it smell like?"

Dirty snow, stale ice and diesel fuel. She shrugged. "It smells cold."

"So glad I'm here, then," Heath said, grinning as he turned to head toward the beach.

She trailed behind him, critically assessing his body since his back was to her and she could get away with it. Where had those muscles come from? Sturdy thigh muscles tapered to strong calves and his ass was a study in male perfection. How was it possible that she'd completely missed the fact that the island boy had grown into a first-class, grade-A choice piece of hunky man flesh?

Maybe she'd noticed but had deliberately ignored the thought because she hadn't wanted to take the chance that something might happen between them. Her cheeks burned at the mere wondering that happened when she played the what-if game in her head.

"How long's it been since you snorkeled?" he asked as they walked to the beach, which was such a short distance from the road that she could literally throw a rock and hit a wave.

"It's been a while," she murmured. Beneath the sweet, heavy air the humidity lurked. Rain was definitely on its way. The rain in Chicago had been cold, driving moisture that could quickly turn to sleet. There'd been nothing about it that she'd enjoyed. But rain on the island…somehow it seemed cleansing. She allowed a small smile as she said, "Hopefully, the technique hasn't changed."

"Nope. Pretty basic. Put this in your mouth and go. Sorry I don't have flippers, though."

She shrugged and accepted the snorkel and mask from Heath. "I doubt I'll be going out too far."

"No sense of adventure?" he teased, eliciting a larger grin on her part. "That's okay. Maybe we'll see some sea turtles."

As Heath walked to the water and dove in, Lora detoured to a large copse of trees and quickly changed into the tiny bikini. She groaned to herself as the scrap of material barely covered her breasts, which threatened to spill out in a wardrobe malfunction if the wind changed.

"Come on, the water's perfect," Heath called out, adjusting his mask on his face.

"Screw it," she muttered, exhaling loudly as she dropped her sarong and tank top to the soft sand and scooped up her snorkel set. Heath had seen her in a bathing suit before; it was an island for crying out loud. People went to job interviews wearing bathing suit tops.

But as she approached the water, Heath stopped to stare, and suddenly she almost lost her nerve.

This had been a bad idea. Lora instinctively went to hide her chest with her arms but Heath quickly recovered and gestured, saying, "Are you going to just stand there or get in? I think I saw a turtle a few yards out!"

And then he disappeared, Lora seemingly forgotten in his turtle excitement.

HEATH WAS THANKFUL HIS FACE was hidden under the waves. Lora was simply stunning in that ridiculously tiny bathing suit. He should've known a suit that fit Lilah would be obscene on Lora. Lora was built like a woman with overflowing curves in all the right places whereas Lilah was more like a petite waif that a stiff wind could knock down. It ought to be a crime for a woman to look like that with her type of personality. Men were lured by that hot body and then sliced to ribbons by her razor-sharp tongue. So she was gorgeous. This wasn't news. *Get ahold of yourself,* he thought, mentally berating himself for longing to stare like a starving man at an all-you-can-eat buffet. It was a short minute later that Lora reached him.

"This feels good," she admitted, smiling. "I'd forgotten about the humidity. You'd think I'd be acclimated by now."

"Well, you've been gone awhile," he said, forcing himself to appear nonchalant and at ease when in fact every nerve in his body was on high alert. He wanted to bury his face in the valley of those barely concealed breasts, but then at the same time he wanted to keep his distance.

"So where'd you see the turtle?" she asked hopefully, and he was grateful to oblige the distraction.

They floated along the water's surface, facedown, watching the angelfish and assorted other fish flit to and fro on a path only they could follow, and Heath felt the troubles of the world slipping from his shoulders. One glance at Lora who was avidly following a school of vividly colored butterfly fish as they darted through the water and he knew this had been a good idea. The woman was strung pretty tight. He couldn't imagine what she did in her fancy, high-powered job but he didn't think it brought her much joy. Lora had an amazing smile when she chose to show it off, but most people remembered Lora as the sour-faced Bell sister because she was too busy acting above everyone else.

They didn't know there was another side to her—hell, he didn't think that Lora remembered that about herself.

He couldn't help but wonder how things might've been different between them if he'd stayed in St. John when his parents had split. Maybe she wouldn't have been so closed-off from him. Then again, maybe everything would've remained the same. He didn't know what had changed for Lora, only that she had. Drastically.

Out of the corner of his eye he saw Lora gesture wildly and point. He swam closer and caught a glimpse of a large sea turtle gliding along the bottom toward the reef. She smiled around the mouthpiece and he saw delight in her eyes behind the mask. That split second when her guard was down, her joy lit up his insides like a Christmas parade. He wished it was always like this. Maybe if it were… *No. Don't go there,* a voice in his head warned and he wisely listened. At least for the moment.

They spent another hour meandering through the water, looking for interesting fish, but as the sun started to sink in the sky, Heath realized half the day had already disappeared. All too soon, it was back to reality. But he wasn't quite ready, not yet.

Lora removed her mask and slipped under the water to rinse her face and then resurfaced. Her eyes sparkled with the dying light of the day as she treaded water. "I haven't seen a sea turtle in so long. I'd forgotten how amazing they are." She sighed and floated on her back, murmuring, "I sure miss this."

"Why do you stay away?" he asked, rinsing his mask, as well.

Lora hesitated and she closed her eyes. Finally, she shrugged as she answered. "Work."

"It's not work that keeps you away," he said, calling her bluff. "It's something else."

She sighed as if caught and returned to treading water, but not quite meeting his stare. "I don't really want to talk about it, okay? Let's not ruin this moment by dragging ourselves through a deep conversation."

"Do you ever talk about what's bothering you?" he asked, curious. "Because it seems to me what you do best is bury things until they smother to death. But you know that doesn't work. Whatever you bury, always resurfaces and when that happens, it emerges as something different, something worse."

She looked at him drily. "Thank you, Dr. Phil. I'll keep that in mind."

"Sure, retreat into sarcasm, but you know I'm right."

"So what if you are? What good is it going to do to complain about things that are in the past? It won't change the outcome. It just reminds you how awful you felt at that moment. It's a rehash of a terrible movie. And, frankly, I don't have the time to dedicate to such foolishness."

"Are you happy?" His question startled her and her hesitation told him everything. "If you're not happy, why not start fresh? Make the choice to accept joy in your life and reject all that other stuff."

She barked a short derisive laugh. "Heath, I'm not the right person to give this kind of advice to. I'm not into the whole peace, love and whatever else people without real careers go around spouting. I love my job. I love my career. I'm good at it. Competitors drool over my qualifications and my adversaries cry into their pillows when they learn they're up against me. I have money in the bank and solid investments to protect my retirement. My condo is paid for and I have very little debt. I can safely say I've made solid business decisions when it comes to myself," she said with the slightest little clip as if daring him to find fault.

"That makes you happy?" he asked. "Because it sounds kind of ruthless, predatory and lonely but not happy. What do you do that brings joy to others?"

Lora's gaze hardened and she lost all the softness Heath had seen earlier as she said, "When I bring a multimillion-dollar client to the company, the joy is written all over my boss's face. And then he shows his appreciation by cutting me a fat bonus check. And when I cash that check, I feel *quite* joyful."

Heath regarded her with open sadness and perhaps a fair amount of pity, too. "The saying 'Money doesn't buy happiness' is true, and you're a living example. You're miserable."

"I am not," she said indignantly but her eyes told a different story. What would it take to reach this woman? To get her to realize that happiness wasn't found in the number of zeros on her paycheck? That family was the true treasure in life? Clearly, he wasn't going to reach her today. If anything, he might've just alienated her further. As if to support that theory, she started to swim to shore, saying, "I've had enough. This conversation is over."

Ah, hell.

He should've left well enough alone.

Now he had an excruciatingly uncomfortable car ride to look forward to.

LORA FELT TEARS BRIMMING in her eyes for no good reason. Who was Heath to presume to give her life advice? She hardly felt Heath was qualified to give advice to anyone. She was successful and people wanted her on their team. At least they used to. Now…her phone was silent and her emails went unanswered. There could be a dozen different reasons why none of her feelers had yielded anything fruitful. It didn't have to mean that she was the social pariah in the marketing circles. Likely…likely, word had spread like a forest fire that she'd openly insulted the CEO of one of Chicago's largest Fortune 500 companies and cost her company millions in revenue.

She wanted to stuff her fist in her mouth for fear of screaming. Somehow, she held herself in check but each step felt shakier than the last. She should've stayed in Chicago, to do damage control. No, that hadn't been possible. Her family had needed her. She had no choice but to come. But that left her with nothing but tatters for a career and no way to fix it while stuck on the island.

And Heath—she cast an accusatory glance over her shoulder at the man as he climbed from the surf—could just go to hell. He didn't know her, didn't have the right to poke around in her personal business and certainly didn't have the green light to start giving her advice.

So whose advice would she listen to, if not her family, or a man who'd known her since she was ten years old? The question snuck up out of nowhere and she almost couldn't believe her own brain had thrown it at her.

Well, she didn't have the answer. Besides, it was a dumb question.

Lora needed to focus on what was truly important and that didn't include philosophical discussions about the meaning of life with Heath Cannon!

And for the tiniest, most infinitesimal moment she'd been enjoying herself. She'd actually started to see what others saw in the man with that killer smile, warm gaze and smoking-hot body. She shook her head as if to shake out the memory of her reaction to him. Not helpful, at all.

To add another layer of complication to the matter, Lora was beginning to think that Grams had been trying to play matchmaker all those years. She'd been oblivious to the fact when she was young but now…there were too many instances where she remembered Grams had helpfully tried putting the two together on tasks. She could only imagine what the woman would've tried if she were still alive.

And if Grams was matchmaking, she could bet Pops had also been in on the plan, too.

"Well, it's not going to happen, not now, not ever," she muttered as she shook out her sarong and wrapped it around her torso, not caring that it was getting soaked, and then jerked on her tank top over that ridiculously small bikini top just in time to watch Heath storm to the Jeep without once looking at her.

Of course, Pops, in his diminished mental state, would giggle like the Mad Hatter at the idea of Heath and Lora linking up romantically. She sent a glance to the heavens and grumbled under her breath, "Grams, you can forget about it. It's not going to happen. I can promise you that."

As if in retort, the skies suddenly took that moment to open up, drenching her in the forecasted tropical rain within seconds.

Lora ran for cover, shouting, "Not funny, Grams. Not funny, at all!"

CHAPTER NINE

HEATH TOOK TO THE DRIVER'S seat and Lora balked that he would make that assumption.

"I drove here," she pointed out stiffly, and he flat-out ignored her. "What are you doing?"

"Ready to put a cap on this day. There's a cold beer waiting for me and you're holding me up."

"We have work to do. Don't you remember?" she asked, irritated that he was willing to blow off his commitments just because he was in a snit. "There are bigger problems than whatever you're going through. Or do I need to remind you?"

"Shut up and get in, Lora," he demanded with exasperation. "Or stand in the rain and get soaked. Either way, I'm leaving."

"Technically, that's my Jeep," she said, feeling mean and spiteful. "So if anyone's walking back to Larimar, it's you."

"Sorry to burst your bubble but this particular Jeep is mine. Check the registration if you don't believe me."

Her gaze shifted to the glove compartment with uncertainty, and then lifting her chin, she jerked the box open and pulled out the single piece of paper in there. And there it was in bold black lettering...the Jeep did belong to Heath. Damn. This was awkward. She climbed in with as much dignity as she could muster and then buckled up. "Fine. It's your Jeep. How was I supposed to know? The resort always had Jeeps for work vehicles."

"And it still does, but when Pops's Jeep died, I purchased this one to replace it since I was the one driving them all the time."

"Oh."

"That's all? Oh?"

She looked at him sharply. "What else were you expecting?"

"Oh, I don't know...an apology?"

"For what?"

"For being a colossal ass," he said, putting the Jeep into first gear.

"I made a mistake," she acknowledged crossly. "Does that suffice?"

"It'll do I guess."

She grabbed the roof handle. "Now, back to the business at hand—"

"Not tonight," he cut in, still glowering. "I'm not in the right frame of mind to deal with you on that matter. I need a fresh start."

"We don't have that luxury," she reminded him, annoyed that he was being so difficult. "We need a new business plan. Yours is flawed."

"Says who?"

"Says the woman who has a degree in marketing as you so *scathingly* put when you were berating me at the ferry. Remember that?"

He exhaled loudly and shook his head. "I remember," he admitted. "But I'm not in the mood to go through ledgers and inventory with you right now. Trust me when I say that it would end badly for us both. Let's just take some time to cool off and hit it first thing in the morning, okay?"

She didn't want to wait, she thought mutinously, which only made her want to insist but she could appreciate his point. If it were anyone but Heath, she would've been the one to make the suggestion. "Fine," she bit out, openly peeved. "But you'd better be ready, bright and early or I will drag you out by your ear because this can't wait any longer."

He shot her a quelling look and a delicate

shiver played with her spine as he answered, "Fine," with equally bad humor. Then he added, as if it were his duty, "You might want to talk with Lilah at least. Sort things out with her. You know she takes things to heart and your disappointment is probably more than she can handle."

Lora rolled her eyes, freshly irritated how Heath felt it necessary to rush to Lilah's defense when she was a grown woman who didn't need a champion—she needed a backbone—and in Lora's experience, adversity built character. "Yes, your knight-in-shining-armor routine is quite touching but I think my sister can take care of herself."

"I didn't say she couldn't," Heath said. "But doesn't it bother you in the slightest that you've come down so hard on your sister?"

Yes. She bit her lip and worried it, the only physical indication his comment had struck a nerve. Of course she felt bad. But if she didn't make Lilah take some responsibility, who would? Pops? Not likely when he couldn't be trusted to make his own damn decisions with any confidence. So that left her—making the tough choices. As usual.

My, my, someone's preparing for a doozy of

a pity party, aren't we? Will there be cheese to go with that whine?

It was Grams's voice, clear as a bell, sounding from Lora's mind and she could only imagine it was her guilt taking the platform. She wasn't a martyr. Far from it, she thought, closing her eyes. However, sometimes she was guilty of taking over jobs from people she deemed incompetent—which was damn near everyone—so that the job was completed to her standard.

"If you raise your expectations of people, it gives them something to shoot for," she said by way of justification. She dusted at the sand on her arm and shrugged. "I just think that Lilah is capable of more than everyone gives her credit."

He didn't argue that fact, which gave Lora cause to look his way. Her surprise at his silence must've shown in her expression because he gave her a grudging nod. "Maybe. But you don't have to be so tough on her. That's all I'm saying."

"Duly noted. Can we drop it now?" she asked quietly. Her head had begun to ache and she wasn't sure if it were the heat and humidity or something less tangible. Maybe it was guilt. She loved her sisters, even when they drove her nuts because she didn't understand them at all. They'd always had that twin thing going on that had always made her feel left out. She risked another glance at Heath but he was focused on driving, resignation in his expression. She could only imagine what he must think of her—likely the worst.

They finished the short drive in uncomfortable silence, the air weighted between them by something heavy that had nothing to do with the humidity.

Was going home this difficult for everyone? Or just her?

THAT NIGHT HEATH SIFTED through glass he'd collected earlier throughout the island. A few places in town always set aside their glass recyclables for him to pick up at the end of the day and then he sorted through the collected bags, separating for compatibility and color. Once finished, he would fire up the kiln to 1700 degrees Fahrenheit and melt the glass to fuse the pieces. Creating fused-glass art was something he'd stumbled upon in his early twenties but he'd found a kinship with the process of recycling someone else's garbage and creating something beautiful.

This task, the focused attention to a single

thing, allowed him to let everything else slide away. When he was sifting glass he didn't have to worry about Larimar or his debt to Pops, or Pops's declining mental state, and most recently, Lora.

But tonight, what usually was enough to soothe him, failed to stop the chaotic mess of his thoughts.

Lora invaded his mind and she seemed stuck there.

He groaned as he dropped a brown bottle back into the bucket, crunching glass as it fell. He stood and stretched, his back protesting from sitting in one position for too long and went to the window. He had a great view of Cruz Bay from his place and it wasn't far from Larimar. It'd been his childhood home—his parents had had the grace to leave it to him when they'd helped themselves to an early grave from living la vida loca for too long—and he'd gutted it to the foundation, ripping out memories along with the walls so he could build new.

So this place was his—not his parents'—and he was proud of it, but tonight, nothing seemed to relax him.

Damn you, Lora, he wanted to mutter. It'd taken him years to get over that woman. How many relationships had he walked away from because the woman hadn't measured up to the fantasy he'd concocted about Lora?

And the kicker? He'd never even kissed her. Yeah, how's that for being a total *clung,* as the islanders would say.

In the beginning, he'd hoped Lora would see him as more than the boy whom Pops had unofficially inducted into the family, but Lora had built a wall around herself, insulated against the world with books and papers. There'd been plenty of times he'd watched her unnoticed as she spent hours curled on the terrace, a book in her hand and an untouched glass of iced tea beside her.

There were a handful of times—likely she didn't even remember, but they were etched in his memory—that he'd seen a glimmer of the girl she'd been before he left the island. Her laugh had lit up her eyes—a lot of people didn't know that Lora had an infectious laugh—and she had a wicked sense of humor. Her quick wit was unparalleled. He'd always secretly enjoyed verbally sparring with her. He'd been a challenge for her because he didn't automatically back down like most did when Lora turned that razor-sharp tongue on someone. And, of course, he'd be a liar if he didn't admit that her looks had always snagged his attention. And time had been kind. A part of him had shamefully hoped that she'd lost some of that dazzling star quality that had always made her stand out even when she was doing her best to hide herself from everyone else.

He'd tried to tell himself to move on, that the girl plainly wasn't interested, but even as his brain had berated his interest, his heart had stubbornly taken no notice.

It wasn't until she'd left the island for college and her subsequent visits became sparse and far between that he'd finally been able to put some distance between his unrequited feelings for Lora and regain some of his dignity.

But now that she was here again, those long-buried yearnings were stirring again and he hated it.

He stifled a groan when he realized he couldn't stop dwelling on Lora. It was his teenage years all over again, and who the hell ever wanted to relive those?

He had no room in his life for a spoiled, cold-as-ice woman with less of a heart than the roughest of sea pirates, so why did Lora remain in his thoughts no matter how hard he tried banishing them?

A knock at the door was a welcome interruption. Billy Janks, a friend and native islander with ancestors who traced all the way to the sordid past of St. Thomas's slave days, smiled his wide, white grin against the dark tone of his skin, as he wiggled two coconuts against his chest like a pair of well-endowed breasts. "Nice," Heath said, opening the door for Billy to pass through. "Fresh?"

"Of course dey are fresh, mon. Why you be dumb?" Billy retorted, his grin never fading. Billy's Crucian was as thick as it came, but having grown up on the island Heath could easily understand whereas a tourist would've been left scratching their head. Not to mention, he and Billy had been friends since he could remember. Billy looked like a Rastafarian with dreadlocks and a long and lanky build, his deep rich island color shiny in the sun that he covered with only the barest of clothing, but he owned his own charter company and made his money taking tourists on pleasure rides around the Virgin Islands. So while Billy may look as though he couldn't rub two pennies together, he probably had more money in the bank than Heath. "How de glass come?"

Heath flicked a short glance at his bucket and accepted a coconut to crack open. "Not good. My head's not in it, I guess."

Billy's brow lifted in surprise. "Why so?" Then his expression turned knowing and he scowled. "She back?"

Heath didn't have to clarify. Billy knew. "Yeah," he said, moving to the back porch so he could crack open his coconut. "She had to come. You know what's happening at Larimar and with Pops. She's got power of attorney for the estate and the only one who can sign legal documents."

"She no good," Billy said, his disdain for Lora evident in his pursed lips. "She break you heart witout looking back. She poison, mon."

"Don't you think that's a little harsh?" he teased his friend. "You don't know her like I do."

"From what I remembah, you don' know her as well as you tink, eithah," Billy said, removing the machete from Heath's hand as he started to position the coconut. "You always suck at breaking coconut. Here, I do." With one quick swipe the machete cracked

the coconut down the seam and split it open.
Then he and Heath settled into the chairs to
watch the night waves roll in. "Why you get
so crazy over dis woman? You find someone
else, less stress. I find you good island girl.
What you tink of Rhonda? She fine, mon."

"And that mama mad sick, too," Heath
countered with a little Crucian slang as he
twirled his fingers at his temple. "What you
trying to set me up with crazy women who'll
likely turn me inside out when she done? And
here I thought we were friends."

Billy let out a healthy laugh. "Plenty true.
Okay, no Rhonda, but any woman is better
than dis Lora. She break your heart again and
again. Is bad, mon."

"Yeah, tell me something I don't know,"
he said, agreeing, but Billy's expression remained skeptical. He chuckled and handed
Billy a spoon to dig into his half. "Relax.
I'm not asking her to marry me. But I need
things to go smooth with Lora so I can get
the gift shop out from underneath Larimar.
As it stands, all my inventory is wrapped up
in Larimar and if I take it out it'll breach my
contract."

"But what about dat space you were going
to lease in town?" Billy asked, scooping the

snow-white flesh from the coconut. "What's happening wit dat?"

Heath closed his eyes, trying not to think of how Lora would react to his plan. "I don't know. Until Lora and I manage to clear the debt Larimar is in, I'm screwed."

"You could walk away, you don' owe dat woman nothing," Billy said.

"No, but I owe her grandfather everything and I wouldn't do that to him."

"You a good mon," Billy said, filling his mouth with the rest of the coconut. Finished, he leaned back in the old ratty lawn chair and closed his eyes, seemingly content. Heath envied his peace of mind. "So you got new glass to show me?" he asked. "Dat las' piece was right fancy. You bettah tan most, you know? And I tell you if it crap, yah?"

Heath laughed softly. "That you would, my friend," he acknowledged. "Thanks, mon." They made small talk and Heath showed off some of his newest pieces, ones he was waiting to showcase in his own store instead of Larimar, and then Billy said good-night and left.

Later, when the humid heat of the day still remained and the fans were doing little more than pushing the heated air around, he tossed in his bed and considered if another swim was in order. He thought of padding down the trail to his slice of beach but even the allure of the water couldn't sufficiently compel him. He knew that the water would clear away the sweat and refresh him but it would do nothing for the thoughts that kept sleep at bay.

If he'd had the balls, he would've just asked Lora out long ago but the timing had never seemed right. Maybe then, he would've gotten her out of his system and today her reappearance would no more warrant a blip on his radar than a tourist that was here and then gone with the next cruise ship.

He glanced at the digital clock gleaming in the dark and groaned when he saw the time. Midnight. Deliberately closing his eyes, he tried forcing sleep to come. Her face—her damn gorgeous face with those witchy blue eyes—jumped into frame. Followed by the memory of her supermodel body. Was it too much to ask for a little unsightly facial hair or a spare tire rounding her middle? Apparently. Lora had neither. In fact, her skin glowed in the island heat and whereas sometimes the island made people sweat like hogs, she simply glistened.

Like a clueless houseguest who didn't have

the sense to know when he or she wasn't welcome, the sudden awareness of his groin made him grit his teeth. An erection? Now? He rolled to his stomach, intent on smothering the stubborn arousal that came unbidden, but the friction only served to make him want to grind into the mattress. He'd never even kissed the woman and yet, by evidence of his body's reaction, he wanted her—bad.

No, he told himself with a growl. Not in a million years.

But don't you want to know what it feels like to be skin to skin with Lora Bell? To taste the salt from her neck? To hear the sounds coming from her throat as you buried your face in the cleft of her soft flesh?

God yes, he answered miserably, hating himself for such weakness, and wondering if he'd ever be free of this pathetic yearning for the woman.

She won't stay, he reasoned with the sly voice urging him into doing something stupid. She couldn't wait to leave. Her life in Chicago was everything she'd ever wanted, which was the exact opposite of anything he could ever offer. So why continue to chase after an illusion?

He knew the answer and it struck an uncomfortable, knowing chord within him. Lora was a sickness deep in his blood, that was neither healthy nor treatable but maybe it could be managed for the short time she remained on the island.

Don't touch her, a different voice cautioned, the same calm, steady voice of reason and logic that ruled his head when he hammered out business deals. It was a voice that he trusted in most instances so why he immediately tensed with irritation at the sound advice was baffling.

You want her. Give in.

"I'd rather chew off my own foot," he said to the empty darkness as if voicing it out loud would give the sentiment strength.

Deep inside laughter rumbled. He swore and bounded from the bed, grabbing his towel as he went.

Looked like he was going for a swim after all.

CHAPTER TEN

LORA WOKE EARLY and after a quick shower she bounded downstairs to find Pops for breakfast. She ran into Lilah in the hall who was carrying a lean black cat with a white belly. The awkward tension was a physical presence that crowded them both.

"Who's that?" Lora asked, curious.

Lilah hefted the cat over her shoulder like a baby and the cat simply accepted this new position as if it were completely natural.

"Maho," Lilah answered. "I found him a few weeks ago." She lifted her chin. "I'm keeping him. Pops said I could."

A cat in the resort? "What about guests who might have allergies. Maho could be a liability."

"He stays in the private section and he sleeps in my room. End of story. I'm keeping him," she repeated, then a tiny smile broke on her face that was clearly meant for the cat and not Lora. "He fetches better than a dog. He's an island *cog.*"

Island cats—like island cars—were a special breed. They were simply different. A cog was a cat-dog. And Lora could plainly see this was not a battle to take on at the moment. She conceded with a smile, hoping her sister would take the gesture as the extension of an olive branch. "I was just going to see if Pops was free for breakfast...want to join me?"

Unfortunately, Lilah wasn't in a forgiving mood, which surprised Lora as her youngest sister had always been so easygoing.

"No, thanks. I have plans," Lilah said, moving past Lora, her lithe hips swaying beneath the soft-pink-and-white sarong, causing Lora a momentary pang of jealousy for her sister's willowy frame. Lora had been *blessed,* and she said that with complete sarcasm, with full rounded curves that were more than a nuisance most times. Her stomach was flat enough—thanks to countless hours at the gym—but her breasts were far too large and often got in the way, and her hips were always causing her to wiggle her way into jeans that hugged almost obscenely.

Frankly, she'd rather have the waifish figure that Lilah had or the athletic build of

Lindy—anything aside from the figure she'd been given.

It was really hard to be taken seriously in the world of business when you were built like a porn star, she thought with an unhappy frown. Men often talked to her breasts instead of her face, and if they weren't trying to get her into bed, they were speculating who'd already slept with her. She swallowed, wondering if the true reason she'd been fired had had nothing to do with her job performance but rather her decision not to sleep with a client to curry favor. She'd sacrificed plenty of her dignity and integrity for that company… Eventually, she'd feel her termination was a blessing, right?

"Lilah," she called after her sister. "We should talk, okay?"

In answer, Lilah gave a halfhearted wave without turning around. Seconds later she was out of view and gone.

"Damn," she murmured. She'd really pissed off her baby sis. She supposed she had been heavy-handed on her. The admission pricked at her conscious and she hated the feeling. Lora had always felt apart from the twins, which given the fact that the girls had shared a *womb,* was probably natural, but she certainly hadn't helped matters she supposed by keeping to herself most times.

Wait a minute…why was she taking the blame? It wasn't as if the twins had gone out of their way to include her.

Oh, great. She was arguing with herself. Shaking her head to clear it and to provide commentary on how she was losing her mind with the island heat, she went to find Pops.

She didn't find him on the terrace as she expected but instead, in the gift shop.

Puzzled, she wandered in. "Pops what are you doing? Everything okay?"

He turned at her voice, a piece of fused glass in his hands. "Isn't it beautiful?" he asked, putting the delicate vase flute in her hand. She accepted it with a quizzical expression, but agreed as she turned it over in her hand. The craftsmanship was exquisite. She thought of the deal she'd struck with Heath yesterday about holding off judgment until she'd seen the inventory. Now she understood why he'd been so adamant. "I always appreciated people who make art like this. Your Grams loves this stuff, too. She's an artist, you know," he said in a proud voice as if sharing a secret with Lora. "I think Lilah is following in Grams's footsteps."

Lora lifted her brow, gesturing to the vase. "Oh? Is this her work?" she asked, trying to look past the part where Pops was referencing Grams as if she were just in the other room.

"Oh, no," he shook his head, accepting the vase from Lora to replace on the shelf next to a series of others in the same style. "Lilah is doing watercolors and pastels but she doesn't sell her work. She's good enough, of course, but you know our littlest sugar bird, she's so private. Maybe she needs a little nudge from her big sister...you know, give her some encouragement. You should see her work. It's inspiring."

Inspiring, eh? She couldn't remember the last time anyone had described her talents in such glowing terms. Ruthless, predatory, heartless...those were the words she was most familiar with. And now that she didn't have a job to warrant those skills where did that leave her? She doubted anyone outside of her circle was interested in hiring a woman who had once stolen a client right from beneath the nose of one of their top competitors. She'd been in fine form by planting incriminating evidence and supplying carefully constructed innuendos that her competitor was ruining the client's brand, something that was suicide for an established company with high stakes. Her methods hadn't mattered as long as she'd landed the account and could deliver the goods.

Damn, she swore silently, shifting in discomfort when she realized she'd been too busy cultivating skills no one in their right mind would crow about. It'd been a source of pride in her private circle to be considered so ruthless but now that she'd been cast outside the circle, those attributes didn't seem so great.

Stop it. She was who she was. Not to mention, if she didn't cease replaying every move, every decision in her head that may have led up to her losing her job, she'd go crazy. And she had a feeling her family could only handle one crazy person at a time. Swallowing, she refocused on Pops. "Well, unfortunately, I don't think Lilah wants much to do with me right now. She's pretty mad."

Pops frowned. "Why?"

Lora hesitated, unsure of how much she could explain without Pops losing his grip on reality. "Um, sister stuff," she said vaguely, hating that she had to censor herself to prevent a meltdown. Quick to change the subject, she began to peruse the inventory, intrigued

by the change she saw. "So, the new artist...
do I know him or her? This is good stuff.
Very pretty." She checked the price on one
item. "And priced well. Does it sell?"

"Better than that awful touristy crap," Pops
said with a burst of lucidity that reminded her
of the Pops she'd left behind all those years
ago. Pops had always been an astute businessman in spite of his eccentric nature. She
supposed she'd inherited her knack for numbers and strategy from him. The knowledge
warmed her inside and a smile followed. He
added, "I always hated that stuff, you know.
It said nothing about the island, nothing that
made it special."

Her smile faded. She'd been the one to suggest that "touristy crap" as he'd called it. It'd
been one of her first suggestions after she'd
graduated college with her master's degree
in marketing. Easy money pandering to the
guests with T-shirts, mugs and visors. "It
made money," she reminded him a bit stiffly,
crossing her arms. "Money that was easily
made because the inventory was cost-effec-
tive. This stuff, while beautiful, is expensive." She lifted a shallow bowl with gorgeous
flared sides as an example. "Tourists don't
want to take home pricey breakables because

no matter how pretty, if it's not packaged correctly, or shipped, it's going to arrive at their home in a pile of broken shards of glass."

"The sales are good," Pops maintained stubbornly. "Just ask your Grams."

Lora bit back a frustrated sigh. "Okay. I'll do that," she said, a wave of unhappiness washing over her. The gift shop was filled with expensive items that were hardly impromptu purchases easily stuffed into a carry-on. She suspected if she went over the books, she'd find the numbers weren't as hearty as Pops claimed. She hadn't had a chance to go over the contract yet but somehow she'd have to break it with the artist and get the tourist-friendly items returned to the shelves, which would only serve to put her and Heath at odds. She rubbed her forehead, her stomach reminding her that she'd been on her way to breakfast. "So who is this amazing artist we've put all our faith into these days?" she asked, her mind already moving to the legal wrangling she might have to put into play to get the shop back on track.

Pops broke into a proud grin usually reserved for his sugar birds and his answer caused her stomach to pitch to the floor.

"None other than our Heath Cannon."

Our Heath.

Good God. Suddenly, it all made terrible sense.

That son of a bitch.

CHAPTER ELEVEN

LORA COCKED HER HEAD and heard Heath's voice as he chatted with a guest or two in the lobby. She took a deep breath and flexed her clenched palms, but it didn't help. Anger—and something else—sang in her veins, blotting out her self-control.

"Real slick, Cannon," she said in a tight voice when he rounded the corner to the office where she stood behind the desk. She'd been searching for the specific agreement that detailed Heath's business arrangement with Pops so she'd have more information at her disposal. So far, she'd come up empty and she'd made a mess, but she didn't care. She was too mad to care.

"What are you talking about?" he asked, wary confusion in his tone.

"The inventory. I saw it." The silence didn't surprise her, though a part of her wanted him to make some sort of protest of innocence. When he didn't, her heart sank just a little.

"Funny how you didn't mention it was your personal inventory on display at Larimar. No wonder you're so protective of it and why you tried putting off this moment for as long as possible. You're despicable," she shouted, grabbing the first thing her hand could connect with to hurl at his head.

He ducked just in time to avoid being brained by a marble pen holder. "What the hell is wrong with you?" he exclaimed. "You can't go throwing shit at people. What if that had hit me?" he demanded angrily.

"That was the point and if I'd had better aim you'd be wearing a marble-pen-holder-sized dent in your big, fat head."

"You're a piece of work," Heath said, disgusted, glancing down at the broken pen holder. "Your Pops is going to miss that. It was a present from your Grams. But then, you already knew that, right?"

Damn it, she swore silently, her hot temper doused by immediate regret. But honestly, Larimar's future had been leveraged for someone else's personal gain, which meant there were bigger problems than a broken pen holder. "I'm sure it can be fixed, which is more than I can say about this mess that you've put us in."

"Listen, I was all ready to go over the financials and talk shop with you about Larimar and my part, but forget it. I'm not your lackey, your subordinate or even your friend, so I don't have to listen to this verbal abuse. You got that, Lora? *I don't have to listen!*"

"Yes, you do," she countered shrilly. "Where do you think you're going?"

"Away from you. I'm going to spend the day on the water. I need to calm down." He walked away, flipping her off as he went. "See ya, babe," he added with a healthy dose of sarcasm that surprised her with its sting.

Oh! That jerk!

That was so typical of a man to just think he could end the conversation because he didn't like the direction. Well, screw that. The conversation was over when *she* decided it was over.

Lora ran after Heath, but he'd already jumped into his Jeep and was rumbling down the road toward the marina. "Lilah! I need a ride!" she called out, almost screaming her sister's name. "Hurry!"

Lilah appeared, thankfully this time without the cat, though she didn't look pleased to answer her sister's call. That would have to wait. For now, she had to catch Heath. "I need you to drive me to the marina," she instructed, assuming Lilah would comply immediately when she heard the urgency in Lora's voice.

Yeah, not so much.

She should have remembered that Lilah had a decidedly deep stubborn streak and she didn't do what she didn't want to do until she was ready to do it. So much for that theory everyone subscribed to that Lilah was the meek one.

"Why?" Lilah asked, sitting behind the counter in the lobby covering for Celly, who was on a break. Lora had been unsuccessful as of yet to convince Pops that Celly wasn't the right fit for the resort. Pops liked Celly's no-nonsense approach to life and had simply patted Lora's shoulder in response to her concerns about the brusque front-desk woman.

"Because Heath is suffering under the misunderstanding that we are through with the conversation, whereas I want to tear him a new one for taking advantage of this family."

"He didn't take advantage of anyone in this family. You need to chill out," Lilah openly scoffed.

Clearly, Lora realized, no help would come

from her sullen sister on this score. "Can you please just drive me to the marina?"

Lilah sighed and shook her head, as if Lora were the one being difficult, and quickly texted Celly to return so they could leave.

"Thank you," Lora said, trying not to tap her foot.

When Celly returned, a sour expression on her face, Lilah apologized, causing Lora to fidget under that assessing stare.

"I don' know why yah have to be so rush-rush 'bout everyting," Celly said, pursing her lips in obvious disapproval. "Das not the *island* way, yah know."

"Not everything can move on island time," Lora snapped. "And this is important."

"Bah. You tink all dah wrong tings is important," Celly said, waving Lora away. Lilah laughed as if agreeing and Lora felt at a distinct disadvantage.

"Can we go now?" Lora asked, freshly irritated.

"Fine, fine," Lilah said with poor humor. "But maybe if you weren't such a difficult, pigheaded person, you wouldn't have to be chasing Heath down to yell at him."

Lora ignored her sister and stalked from the lobby, eager to get away from Celly's judgment and the feelings that the older woman created.

"I don't like her," Lora said once they were in the Jeep. "She's bad for business."

"That's a bunch of baloney. You don't like her because she doesn't take any of your crap."

"It's nice how you always take everyone else's side but mine," Lora muttered.

"I call them as I see them. Besides, Celly is great. The guests love her. And so does Pops."

Lora gave up on that particular argument, needing to prioritize. Another thought came to her. "Heath probably loves the woman, too, doesn't he?"

"Pretty much."

"Well, she's not very nice if you ask me," Lora bit out, hating that everyone but her was enamored with the older woman. "And I don't think Grams would've liked her, either."

Okay, that part was probably not true. Likely Grams would've gotten a kick out of the woman's blunt nature. Grams had always said that was part of the local charm. The natives rarely held back, whether it was polite or not. "Where'd Pops find her anyway?" she asked, still glowering. "Nurse Ratchet wasn't available?"

Lilah shot her a look that said *tread carefully* and Lora took the hint. The Jeep lumbered down the hill, the engine laboring as she downshifted. "You're always so sure of people's worst. Why is that?" Lilah asked.

"Because I'm not naive."

"I'm not naive and I try to think the best of everyone."

Lora sighed. "I'm glad that approach to life works for you, Lilah. It never did for me." Unable to resist, Lora added, "So, how do you think the best of our father who abandoned us when we were kids?"

Lilah lifted her chin and said, "Actually, I try to. I'm sure he had his reasons. And until I know what those are I won't judge him."

Lora barked a short laugh. "You're right— you go way past naive and have landed straight into ridiculous. He's a rat. There's nothing noble or justifiable about his actions. Sometimes people are just who they seem to be—rotten."

"And I take it you believe that of Heath?"

"The evidence is pretty damning."

"Depends on how you perceive his actions," she countered mildly. "And if you know Heath, you would know that he would never do anything to hurt this family. Even you, though you're certainly on the fringe."

Lora shot her sister a stony look and bit out, "Just drive, please," before she started yelling at her sister and making things worse.

A hitchhiker stood pointing in the direction they were headed and Lora felt Lilah slow the car. In St. John, hitchhikers didn't stick their thumb up, but rather would point in their desired direction. The first time she'd seen that Lora had giggled when her Pops had explained that on the island sticking the thumb out was the equivalent of something very rude, hence the pointing fingers. But it had been a long time since she'd made a habit of giving strangers a ride. In Chicago inviting a stranger into your car was like tempting fate to send a serial killer your way. "What are you doing?" Lora asked incredulously.

"She obviously needs a ride and we're headed that way," Lilah answered, as if that should've been obvious.

"We don't pick up strangers," Lora said, horrified at her sister's lack of common sense.

"Relax. Don't you remember a thing about growing up here?" Lilah asked, a bit exasperated. "This is the island way. You'd better start getting with the program if you're hoping to understand how to fix things with your marketing savvy. I mean, isn't knowing your product important information when you're trying to market something?"

"Of course," she admitted. "But I'm not marketing an island. I'm trying to get more people to Larimar."

"Which is on an island. Duh."

Lora ground her teeth but buttoned her lip. Arguing with Lilah wasn't going to gain her any ground and Lora chose to focus on one adversary at a time.

Lilah smiled as the young woman climbed into the back of the Jeep with a grin. "Thanks! Much appreciated," she said breathlessly. "You headed to town?"

"Yeah, the marina."

"Excellent." She glanced at the two women, asking, "You sisters?"

Lilah grinned. "How'd you know? People say we don't look anything alike."

"It's in the jawline. I can see the resemblance. I have an eye for that sort of thing."

Lora wanted to roll her eyes at the small talk but pasted on a fake smile, nodding as was appropriate, otherwise keeping to herself.

"You from here?" she asked. "I'm Penny. I love this island. I just moved here and I'm still learning all the local customs and what-not. Every day I pinch myself because I've got a view of paradise outside my window. What could be more amazing than that?"

Lora feigned interest. "What do you do for a living?"

"Oh, I used to be a paper pusher, you know, human resources analyst at a big company in California, but one day I just said, 'forget this,' and I left the rat race behind. Now I'm a waitress at the Rush Tide Bar and Grill. And I don't regret a second."

Lilah grinned. "Our family owns Larimar," she said.

"That gorgeous resort on the hill with the private beach? Man, growing up there must've been like waking up in paradise every day. I wish I'd discovered St. John earlier in my life. I mean, I'm only twenty-five but still, I cringe when I think of all the time I wasted elsewhere. This is my new home and I'm never going back."

Lora couldn't argue the island's attributes, but she'd never truly understood how people could just leave an entire life behind to start new somewhere else. When it had happened to her, she hadn't had a choice in the matter.

Although she couldn't really complain. Growing up at Larimar had been wonderful.

"It's gorgeous for sure," Penny went on. "I happened to wander in when I took a wrong turn on my way to Hawksnest and wow! It's like something you see on a postcard, but then everywhere you look in St. John is like that. And you have a bomb gift shop. I mean, simply amazing artisan stuff in there."

Lora's ears perked, curious. "Did you happen to buy anything?" she asked.

Penny's expression turned rueful. "I wish. I can't afford art like that on my salary. But I sure like to look at it."

Lora held her smile in place by the thinnest thread. Inside she was simmering all the more because Penny had just inadvertently made Lora's case that the gift shop was bound to fail.

Lilah made the pit stop at the plaza and dropped off the amiable young Penny from California and then Lora.

"Hey, try a little sugar," Lilah suggested.

Lora gave her sister a patronizing look as she said, "Sure. I'll give it a whirl." When in fact she planned to shout at Heath for all the reasons she'd banked since landing on the island. "Thanks for the ride. Keep an eye on Pops, okay?"

Lilah, clearly displeased with being dismissed, agreed with ill humor. "Whatever. Bye."

Lora thought to soften her parting comment but Lilah didn't give her the chance. She was gone before Lora could open her mouth. *I'll fix it later,* Lora thought to herself, and then strode to the dock where she could see Heath aboard a beautiful sailboat christened the *Jumbie Moon* or *Ghost Moon.* She stopped short to wonder who owned the boat and for a horrible minute she thought the worst. Had Heath taken the money from Pops to purchase this expensive toy? But even as angry as she was with him, she couldn't bring herself to make that accusation. Heath saw her and glanced away, causing her to grasp onto the boat and jump aboard.

"Hey! You're not supposed to come aboard without the captain's permission and I sure as hell didn't grant it to you."

She ignored that. "I told you we were going to talk and here I am. You're crazy if you thought you could just run away from this discussion. My family's legacy is on the line, so you're just going to have to suck it up and act like a man, because we've got issues to hash out. Not once did you come forward and admit that the inventory in the gift shop was your art. Not once! Don't you think that was important information?"

"What difference does it make what I sell in *my* gift shop? I'm leasing the space in Larimar and I pay rent every month, so if I want to sell candles and mugs shaped like penguins, it's my prerogative as long as I make my obligations. Which I have!"

"That's a bunch of bull," she countered hotly. "You may pay your lease with the money that Pops lent you, but you're not doing anything to pay off the loan. I checked. There haven't been any payments on the actual loan yet."

At that he looked uncomfortable. "It's taking a bit longer to make a profit than I thought it would," he admitted in a grumble, and then added firmly, "But things will turn around. I've got some ideas—"

"Larimar doesn't have time for your ideas! Larimar needs cash." Heath met Lora's stare and angry sparks flashed between them. "Come back to Larimar with me so we can finish this conversation in an appropriate place," she said, noting how neighboring boaters had taken interest in their conversation. She lowered her voice, saying, "The last thing anyone outside the family needs to know is that Larimar is in trouble. People will start descending on Larimar like a pack of wolves to buy it at a loss. And that's not going to happen."

She turned to disembark, expecting Heath to follow, but she should've known he wouldn't be that docile.

"I said I was going to spend the day on the water," he said to her back. She turned to face him, shocked. His jaw was set and he was clearly not leaving that boat. "My friend Billy was nice enough to lend me the boat because I needed some downtime. I told you I had a personal interest in the gift shop and that Pops had invested in a business opportunity with me. It wasn't a secret. You didn't ask for details."

"Omitting the truth is the same as lying in my book," she returned, her voice wavering with anger. "I demand that you come back to the office with me and discuss this situation."

"No can do," he refused firmly. "However, unless you plan to come with me, you'd better disembark, because this girl is heading out.

Hurry and make a choice. I'm setting sail in two minutes."

Lora decided to call his bluff. He wouldn't really leave with her on the boat. She crossed her arms over her chest. "Guess I'm going for a boat ride, then."

"Suit yourself."

And to her dismay, true to his word, within two minutes they were pulling away from the marina.

Oh, damn... Lora realized too late Heath hadn't been bluffing.

CHAPTER TWELVE

HE DIDN'T THINK SHE'D STAY but he supposed he'd underestimated her resolve when she put her mind to something. But now he was stuck with her and he wasn't sure how he felt about it. By her expression, neither did she. "Listen, it was your choice to stay so I don't want to hear any crap about how I choose to spend my day, got it?"

"As long as you can answer my questions I don't care what you have planned," she said with a false sweetness. He shot her a look and she smiled. "Besides, I can conduct business anywhere…a boat, a plane, a toilet stall. I've done it all."

"A toilet stall? I don't believe you," he said.

Her thin smile dared him to question her. "I don't let anything get in the way of business."

"Not even family?" he asked. He could understand how intimidating she could be from the other side of the boardroom and oddly, he found it sexy as all hell. Her take-no-prisoners approach made him want to know if she took control in all aspects of her life, including the bedroom. Was she the kind of lover who threw her partner to the bed with a growl and stripped him without hesitation, taking what she wanted without apology? Or did she shed that need for control and let someone else take the lead for those moments when there was nothing between them but skin and sweat? He nearly stumbled at the track his mind had taken without his permission. He pushed his dirty thoughts away as he realized he'd just stumbled into the no-man's-land of dangerous fantasies and stalked away with a growl of self-recrimination for attempting to bluff a woman who ate corporate flunkies for lunch.

Lesson learned.

Of course, the bigger question was, how was he going to spend an entire day alone with Lora on a boat in the middle of the ocean, without putting his mouth on hers at least once?

Excellent question—and he didn't have a clue for an answer.

"Where are we going?" she asked. "Obviously, I don't have my passport with me so

I hope it's not toward the British Virgin Islands."

He smirked but shook his head. "Just a little sail around St. Croix and Water Island. Though I'd planned to be gone all day. That okay with you?"

Her expression faltered, which told him, no, it wasn't okay, that she didn't like the idea of being cloistered on a boat with nothing but the sea and himself any more than Heath did. But there was no turning back now. She recovered in a heartbeat, though, saying with convincing bravado, "Good. That should give us plenty of time to get to the bottom of your business arrangement with my grandfather." She took a seat, safe from the sail, and affected a relaxed expression with her face toward the wind. "It's a lovely boat," she remarked abstractedly, running her hands along the teak paneling. "Who did you say the boat belonged to?" she asked.

"Billy Janks. Maybe you remember him?"

She searched her memory, then remembered, wrinkling her nose in distaste. "Vaguely," she said. "It's a nice boat. He must be doing well."

"He owns this boat and many others. He started a charter company," Heath answered, his mouth turning up in a short smile. "He might even be a millionaire by now," he said.

"Billy Janks?" she repeated, surprised.

"He's got a head for business. He's the one who convinced me I ought to start selling my work."

"Oh. So you two remained close?"

"He's my best friend," Heath answered without hesitation. "He's been there through thick and thin, just like Pops. I consider them both family."

Lora wisely remained silent while she digested his admission. Heath maneuvered the boat free from the bay with the motor and then once they were clear, he made short work of unfurling the sails. He was glad for the distraction of readying the boat for open water. Panic at being alone with Lora was starting to color his every thought. How many times had he wanted this very thing when they were teens? Too many to count. But it felt all wrong. In his fantasy, she was the adoring girlfriend, not the angry harridan ready to impale his head on a stick. He could understand where her anger was coming from but it killed him that she automatically thought the worst of him when it came to Larimar.

He only wanted the best for Pops and the

family, even Lora. Well, at the moment, Lora only marginally. How could she be cut from the same cloth as the rest of the Bells? And why the hell did he still have feelings for her? That was the bigger question. He'd tried to root her out, tried to move on, but she haunted him without reason. There was something about her that turned his clock in a big way. Clearly there was something wrong with him. Yeah, that was it. He was cracked.

"WHEN'D YOU START working with fused glass?" Lora asked as Heath took to the wheel. He looked magnificent; hair lifting in the warm Caribbean breeze, blond highlights glinting in the sun, and a chiseled and tanned body that teased her from beneath his loosely buttoned white shirt. Why'd he have to look so good? She pulled her cover-up off to catch some sun. Her skin was Chicago-white and could use a little Caribbean color. She wasn't blind to his reaction, either. Her skin warmed and her breathing quickened but she pretended she hadn't noticed.

"Uh, well, in my early twenties," he answered with a faint scowl. "I took a workshop up at the eco hotel above Maho Bay and something about the process really spoke to me. I was hooked almost immediately."

"What do you enjoy about it?" she asked, making conversation—something she distinctly hated—if only to keep her mind and hormones in check. If the situation was less complicated between them, perhaps they could've indulged their physical attraction and moved on, but there was no way she was going to risk such intimacy with a man she'd be forced to see for the rest of her life. She doubted Pops would take kindly to her *disowning* their adoptee because she'd finished shagging him and no longer felt comfortable sitting across the dinner table from him at Christmas.

"I don't know, it's hard to explain," he said with a noncommittal answer. "It just appeals to me."

"Is it difficult?"

"Yeah, it can be. The learning curve is steep. I started off with a lot of worthless junk that shattered easily. The trick is knowing what is compatible and what isn't."

She smirked. "Isn't that the trick to everything in life?"

He glanced at her, his gaze sharp and hungry and for a moment she was paralyzed by that heated stare. In a lightning flash she saw him above her, worshipping her body, lavishing it with all the attention his tongue could provide, and she couldn't breathe. Fortunately, he broke the spell as he said, "Yeah, but you learn pretty quick what isn't meant to be and you resist the urge to throw the pieces together that will likely make an ugly mess when you put the heat on."

Was that a metaphor for the attraction they both felt yet knew they ought to ignore? Was she reading a message into something that wasn't there? Annoyed with herself, she looked away, putting her face to the sun, her heart hammering. "Well, obviously you have it figured out. Your work isn't half-bad."

"Coming from you...that's high praise."

She turned back to him and caught that bad-boy smirk lighting up his face and she wondered, how in the hell had she been blind to Heath's obvious good looks? Suddenly, she realized with painful clarity—she'd made a huge mistake stepping foot on this boat.

And it was too late to do anything about it. So she did the only thing she knew to bring everything back into focus—attack.

CHAPTER THIRTEEN

"Why'd you do it?" she blurted without finesse or tact, and Heath didn't pretend ignorance. Lora was like a hound on a scent and she wasn't going to let go until her teeth had sunk into her quarry. He sighed, focusing on heading for open water instead of meeting that accusatory stare, trying to put into words how the deal with Pops had come about, without making things worse. She waited for him, her gaze full of reproach and disappointment. It was the disappointment that cut at him, putting him on the defensive, blotting out all the sensible and responsible ways to handle her honest question.

"Do what? Have the audacity to start my own business? To try and become something more than Larimar's handyman?"

Her gaze narrowed. "You know that's not what I'm asking. I couldn't care less if you wanted to do more than fix toilets and pick bananas for the rest of your life. What I care about is what you did to my grandfather."

"Why do you assume I did anything wrong?" he shot back, his mouth tightening as if trying to prevent him from sticking his foot in it. *Just tell her what happened and how wretched you feel about the whole deal,* a voice reasoned. But stubborn pride had control of his tongue and he seemed on a collision course with an inevitable catastrophe.

"You signed a business deal with my grandfather who clearly wasn't in his right mind. I'd say that's pretty wrong," she said in a hard voice. "You're the man Pops put his trust into and now we're on the verge of losing the family business. How do you sleep at night?"

"Just fine," he lied. Most nights he tossed and turned, wondering how he could pay Pops back in half the time of their agreement but Lora was right; he hadn't been able to make a single loan payment yet. He needed more time but that was something they didn't have a lot of. He'd had no idea how difficult it would be to start making a profit. He'd just believed in his work and went for it with Pops's support. In hindsight, he probably should've done more research but he sure as hell wasn't going to admit that to Lora so she could gloat. "How about you? How well do you sleep knowing you abandoned your family when they needed you the most."

"Touché," she acknowledged coolly, refusing to take the bait. "Had I known the wolf was at the door, I would've come running."

Was she calling *him* the wolf? Or the IRS? He narrowed his gaze with open aggravation. "I didn't take advantage of Pops."

"Looks different from where I'm sitting."

"That's your problem. Not mine. My conscience is clear."

Why was he being such an ass? Did she truly bring out the worst in him? His mouth locked as if to say, *save yourself, man, and shut your yap,* but he was angry. She could drive a man to violence. For a split second he envisioned kicking her butt off the boat and sailing away, but he'd have a hell of a time explaining that one to Pops no matter that the man was losing his grip. He choked down another hot retort dancing on his tongue and he reached for some sort of truce. "Lora…I… didn't know he was ill," he finally acknowledged, avoiding her stare. "He hid the fact that he was losing time from all of us. Honestly, I never thought to ask Pops for the capital, he offered and it seemed like a good opportunity for both of us." Was he really putting himself out there for her scrutiny, and worse, disbelief? Yes…he had to. Contrary to what she may have cooked in her head, he was an honorable man. "It wasn't until a few months after signing the paperwork and spending the money that I discovered that Pops might not have been…"

"Capable of striking such a deal with you?" she finished for him, lifting a brow.

"Yes, damn it," he growled, hating that she wasn't giving him an inch. His simmering anger, equal parts guilt and shame, returned to the surface to singe his good intentions. The fact was, he'd been so excited about the prospect of getting his business off the ground, he'd ignored the tiny misgivings that had fluttered at the edge of his consciousness. He should've waited, talked it over with Lora at the very least. But he hadn't. Bad judgment aside, there was no malice. Of that, he was solid. "Do you really think I'd screw Pops over like that? Intentionally?"

She hesitated, clearly torn and unhappy about it, too. Good. It was about time she recognized the fact that he wasn't the enemy she painted him out to be. Her mouth firmed and he lost all hope. "It doesn't change the fact that Pops wasn't capable of going into business with you. He drained the reserve account to give you your capital. Pops wasn't a wealthy man. Everything he had was sunk into Larimar, and now Larimar is in danger of being seized by the government and, frankly, I'm sorry that you don't like to hear it, but you're at fault. The bottom line is, I need to know your plan for fixing this mess or else... I'm going to take you to court."

HAD SHE JUST THREATENED Heath in one breath while secretly wincing at her cold tone with the other? Yes, that was her, delivering the death blow without blinking an eye, the cold bitch from Chicago, living up to her reputation.

She faltered a fraction when Heath stared in stunned silence, as if not even he could believe she'd taken it to that level. Gone was any semblance of desire from his eyes and she was seized by the irrational urge to apologize. Had she been too callous? Why was she even questioning herself? Heath was responsible for Larimar's current predicament and it was up to her to fix it. Holding hands and singing around the campfire wasn't going to convince the IRS to back off. Only hard cash would do and it was up to Heath to find it.

"Tell me—"

"Stop talking."

The curt demand shocked her into silence. But only for a moment. "Excuse me?" she said. "Don't presume to talk to me like you have the right. I'm not your friend. I'm your business partner and as such I demand a little respect."

"I would never presume to talk to you like a friend at all," he returned coldly. "Because you're the furthest thing from a friend that I can imagine. As far as I'm concerned, you're nothing but a suit to me, another person coming at me for money. Don't worry, *sugar bird.*" The way he sneered her nickname made her feel sick inside but she held her stung reaction in check. "I'll get the money. But not for you. For Pops and the twins. For *them* I'd do anything. You, on the other hand, can go to hell." She opened her mouth but he cut her short. "If I were you, for the sake of self-preservation, I'd keep my mouth zipped because it's a long swim back to the island."

She blinked back the sting of tears, horrified at how deeply his words cut. Why did she care what Heath Cannon thought of her?

She didn't. Right? What mattered was getting Larimar back on track. That's why she was here. Not to coddle a grown man. Yes, all those things, but the truth stared at her without mercy. She hated the look of raw disgust radiating from those beautiful green eyes. It made her want to apologize and that, she plainly would not do.

HEATH WAS TEMPTED TO WRENCH the wheel and steer them back to port, but for some unknown reason he stayed his course, taking them deeper into the crystal blues and greens of the Caribbean waters. Wisely, Lora remained quiet but he saw the storm behind her expression.

She was only looking out for her family's best interest, he argued with himself, willing his temper to recede. If anyone else had done this to Pops, he would've rearranged that person's face. He understood her anger, her fear. He supposed what rankled him the most was her belief that he, of all people, had willfully taken advantage of the one man who'd ever shown him love and affection without expecting anything in return. Pops had shown him kindness, taught him how to be a man, and welcomed him into a family that wasn't his own. The fact that Lora distrusted him so quickly hurt. Didn't his past actions warrant a little latitude? Yes, he may have made a mistake and he was willing to take responsibility for that but to jump to the conclusion that he was trying to deliberately swindle Pops struck him deep in the heart.

All of these things smacked of concrete evidence why he ought to stay away from her. But the heart wants what the heart wants, so Grams used to say. And damn it all to hell, his heart—stupid as it was—wanted Lora.

And it always had.

LILAH GRABBED HER PHONE and took it with her to her private patio. It was noon in California, which made it three o'clock in the afternoon in St. John, but there was no guarantee that her sister Lindy was awake even at this hour. Still, she had to talk to her.

It rang twice and Lindy picked up, the sound of her twin's voice instantly making her smile. She missed her so much. They weren't identical but they'd often been able to confuse people by playing the switcheroo game. It wasn't until the differences in their personalities had manifested into clear differences in their appearances that they'd stopped fooling people.

"Hey, Li," Lindy answered, her voice just a bit sleepy which told Lilah she'd been right about her sister's sleeping habits. "What's shaking?"

She'd planned to chitchat first but hearing her sister's voice opened the floodgates and tears weren't far behind. "You need to come home. Larimar is in trouble."

"What?" Lindy repeated, suddenly awake. "What are you talking about?"

"Remember how I told you that Larimar had some issues with the taxes?"

"Yeah, and you said it was no big deal and that Heath was going to take care of it," Lindy answered. "What happened?"

"It's a bigger deal than I let on. I had to call Lora home. We're going to lose Larimar and it's my fault."

There, she'd said it. Only with Lindy could she be so honest. The guilt over her part in the resort's troubles spilled over in a wash of tears. "I tried to fix it. I thought we'd get it figured out but Pops hasn't paid taxes in years and there was no way to raise as much money as the resort needed. And now Lora is here and she's blaming Heath for everything and I can't handle Lora all on my own. I need you here, Lindy. Larimar needs you, too."

The long beleaguered sigh said it all but Lilah knew her twin wouldn't let her down. "This is bad timing, Li," Lindy said, and Lilah could almost hear her sister biting her lip as the difficult choice ate at her. "What can I do that Lora isn't doing already?"

"It's Pops, actually," Lilah said. "He's been losing time, but that's not the worst of it. He talks about Grams like she's still here and Lora isn't dealing well with that. You know how close she was to Grams. I think it's just too much to handle. You could help Lora with Pops. Right now, I'm taking shifts at the front desk but we need more help so we don't have to hire out. The money we save in employee costs can be applied to the debt."

"Hmm, so work for free?" Lindy mused, mildly amused. "Sounds like the acting jobs I've been getting lately." She sighed. "So, Lora on the rampage?"

Why lie? "Yes."

Lindy's chuckle was laced with sarcasm as she said, "Good times. I can hardly wait."

Lilah laughed for the first time in what felt like weeks and said, "I miss you, Lindy. Say you'll come home at least for a little while. I can't deal with Lora on my own. You know how she gets and right now, she's like the high-octane version of Lora."

"I guess I could take a few weeks off… I'd been waiting to hear if I was going to get a callback for this commercial but something tells me it's not going to happen."

"What was the commercial for?" Lilah asked, still mystified that her sister was in the big, bad, glitzy world of Hollywood when Lilah could barely handle a trip to St. Thomas without a stomachache.

"Um, tampons."

"Tampons?"

"Yeah…not very sexy but it was a national campaign, which means if I'd landed it, I could've gotten residuals for years. Can you say 'cash mo-ney'?" Lindy laughed.

"Yeah, but then you would've been known as the tampon girl. Not exactly the nicest nickname I can imagine. Why can't you land a Victoria's Secret campaign? That seems more your speed."

"I'm flattered, Sissy, but they use their own models for those campaigns."

"Well, there has to be some sort of underwear company you could audition for. You're always half-dressed, anyway, which on the island is no big deal but I imagine in Hollywood, it raises some eyebrows."

"Nah, not really," Lindy quipped, eliciting more laughter but soon she sobered and said, "Okay, I'll come. But listen, I can't come until next week. I have a few things to do first. Until then, stay strong and don't let Lora bully you. Stand up to her and tell her to shut her trap if she starts in on you. That's what I do and it seems to work."

Lilah smiled. If only it were that easy. "Okay," she agreed, though she doubted she'd say much of anything to Lora if she could avoid it. She'd already said her piece and besides, Lora didn't listen to anything she didn't want to hear. "I can't wait to see you."

"Me, too, Li. Stay loose. I'll be there before you know it."

They said their goodbyes and Lilah hung up, relieved that Lindy was coming. The separation was hard enough, but add the stress of her older sister stomping around like a bull in a China shop, determined to do things her way or the highway, and Lilah felt the distance between herself and Lindy like a physical thing.

Lindy had invited Lilah to come stay with her in L.A. but the idea made her want to run the other way. Los Angeles was not a place on her bucket list to visit. She doubted she'd fit in with the superficial crowd that Lindy ran with and Lilah wouldn't want Lindy to feel she constantly had to look out for her. So she'd declined, but there were so many times when she missed her sister so much her heart ached.

At least having Lindy here would serve as a buffer for the storm that was coming between Heath and Lora. Lilah could feel it building, threatening everything they were trying to save.

CHAPTER FOURTEEN

"YOU HUNGRY?"

The abrupt question after an hour or so of tense silence caused Lora to jump but she quickly recovered to answer with a cool "No."

But he wasn't going to accept her answer and pushed some more, much to her annoyance. "Listen, we both said some things that were mean, let's start over."

"And how do you propose we do that?" she asked.

"We'll sit and enjoy a meal together like two normal people out on a beautiful day in paradise," he answered reasonably. "I mean, look around you. How can you let such negative crap intrude on the natural beauty of this place? And I, for one, am starving and ready for breakfast."

She hated to admit it but her stomach was growling, too. But she was also still angry. And, oddly, hurt. "Why does everything revolve around food for you?" she asked, dismissing him and his offer with a look. "I'd rather return home, if you don't mind. There are pressing matters that need attending and I don't have time to float around with you on a pleasure cruise."

"Then you shouldn't have hopped aboard," he reminded her. "And to answer your question. I love food because when I was growing up, there was never enough of it. The meals I had at your family's table were the only square meals I had aside from what I could scrounge on my own. But you know, the resources of a child aren't that many, so I went to bed hungry more times than not."

A flush of shame heated her cheeks and she wanted to sink below deck for being so insensitive. She couldn't imagine not knowing where her next meal was coming from or going to bed with a belly cramped from hunger. Her grandparents had given them a wonderful life and she'd been blessed in so many ways. She really didn't know much about Heath's background because she'd never thought to ask. What a self-absorbed kid she'd been. One might say she hadn't changed much.

She risked a glance at Heath, reluctantly noting how at ease he appeared at the helm, his hair lifting in the breeze as if being teased by invisible fingers, and she choked down her previous anger for the time being. He was right, it was a beautiful day, and she hadn't enjoyed a vacation in years. She mentally squared her shoulders and made the choice to put aside the problems between them and enjoy the day. "I could eat," she ventured, holding her breath for his reaction. "Did you bring enough for two?"

A smile broke on his mouth as he said, "I always bring more than I need. Old habits die hard."

She returned the smile, albeit a bit tentatively for this was all virgin territory for her, and said, "All right then, let's eat."

HEATH SENSED HE'D scored a major victory between himself and Lora, but he wasn't sure in which fight. He hadn't told her about his relationship with food to elicit pity—not that she would give it—but he saw no value in shirking the truth. He loved food because as a kid he hadn't had much of it. So, yeah, sharing a meal with Lora seemed the best way to offer a truce—and he wasn't about to ruin his meal with awkward or angry silence. Besides, Lora was wound tighter than an islander's braid and she could use a little loosening up.

After securing the boat and dropping the anchor, he went below deck and brought up the food he'd packed earlier. Sandwiches, fresh fruit and, of course, cold beer.

She accepted the beer with a small smile as if she wasn't going to waste her breath denying that she actually enjoyed a beer and he swigged his own. Then, after a healthy bite of his sandwich, he sighed, happy with the moment. He purposefully chose to overlook the fact that she'd plainly threatened him with court and focused on how good it felt to simply live in the moment. He knew it wasn't that cut-and-dry—that there was plenty that needed to be straightened out and addressed—but seeing as they couldn't do anything on a boat, he let it go. He wished every moment could be this easy between them. The sun glinted off her dark hair, picking up threads of lighter brown that gave away her true color. At first glance it was easy to assume her hair was black because it was so dark, but in truth, Lora's hair was a rich assortment of colors ranging from deep auburn to soft mocha. She'd always had glorious hair and that hadn't changed. The long tendrils trailed in the wind, dancing on the mild air currents, and his heart spasmed, kicking up a beat. He returned to his sandwich, wishing he had the courage to finally do what he'd wanted to do so long ago and kiss her.

"Your job in Chicago, what exactly do you do? I know you're in marketing but aside from that...what is that?" he said, hoping to derail his current train of thought before he did something stupid and uninvited. "Pops never really said, just that he was real proud of you."

"If I were to boil it down in the simplest terms, I help create and maintain brands for multimillion-dollar corporations so they can make even more millions," she answered, though her expression had clamped down, sealing off any hint of pride or joy. *Curious.* Something didn't add up but she didn't elaborate, and instead changed the subject. "Whatever happened to your parents?" she asked.

"They died of drug overdoses over in St. Thomas about five years ago. I got a call from the police saying they'd been identified after a raid on a known drug house. They'd been dead for at least a day but no one in the house had noticed because everyone else there was so drugged up," he said, his tone matter-of-fact. Their deaths had never been painful because he'd lost them to drugs long before they'd died. In fact, he'd been relieved and he refused to feel bad about that. "But they left me the house and it was paid for, so at least I had a roof over my head."

"I hadn't heard anything about that," she admitted.

"I didn't see the point in telling anyone. It wasn't as if they'd been in my life up to that point. They walked out on me when I was ten. Frankly, I was surprised they'd lasted that long. Their path had been decided long before that moment."

His candor plainly shocked her but he'd long ago stopped questioning the *why me* aspect of his life. It is what it is, as he liked to say.

"I'm sorry," she murmured, likely because that was the appropriate response to that sort of admission but he shrugged it away.

"Don't be. Their dying was the best thing that ever happened to me."

At that she looked horrified. "How can you say that?"

"Easily. Before you get your feathers ruffled, my parents were nothing like what you've known as parents. They were so deep in their addiction all they cared about was their next fix. They were crackheads. Plain and simple. And crackheads don't feed their kids or care if they're safe. And if you have the misfortune to get in the way of their drugs, you get this—" he paused to show her the long, faint scar running up his forearm "—for your troubles."

She swallowed and appeared stricken by the sight of the scar his father had given him with a razor when Heath had mistakenly thought that if he simply threw away their drugs, they would get better. The naive ignorance of a seven-year-old. A mirthless chuckle escaped and he took another bite of his sandwich. "I know you lost your mom to cancer and that you loved her very much. Our situations are nothing alike."

She processed his stark honesty and then said, "Well, I'm still sorry. Not that they died, but because no kid should live that way."

"Agreed. Which is why when I have kids, I'm going to be the most hands-on dad on the planet. I'm going to be there for every event, every milestone, and I'm going to make sure that my kid never goes to bed hungry. That he or she never knows what it's like to open the refrigerator and stare at nothing but moldy bread and an ancient bottle of mustard. My kid will always know he or she is loved because I'll tell them every day of their lives."

He might've shared too much, but it was something he felt very passionate about and she'd inadvertently triggered a sensitive spot. For a heart-stopping moment, he pictured little girls flocked around him who looked just like Lora with their long, streaming hair and varying shades of blue eyes. The fantasy squeezed his heart and made breathing difficult. He wanted Lora to be the mother of his children. He might as well wish for the moon. Neither was likely to happen.

"This is a very good sandwich," she murmured, her voice catching as her gaze bounced away from his, confirming that he'd shared too much. "But it takes more than love and sandwiches to be a good father. You have to be able to provide for them, too. And sometimes that pressure can do things to a person's convictions. Sometimes, it makes you forget all the promises you'd made in the beginning."

HER OWN FATHER HAD BEEN charming, sweet and loving—until he left. And then she never saw him again.

"Kids are a huge responsibility and once the novelty wears off, some guys can't handle the day-to-day and split, leaving the mothers to fend for themselves."

"Yeah, but real men don't do that," he countered, his gaze dead serious. In that moment, she was certain he'd never abandon his children like her father had abandoned his. But hadn't her own mother been certain she'd married and had kids with a solid man? It's hard to know for sure when you're in love. Those endorphins do kooky things to a person's brain. She'd rather not risk it at all.

"A real man takes pride in his family and does everything in his power to protect them," Heath continued.

"So they say," she quipped lightly, ready to move on. This wasn't a subject she felt comfortable discussing. "You never truly know another person's character until they face adversity. A series of lost jobs, financial stress, trust issues…it's a house of cards waiting to fall."

"Was that what happened with your parents?" he asked, keying into what she hadn't said.

"Yes," she answered, then shrugged. "At least, that's what I managed to glean from childhood memories. My dad split when I was nine and my mom died of cancer a year later. It wasn't exactly a time of great sharing. But I remember the fights right before the big exit."

"Is he still alive?" he asked.

"How should I know?" The bastard could rot for all she cared. "He hasn't deigned to keep in touch and neither have I." The subject of her father was an off-limits topic of conversation that she kept locked down and inaccessible. The fact that Heath had even managed to pry her lips open on the subject was surprising. She leaned back and closed her eyes, hating how unsettled she felt. "Lilah had asked me to hire a private eye to find him but I didn't feel it was necessary or healthy to start poking at that particular beehive. What if he'd started a new family? Frankly, I wouldn't care but it would devastate Lilah. She's fragile like that."

"She's stronger than you give her credit," Heath said, causing her to snap open her eyes and stare. He shrugged as if he didn't care that she hated when he openly disagreed about her family. It was her damn family, for crying out loud. "You can't baby her one minute and then expect her to shoulder the load in the next. It's not fair and it sets her up to fail."

"Can you even stop yourself from picking a fight with me?" she asked wryly. "I think I know my sister better than you."

"That's where you're wrong. You haven't been around and when you were around, you were pretty wrapped up in your own world."

She shifted in discomfort. Why'd he have to be so damn right all the time? "Next subject. Or else you might find yourself overboard."

"Can you sail?"

"No."

"Then I'm not worried."

At that she laughed. He had a point. "So what are we going to do? We can't talk about our pasts without stepping on something painful and best left forgotten, can't talk about the present because there's a whole lot of dangerous territory there, too. What does that leave us, aside from chitchatting about your culinary skills? I mean, don't get me wrong, that was a pretty good sandwich but not so good that we can spend all day talking about it."

"You can ask me anything. I will always be honest with you, even if it's something you don't want to hear."

She regarded him with something akin to silent wonder. For someone who'd lived through a terrible childhood, he certainly didn't let the scars show. She didn't like to talk about her parents because it hurt to remember. By all accounts, Heath ought to shy away from the topic of his upbringing but he was offering to share if she chose to ask. She wanted to ask him if he'd ever had feelings for her. But the question stuck to the roof of her mouth, refusing to be asked. Was it fear that her sister had been wrong and that Heath had never felt anything for her? Why would she care either way? When she realized the moment had stretched too long, she forced a light smile and said, "If we're taking a break from everything else today, let's stick to that plan and make a pact to keep the questions to the superficial and polite. It's a beautiful day and I'm going to take advantage of the sun. Do you happen to have some sunscreen I could use?"

Heath seemed disappointed, as if he'd wanted her to ask him something of substance, but he nodded and went below deck to grab the sunscreen. It gave her the time she needed to settle her nerves so Heath didn't notice how her hands trembled.

He returned and hesitated. "Should I...?" he asked, gesturing to her back.

She paused, knowing that if she didn't have protection on her back she'd fry like a dough-nut in hot oil, but she wasn't sure she wanted Heath's hands on her skin. And not because she loathed the idea, but rather because she found the idea exciting and taboo. This bur-geoning attraction to Heath was coming out sidewise, she thought irritably. If only she'd had a boyfriend in Chicago to keep her hor-mones in check. But it'd been a while since she spent some serious time with the oppo-site sex without business between them. She wasn't sure she remembered the moves to that particular social dance.

"It's just sunscreen, Lora," Heath said wryly.

"I know that." As if to illustrate that point, she nodded and presented her back. She could certainly handle Heath lathering a little cream on her back. It wasn't as if one single touch was going to ignite a firestorm of un-restrained lust, she chuckled to herself. The very idea was preposterous.

At least that's what she'd thought. The minute Heath's hands slid over her shoulders, an unwanted tingle made her aware of their close proximity to one another. She clenched her teeth, determined to ignore the dangerous fluttering in her stomach that felt too much like the beginning of arousal for her comfort.

But his hands felt good. Much too good. Was that a moan that'd just popped from her mouth? Her bones were melting beneath his touch. Yes, it was most certainly a moan because another followed the first in quick succession.

She turned to say something—anything, who knows—but she was stopped short by the dark intensity in Heath's eyes. Had anyone ever looked at her with such hunger? Such raw desire? Her breath tangled in a knot and she knew he was going to kiss her.

The question was…would she stop him?

CHAPTER FIFTEEN

POPS WANDERED INTO THE LOBBY and saw Lilah behind the reception desk. Lilah looked up and smiled when she saw him.

"Hey, Pops, what are you up to today?" she asked.

He grinned and hefted the drink in his hand. "Just doing what I do best… Have you seen your Grams? I need to talk to her about this situation with Heath and Lora."

Lilah's smile didn't falter but inside she cried a little. Pops had always been her knight in shining armor. She didn't remember enough about her biological father aside from snippets in her memory, so Pops had taken the place of a father figure. To watch him decline right before her eyes was a hardship that she wouldn't wish on her worst enemy. But in spite of her pain, she played along for Pops's sake and said, "I think she said something about needing to get supplies from St. Thomas. She said she'd be gone all day."

"Dang that woman, I wish she would've told me. I could've gone with her. There's a few things I need, too."

"Well, maybe Heath could get what you need," Lilah suggested. "Besides, I think there's a small storm coming. You don't want to be out there when it hits."

"Yes, I suppose you're right. I'll have to ask Heath when he gets back," Pops agreed, then he turned to Lilah, his expression troubled. "What happened to…" He paused, searching his memory with obvious difficulty. "You know, that girl…"

"Celly?" Lilah supplied. "Well, she's working part-time so I could get some more experience behind the counter. Is that okay?"

Pops's uncertainty faded away at Lilah's admission and he beamed. He loved the idea that his sugar birds were becoming more involved with the resort and Lilah knew it would distract him. "I think that's a great idea. How are you liking it? You picked a good time, too. Hurricane season is slower, less stress."

"Yeah," Lilah nodded, wondering how Pops could look every bit as normal as he ever was, but inside his brain was slowly dying and taking reality with it. Lilah drew a deep breath and smiled. "I love you, Pops."

"I love you, too, sugar bird."

She warmed, loving the little endearment. Everything seemed more precious now, more so than she'd ever realized.

"Where is Lora?" he asked, glancing around. "I haven't seen her all day."

"She went to find Heath. She seemed pretty mad. Like usual," she added under her breath.

"Don't be so hard on your sister," he admonished, which to Lilah felt pretty absurd. Lora didn't need anyone to defend her; Lora could take care of herself. "She's under a lot of pressure. I don't think she's having a good go of it with that job of hers. She needs some island time to relax, soak up the sun and get back to basics. You can help her with that. You've always been able to go with the flow."

"That's about all I can do," she said with a self-deprecating chuckle.

"Ah, sugar bird. It's all going to work out," he said as he caressed her cheek. She leaned into his soft, weathered touch and wished she shared his conviction. Of course he believed everything was going to work out. In his world, his wife hadn't died a painful death and was simply on a shopping outing.

She pulled away but offered a brief smile. "Thanks, Pops."

"You bet. Let me know when your Grams gets back, will ya?"

"Sure, Pops," she promised, biting back a sigh. She couldn't wait for Lindy to get here. She didn't know how much more she could take without losing her sanity, too.

HEATH KNEW HE SHOULDN'T but if he was anything, he was an opportunist, and one thing life had taught him was that you took advantage of the moment because you never knew when it might come again. And frankly, even if he'd had the good judgment to pull away, his body simply wouldn't let him.

This was the moment he'd dreamed about. Sure, the idea had faded over the years but it hadn't taken long for the desire to kiss Lora to pulse to life. And it was damn torture trying to deny his feelings.

"Heath…"

The soft sound of his name on her lips, unsure and hesitant, broke through his haze and he stopped short of pressing his lips to hers. "Yeah?" he asked, almost painfully.

"I don't think we should do this…"

He swore silently. Of course she was right,

but he didn't care about right. He wanted her so badly, his whole body shook with it.

He pulled back a fraction and he saw indecision in her eyes, which mollified him a bit. At least she was struggling with herself, too. He'd hate to think he was alone in this quagmire.

"We should address what's happening between us and get it out of the way," she suggested, and he wanted to snort in derision. His hormones were still kicking healthy doses of testosterone through his veins. Talking about how he wanted to strip her down and plunge inside her didn't seem very helpful to him.

"I have a better idea," he said. "Let's just play it by ear and see what happens."

At that her gaze narrowed and she actually pushed him away from her. "That's exactly what I *don't* want to do."

"What's wrong?"

"Do I look like the kind of woman who just *goes with the moment?*" she asked with obvious distaste. "Let me tell you where that kind of irresponsible behavior puts you. It puts you in bad situations where you end up used and abused and I'm never put in that situation. Ever."

The lust clouding his reason melted away

and he stared at her, insulted that she would insinuate he would ever treat her that way. "I don't know the kind of guys you typically hang out with, but I don't treat women that way," he said. "And furthermore, if you weren't so damn uptight you might learn that going with the flow can actually be a lot of fun."

"Only for those without a care as to how things work out in the end."

"And you think I'm like that?"

She shrugged. "Well, the shoe seems to fit. You struck a deal with my grandfather that benefited you without caring to see how it might affect my family."

"I told you I didn't know about Pops at the time," he said between gritted teeth. "Do I have to have it tattooed onto my forehead before you believe me?"

"It doesn't matter what I believe. The facts remain the same, which is why if you were thinking, you'd realize that indulging in some sort of physical attraction between us would be terribly ill-advised in the long-term."

He jerked his fingers through his hair, more than sexual frustration lacing his voice as he said, "Right, Lora. As usual, you're right and everyone else is an idiot. Thank God we have you to make sure no one makes any damn mistakes."

There was a boom of thunder that caused both Heath and Lora to look to the sky. While they're attention had been on each other, a tropical storm had blown in and was quickly headed their way. Heath swore and Lora rushed to grab her cover-up and pull it on. The wind had already kicked up and as he contemplated heading back to the island, the rain started pelting them. Lora shrieked and he hollered for her to go down below while he readied the sails to handle the barrage.

"Are you sure you can handle this?" she yelled, hesitating, but he waved her away, too focused on the wind that was building along with the rain. It wasn't unusual to weather a quick tropical rainstorm during hurricane season but he was a little concerned over how the skies had darkened and the wind had begun to howl. He had two choices, try to outrun the bad weather or anchor up and wait it out. It looked as if the storm was heading right in the direction he needed to go if he were to pull up anchor and sail for shore, so he opted to wait it out. With luck, most tropical storms moved quickly in and then out.

He double-checked his lines and then

headed below deck to start the engine and put it into neutral.

"What are you doing? Don't you need to be steering or something?" she asked, the tension radiating from her shoulders and reflecting in the tightness of her voice.

"We're going to wait it out. The storm is heading toward St. John. I'd rather weather some choppy waves and rain than try to outrun the storm when it's going in the same direction. Don't worry, we're anchored tight and Billy's boat can handle a little rough water. She's built to last."

"How rough of water?" she asked.

"Nothing to worry about," he assured her, and hoped that was the case. He checked the gas level for the engine and noted the tank was nearly full. "It's going to be fine. At least the storm's not gunning for us. That could be a little stressful."

"A little stressful? I think this is a lot stressful," she said, rubbing her arms and cocking her head to listen to the thunder rumble and the rain hit the deck. "Please tell me you've done this before."

"Sailed rough water? Yes. Alone? No. But it's going to be fine. I promise."

"So now what?" she asked in an almost

desperate tone. "I'm not good at just hanging out. I'm already about to jump from my skin and I've only been down here a few minutes. How long do you think it's going to take?"

"I don't know. I didn't check the weather report before I left."

She arched her brow. "Isn't that, like, rule number one when you're sailing? Followed closely by making sure there are life vests on the boat?"

Yeah, he should've checked. "Slipped my mind. But you're the one who's stressed, not me." She nibbled her lip and he tried not to notice how attractive she appeared under such unlikely circumstances. Perhaps it was because she was always so hard-boiled, so matter-of-fact that seeing her react to a situation where she had to rely on someone else allowed him to see the vulnerable side of her. "I won't let anything happen to you, Lora," he said, and he meant it. "Will you trust me?"

HE WAS ASKING A LOT, she thought as her mind escalated the situation with each peal of thunder. But even as she started to shake her head, she caught his gaze and felt his sincerity through her bones. He would protect her. She suppressed a shudder and for a wild moment she wished she'd let him kiss her.

"Okay," she agreed, hating that she felt so scared over a silly storm. "Say something… I need to get my mind off what's happening right now." *Or better yet, forget what I said earlier and just get over here and kiss me until I can't think any longer.* "Tell me about what you've been doing since I left. How come you haven't met someone and started a family or something?"

His expression fell and she imagined that's what she'd looked like when he'd asked about her job in Chicago.

"I'm sorry, that's so personal. I'm just nervous," she apologized, moving to the rear of the boat to sit on the bed. The boat was small so when he followed and sat beside her, she didn't comment, just simply scooted to give him more room. "Tell me your business plan for recouping my grandfather's investment," she said, focusing on the one thing—business—that could narrow her thoughts in a predictable and manageable line.

But Heath wasn't going to go there. He firmly shook his head and said, "If all there ever is between us is business, we can't ever hope to be friends."

"Do you want to be friends?" she murmured, shooting him an unsure glance. "I don't have much experience in that area. The people in my life are placed in clearly marked compartments—family and business associates. I'm not sure I have friends. And I don't think I know how to be one," she admitted.

"I have lots of friends. I can teach you. I remember you being an excellent student. Straight-A girl, right?"

She risked a smile. "Even through college. Grams used to say I was obsessive. And she said it like it was a bad thing."

"There's nothing wrong with attention to detail," he said softly, his gaze roaming her face. Another shiver threatened to rock her body and once again the moment changed between them. They were too close, the situation had heightened the feelings zipping between them. None of it was real, she reminded herself, trying to pull free from the threads winding around them, drawing them ever closer.

"I think we should kiss," he said in a husky tone that caused goose pimples to erupt up and down her skin.

"I thought you said we should try to be friends," she reminded him in a breathless whisper as he leaned in and she moved forward to meet him.

Seconds before their lips touched, and her eyelids fluttered shut, she heard him say in a playfully sexy voice, "How about friends with *benefits?*"

CHAPTER SIXTEEN

THIS IS INSANITY, LORA thought dizzily as she fell back against the bed, Heath's mouth moving in concert with her own. And yet, crazy as it was, Lora was in no hurry to stop. If anything, she hungered for more.

She slid her tongue against Heath's, reveling in the sensation, lifting her hips to press against his, gasping as she felt the urgency in his hands as he touched her body.

The feel of Heath's mouth and body was the only thought running through her mind as she lost herself to the sensation of being thoroughly kissed. There was nothing tentative or submissive about his touch. He plundered, took and demanded—and it thrilled her senseless.

The storm continued to rage, buffeting the sailboat and rocking them with the waves that crashed around them but Lora could focus on only one thing—getting her clothes off so she could be skin to skin with Heath.

She panted, writhed, and when she thought she might completely lose herself, he pulled away and jerked her hands above her head, stretching her until she was helpless to change position.

"Say you want me," he demanded in a silky voice that slid along her nerve endings and then lit them on fire. He nuzzled her right breast and then nipped at the tip that had instantly pebbled beneath her thin bikini top. She gasped and bit her lip as if to prevent herself from giving in but he was relentless. "Say it," he growled, grazing her nipple with his teeth. She bucked and he pressed against her, grinding his erection into her pelvic bone and causing her to moan. *She wanted him. She wanted him.* The knowledge slicked her insides and she twisted, silently begging him to touch her, somewhere—anywhere— but he simply tortured her with featherlight grazes that teased. He moved up her body to stare into her eyes, forcing her to meet his heated gaze. He freed one of his hands and pressed his palm against her pubic bone. The delightfully carnal pressure made her moan and open her legs in silent invitation but he wouldn't give in until she said the words.

"Say it," he whispered in her ear, tickling her with his voice.

"I want you," she gasped, giving in, twisting. "I want you, damn it!"

He chuckled and released her hands only to strip her bikini bottom off with lightning-fast speed. She followed by ripping her cover-up and top off. She rose on the bed and pulled the drawstring on his linen shorts. She sucked in a tight breath when she saw he was nude underneath. Her memory hadn't embellished his size and she couldn't help but stare. Good God…was that natural?

"I'm glad you like what you see," he said, his voice raw, primal as his own gaze feasted on her breasts, her flat stomach and lower. "You're more beautiful than I ever imagined…" She warmed at his perusal but she didn't have time to respond before he pulled her against him, turning her so that her back was to him. He splayed his fingertips over her belly and slid down to cup the hot aching core of her. "So perfect…" he murmured, slowly dipping his finger inside her, testing. She sank against him, swallowing her moan, trying to focus, to return to herself, but he must've sensed her innate refusal to give in and withdrew his finger. He threaded his fingers through her hair and then gripped it hard, the sensation sending rockets of need straight to the place that pulsed and spiraled, waiting.

"I've always wanted you to be mine and in this moment, right now, you are," he breathed against her ear, causing her to shake. She'd never had a lover demand so much of her. Most had been attentive but way too polished to ever dominate her. If anything she'd dominated them, taking her pleasure and then moving on, simple as any other task on her to-do list. But not so with Heath. She breathed hard, her whole body trembling as his lips traveled the sensitive shell of her ear. "Tell me, Lora…what do you want me to do to you?"

HE COULD FEEL THE SUBTLE shakes and tremors coursing through her body and it only fueled his need to have all of her. He felt the clock ticking, that time was not his friend. He wasn't naive in thinking that Lora would soften toward him just because they'd been intimate, and so he was going to wring every last cry from her throat and savor the taking. Maybe if he got her out of his system he could finally move on and find a less difficult woman to want. It was a thought, even if the likelihood of it coming true was remote.

The smooth lines of her body felt like silk beneath his fingertips, and the soft, sparse curls of her pubic mound tickled. He wanted to bury his face in all that womanly flesh and feel her come against his tongue. But first...

He surprised her by bending her over the bed, and lifting her hips so that her plump, perfectly shaped ass rose to meet him. He heard her sharp intake of breath and then she arched as if in invitation and he nearly lost it right there. He reached with shaking fingers and jerked a condom out of the drawer where Billy kept his stash and after quickly sheathing himself, slowly slid inside her hot body. A guttural moan escaped from his lips as her flesh clamped around his and he pushed until he was deep inside. She cried out and curled her palms into the comforter, moaning as he pulled out only to slide back. He kept this slow, torturous rhythm until he thought he was going to die from a heart attack. Then he started to pump harder. She matched his thrusts by pushing against him. Before long, he felt the deep pulling in his balls and he knew he was about to come. He gripped her hips and with one last thrust he came so hard he thought he saw stars and his knees threatened to give out. He collapsed against her and for a long moment it was just the harsh sound of their breathing. Then he rolled away and pulled the condom free and put it in the trash. She'd rolled to her back, her stomach lifting and falling from the exertion, though he wasn't sure if she'd reached her climax.

He climbed her body and pulled her arm free from her eyes. Her face was flushed and she was still breathing heavy. She looked at him with something akin to surprised wonder and he had his answer.

When she could speak, she said, "You wore a condom?"

"Yes."

She nodded in relief. "Good." She started to roll away but he stopped her with a frown. She turned to look at him. "What's wrong?"

"Not yet," he said firmly. When she looked at him in question, he pushed her back down and straddled her. "When we return to Cruz Bay, I know you and I will be at odds again. It's the nature of our relationship, but right now, we have this moment and I'm not ready to let it go just yet."

She nodded, understanding. "So what do you propose? We can't spend all night out here. Everyone will worry. And no matter how much we enjoy ourselves it's not going to change the reality of our situation."

"I know. But we can have this moment. And that's what I intend to do."

She closed her eyes and he bent down to suck her nipple into his mouth. She arched into him, clasping her arms around his neck. "Heath…" she murmured on a groan, and he lavished her breasts with equal attention.

"You have the most amazing breasts," he told her, nuzzling the soft, plump flesh and teasing the tips until she writhed and squirmed. "I could spend all day right here."

But that wasn't entirely true. He was aching to go lower, to taste her, to know her completely.

He moved down her body and opened her legs, baring that prized spot. She whimpered something and tried to close her legs but her sudden show of bashfulness was like a shot of aphrodisiac straight to his groin. He placed long lingering kisses on her inner thighs and then hooked her thighs over his arms, dragging her closer.

She lifted her head and braced herself on her elbows, her cheeks pinking in the sweetest, most unexpected way as she said, "You don't have to do that…"

"I want to," he answered. She thought it was an obligation. If she only knew how he couldn't wait. The moment his tongue delved inside those soft, pink folds, he knew this was the place he could gladly spend forever. And judging by her reaction, he didn't think she'd mind.

LORA GASPED AS SHOCK WAVES coursed through her. She'd never been a fan of oral sex; in her experience, it was messy and embarrassing, and frankly she'd never been with anyone who'd convinced her otherwise.

Until Heath.

She clutched at his head, urging him on and writhing as he held her in place, his wicked tongue and lips doing things to her she'd never imagined were possible.

"I can't… This is… Oh…oh…" Her entire body clenched and she thought her heart may have stopped as every muscle contracted and she cried out Heath's name in a keening wail that surely everyone on St. Croix heard.

Little pulses rocked her body and radiated to every nerve ending until she felt wrung out and completely sated.

Heath moved to lie beside her, leaning on his elbow to look down at her. For a moment she couldn't meet his stare; this was the embarrassing part. But once she caught her breath, she turned to him and smiled like the Cheshire cat. What else could she do? She felt wondrously drowsy and deliciously relaxed. Not even the most expensive spa treatment had yielded this type of contentment.

"If you could bottle that up and sell it, you'd be a rich man," she said playfully. He leaned down and pressed a kiss to her lips. He smelled faintly of her own musk and instead of being grossed out, she was turned on by the scent of her body on his lips. "This could be a problem," she amended huskily.

"Which part? The part where we both can't keep our hands off each other, or the part where we're destined to forever be on opposite ends of the spectrum as far as life goes?"

"Both. But mostly the first part."

"I think I can deal with it."

"I'm not sure I can," she said truthfully. This changed everything. And when she came to her senses that would weigh heavily on her conscience.

He shrugged. "Let's cross that bridge when we come to it."

"Do you ever worry about anything?"

"Plenty." He kissed her again. "But for the moment…all I'm worried about is having enough time to grab a bite to eat and then make love to you one last time before we head in."

"What about the storm?" she asked.

He paused to listen. The rain had stopped pelting the boat. "Sounds all clear. Guess it was a good thing to wait it out after all."

She paused to listen and then said with a smile, "Well, we'd better get some food down that gullet so we can burn off those calories because—" she pushed him over so she could straddle him this time "—I believe it's my turn to be on top."

CHAPTER SEVENTEEN

LILAH CLOSED UP THE FRONT DESK and put the phone on night service then went to see if Pops wanted anything to eat from Sailor's because she was starving and ready to eat her weight in beef.

The resort was empty as the last guests had just checked out and Lilah was glad. Hurricane season was her personal favorite because the flow of guests trickled to a manageable stream and everything became more relaxed. If it weren't for the unpredictable torrential rains and high winds that also came with the season, she'd say it was downright perfect.

She and Grams used to sit on the patio and watch the lightning streak across the sky, listening to the rain douse the beach. The sound of the rain hitting the water soothed her like none other. If only Lora had learned to appreciate the wonders of the island. Maybe she'd be less high-strung. Lora thought Lilah never worried about anything but the exact opposite was true. Lilah worried a lot. It's just that Lilah kept her worries private. She'd known Heath was struggling to make a go of the gift shop and it killed her because Heath was a true artist. His work was good enough to go in any gallery in the plaza but he didn't have the right connections, not yet, anyway. She'd tried to talk him into opening his own gallery in town but he'd been unsure. Taking over the gift shop had been the safe bet. At least, he'd thought it was going to be. Lilah's heart broke for Heath because she knew that he was under a lot of pressure.

But with that said, she really didn't want to see Larimar get sold right out from beneath their feet. Lora and Heath needed to work together or else they were all in big trouble.

The question was, could Lora work with someone else, most of all Heath? The two were like oil and water.

She sighed, glad Lindy was coming in a few days. Lindy would help Lora see reason. At least that was Lilah's fervent hope because Lilah had never been successful at reaching Lora.

"Pops," she called out, heading to the private section of the resort and into Pops and Grams's residence. "You in here? I'm heading to Sailor's…do you want me to get you a burger?"

She wandered the expansive apartment and smiled as warm memories of when Grams was alive followed. Grams had been the most amazing grandmother anyone could have. She was a bit unorthodox, which is probably why Lilah identified with her so deeply, even though Lora would say she was closest to her.

Lora had always thought she'd cornered the market when it came to Grams, Lilah thought with a sniff of annoyance. Which was patently ridiculous when you consider they'd been polar opposites. Of course, that begged the question, why couldn't Lilah and Lora get along, then? It always felt as if Lora was perpetually irritated with Lilah and Lindy, but Lindy couldn't care less what Lora thought. Lilah wished she could be as flippant about her older sister. Ugh. Her head ached just thinking about the situation with Lora. There were no easy answers and she was hungry.

"Pops?" she queried one last time before concluding he wasn't in the apartment. She went to the private terrace and found it empty, as well. A growing sense of disquiet followed the realization that Pops had left the resort.

She went out to the garage and found that one of the resort Jeeps was gone.

"Shit," she muttered, biting her lip. "Where'd you go, Pops? Lora is going to kill me."

LORA CLOSED HER EYES and let the wind caress her face as they returned to Cruz Bay. She was still loose and relaxed, and she couldn't quite help the small smile that kept finding her mouth. Dusk was upon them and the sunset was like a fire in the horizon. The air smelled sweet and fresh after the rain and she wished every night was this perfect.

She stole a look Heath's way as he steered the boat home and her breath hitched in her throat as her cheeks heated. She could smell him on her skin—a heady combination of masculine musk and sunshine—and she had to resist the urge to deeply inhale the intoxicating scent.

Lora narrowed her gaze at him in open speculation. Could they enjoy a sex life apart from their business relationship? Her toes twitched as desire curled in her stomach, igniting the embers of what had already burned through her body. She looked away, fearing he'd see in her gaze what she wasn't ready to share.

She didn't want romantic entanglements but she'd enjoy spending her nights with someone she clearly shared a connection with while she was here sorting out this issue with the resort. The question was, could she and Heath manage to keep their relationship sexual after-hours and strictly business during the day?

"Were you serious about the friends-with-benefits suggestion?" she asked, curious as to his reaction.

"Were you serious about being friends?" he countered with a sardonic grin that was entirely too sexy to be taken seriously. She frowned, determined to stay focused. He sobered reluctantly, regarding her with a somewhat guarded expression. "Why do you ask?"

"Well, clearly we have some physical connection and I wouldn't be opposed to—" she drew a deep breath, surprised at how difficult it was not to squirm like a teenager faced with her crush "—continuing if we could come to some sort of arrangement."

"Arrangement?"

"Yes. Let's be frank. Sex with you is very... good."

"Just good? You really know how to massage a guy's ego," he said wryly. "Please continue. I'm interested to hear where this is going."

She glared. "A little maturity, please? What I'm saying is, yes, the sex is fabulous, okay? Is that better?" If she were being honest, she'd have to say it was the best sex of her life, but there was no need to inflate his ego any further. Besides, she'd never live that admission down and she'd rather keep the information to herself. "So here's the deal. I propose we enjoy each other's company in the evening but during the day we keep to strictly business. So no kissing, touching, no endearments— good God, please no endearments. I find them embarrassingly trite. Nothing that would give anyone the impression that we're being anything other than civil to one another for the purposes of saving the resort. Does that sound amenable to you?"

She paused and awaited his answer, but it was hard to gauge his reaction to her proposal. The light was fading fast and his silhouette was all she could make out, but somehow she sensed he wasn't happy with her suggestion.

She stiffened when the silence stretched to an uncomfortable pause. "I thought you might feel the same way. You seemed to be enjoying yourself, if I recall correctly."

"Why does everything have to be squashed and packaged into a neat and tidy compartment? Here's a newsflash—sometimes life is messy and complicated and it doesn't fit into a nice little box for your convenience. And to answer your question, no, your offer does not sound amenable to me. It sounds like a damn business arrangement that I'm not interested in signing on for."

She stared, glad for the gathering darkness when her eyes began to sting. "I see."

"No, I don't think you do, Lora," he disagreed hotly. "I don't think you could see what is right in front of your face."

"What are you saying?"

"Forget it."

"That's not fair. You insult me and then button up? I don't think so. Say what you mean. I think I can take it," she shot back scathingly. Certainly she'd suffered through worse than whatever Heath had to dish out. "Go ahead. Don't hold back." But in spite of her hot words, there was a small part of her that worried about what Heath might say. She didn't want to admit it, but his rejection hurt…a lot.

"Lora…I'm not interested in your deal, okay? Let's leave it at that."

"Fine," she said, turning away. But it wasn't fine. Not by a long shot. She wanted to know specifically why Heath found her offer untenable. "For what it's worth, I thought most men jumped at the idea of being in a no-strings-attached sexual relationship."

"Well, what can I say? I'm not like most men," he quipped darkly.

You can say that again, she thought with a frown. She opened her mouth to retort, but he cut her short. "Let's just cut our losses and forget this ever happened? Okay? From now on, strictly business. That work for you?"

It should work. It should sound perfect. But it struck a discordant chord within her heart that reverberated uncomfortably throughout her body. She straightened. "Of course. That's perfectly acceptable. I assume you'll remain silent about our…"

"Hookup?" he asked, the sarcasm causing her to wince inwardly.

"Y-yes."

"Yeah. No one will know from me, sugar bird."

She ground her teeth. "Stop calling me that. Only Pops can call me that."

"My apologies. Lora. Or do you prefer Ms. Bell?"

"Now you're just being an asshole," she said, feeling miserable inside but refusing to let it show. She could sort out the confused jumble of her feelings later. Right now she just needed to keep it together until they got back to Larimar. "How much longer?" she snapped.

"Fifteen minutes."

By the tone of his voice, she wasn't alone in thinking that it might be the longest fifteen minutes of their lives.

HEATH DIDN'T KNOW THE TRUE source of his anger, but at the moment it didn't matter. He was well and truly *pissed off*.

He swore silently. There was no one on this planet who could rile him faster than Lora Bell.

Had they not just shared the most amazing physical and emotional connection together? Apparently he'd been alone in that cosmic union. To Lora, he'd simply been another notch on her belt. If he weren't so jacked up over the whole situation, he might've found the ironic humor in it all. And now she wanted to make an arrangement with him, as if he was some kind of good-time guy, ready and waiting whenever she had an itch she needed scratching?

Hell no. He was better than that. Right? Yes. Unequivocally. He just had to find a way to forget the feel and taste of her skin, and above all, the way his heart had sang like a bird when she'd been in his arms. Should be easy as long as he remained angry. When he was mad, he didn't care two figs that she was the epitome of his perfect woman in face and form, or that being with her for that heartbeat of a moment, he'd been deliriously happy.

So…yeah. Angry. Angry was good.

"Heath—"

"We're almost there." He cut her off, not caring that he was being rude. "I'm okay with silence, if you don't mind."

"Why are you acting like this?" she asked crossly, but he thought he might've detected the barest hint of hurt couched in her tone. He ignored it.

"I guess I misjudged the level of enjoyment we were both having," she said with a sniff.

Was she joking? He wanted to tell her he wasn't that good of an actor, but that would give her an opening to worm her way into his head and somehow convince him to forget everything he believed in, sell out his soul and slide into her bed with no questions asked. He ground his teeth and focused on getting them home.

"This is so ridiculous," she muttered, her frustration mirroring his own but for different reasons. "I would've never slept with you if I'd known you were going to be so melodramatic about it."

"God, woman, can you just shut the hell up, please?" His best intention to remain quiet shattered as his ire boiled over. "You want to know why I would never consider your little arrangement? Because I'm not interested in soulless little sexual encounters where there's nothing more intimate than blowing your nose into a tissue and tossing it into the trash. Forgive me, but I'm a little more sensitive than that. I prefer my bed partners to be actively engaged, both mind and body."

"Are you saying that you've never had a one-night stand?" she mocked, then added with a healthy dose of sarcasm, "Give me a break."

Of course he'd had one-night stands, but why should he admit that to her when it would only serve to make her case and force him to tell her why he didn't want a mean-

ingless fling with *her*. If she wasn't ready
to be openly romantic in clear view of God
and country, she sure as hell wasn't going to
tolerate his admission that he wanted more
than her body—he wanted her heart, too. And
frankly, one nut-squashing episode per night
was his current limit. "Forget it," he muttered.
"This conversation is going nowhere."

"Yes, it is," she agreed angrily. "And you're
a jerk."

Yeah, well, he was also an idiot.

"You know, you're right about one thing—
if I'd known you were going to be like this
after we hooked up, I'd have steered clear,
too."

"Glad we finally agree on something," she
said with ice in her tone. "Now that I think
about it, silence is probably the best idea."

"Amen to that," he said stonily. "A-freak-
ing-men."

CHAPTER EIGHTEEN

LORA AND HEATH ENTERED Larimar, both heading in separate directions when a frantic Lilah waylaid them.

"Pops is gone," she blurted, getting straight to the point.

Lora immediately shelved her hurt over Heath and his rejection, her heart stopping at her sister's words.

"At first I wasn't too worried because sometimes he likes to take little jaunts into town to get stuff, but we've been trying to keep him from driving too much because he forgets where he's going or forgets which side of the street to drive on, so it's just safer for everyone for him to take a taxi or have one of us take him to town."

Lora willed herself to calm, knowing that railing at her sister for losing their grandfather wasn't going to help matters and would likely cause Lilah to break into a useless, blubbering mess, but deep inside a cold knot of worry had begun to form.

"Where does he usually go when he goes to town?" she asked. "What about Celly? Does she know where he goes?"

"I already checked all those places and Celly went home early today," she wailed, a note of cross exasperation in her voice. "Don't you think I would check there first? He's gone! Like vanished."

"People don't vanish," Lora corrected, quickly losing patience with her sister's immediate panic. "He's probably just—"

"He's *gone*. You think I wouldn't know the difference between him disappearing for a few hours and him missing? You haven't been here, Lora. Sometimes he wanders, but he always manages to find his way back home. But I've searched everywhere! What if he fell into the ocean and hit his head? He could be dead for all we know."

"Stop it," Lora demanded sharply, hating that her sister's fear was contagious. The fact was she didn't know much about dementia or even what stage her grandfather was in. She hadn't had time to talk to his doctor, and since he'd seemed mostly fine, aside from the fact that he conversed with his dead wife, she'd put it at the bottom of her priority list. *Damn! Wrong move.*

Lora wrapped her arms around herself, determined to hold it together in the face of her sister's total unraveling. Someone had to keep it together, but Lilah's fear had started to eat at her ability to think straight. If anything happened to Pops she'd never, ever forgive herself. And to think of what she'd been doing when he disappeared... *Oh, God.* Fresh shame flooded her cheeks and tears stung her eyes. He had to be all right. *Stop freaking out! Keep a cool head,* she admonished herself. *Everything will be fine.* Before she attempted to calm her sister, Heath stepped in, gently grabbing Lilah's shoulders to get her attention.

"Li...it's okay. We'll find him. The island is only so big and there are only so many places he can go. I'll start making some calls. Why don't you and Lora take a second look in town? He might've got a hunger for something to eat. Did you check Sailor's?" She jerked a nod, but Heath's voice had in fact calmed her down. Lora choked back her resentment over how easily Heath could relate to her sister and tried to focus on the problem at hand. Seeing as he was so much better at handling hysterical women, Lora took a backseat to Heath for the moment. Heath rubbed Lilah's shoulders, then released her. "It's going to be all right. We'll find him."

It sounded like a promise, and even though she knew that logically he couldn't make a promise like that, she liked hearing it as much as Lilah. Lilah nodded again and looked to Lora, her eyes red and worried. "So you want me to drive?" she asked.

"Sure," Lora said, following her sister out. She resisted the urge to look back to Heath with the need to say something—such as a thank-you for stepping up so readily—but given how their last conversation had deteriorated so quickly, she opted to simply remain silent and focus on finding Pops.

Once in the Jeep, Lora said, "I know it wasn't your fault about Pops." Contrary to popular belief, Lora hated the gap between herself and her sisters, but she seemed helpless to bridge it. Most times it seemed easier on everyone's part to just leave it be. Some things couldn't be fixed. But even recognizing that fact, Lora still wished for something different. And maybe it was because of that small, buried hope, she was trying to offer some kind of comfort to her sister. She knew

Lilah was beating herself up and Lora hated that it wasn't natural for her to simply put her arms around her baby sister and comfort her as Heath had so easily done earlier.

Lilah shot Lora a wary look but accepted her comment with a watery sniff. "I know. I'm worried about him, though. I've been looking all afternoon. He's never been gone this long. I tried calling you, but your phone went straight to voice mail. Where were you all day?"

Lora remembered guiltily that she'd left her phone in her room because she hadn't had any pockets in her cover-up. She hadn't expected to be gone long—certainly not all day and evening—and she definitely hadn't expected to…well, she suddenly understood temporary insanity. She cleared her throat. "I was with Heath. We were discussing the situation regarding Larimar."

"All day?" Lilah asked incredulously, finding Lora's admission odd. Lora shot her a quick look, and she realized she must look guilty, because Lilah frowned with open confusion. "You can hardly spend five minutes with Heath without turning into a shrew. Why would you spend all day with him?"

"In business, sometimes you have to spend

time with people you'd rather not," she answered sharply, as if it was a simple situation with a simple answer. "He wasn't willing to change his plans for the day so we could discuss the circumstances facing Larimar, so I joined him. This is a good lesson for you, Lilah. Sometimes you have to turn a situation to your advantage. It's a lesson that works in life and in business." Lilah shot Lora a look so full of irritation that Lora was taken aback. "What? I'm just trying to share some advice with you."

"I don't need *business* advice from you, Lora," she said. "I need a big sister's advice. You know, from your heart for once. Why can't you just be my sister?"

Lora sat stunned, unsure how to respond. She didn't know how to be *just* a sister. She'd never tried to get to know her sisters beyond the superficial. What if Lilah realized she didn't like Lora? "I'm just trying to be helpful," Lora murmured, looking away. "Maybe we should just drop it."

"Fine," Lilah said on a sigh, clearly frustrated. "Keep an eye out for Pops. I'm going to circle the plaza."

Lora nodded and blinked away the tears that flooded to the surface. She wasn't usually so emotional, but it seemed coming home had unleashed something inside her that was terribly vulnerable and needy. And it was frightening to feel this way. She focused on searching for her grandfather, scanning faces in the crowds as they slowly circled the small plaza. After the third pass, Lilah said, "He's not here. We should head back to Larimar in case someone's called."

"Heath is at the resort—he'll let us know if anyone called. Let's take one last pass."

Lilah reluctantly agreed and twisted the wheel to go again. "He's never done this," she said. "He's never just taken off without telling someone where he was going."

Lora nodded, her heart hurting. "I can't believe this is happening to Pops. When I was a kid I thought he was indestructible. Grams, too." Even though Lora had learned how fragile life was at an early age, somehow she'd thought Grams and Pops were untouchable. "He has to be around here somewhere. He couldn't just disappear. What about friends? Anyone who he might want to visit?"

Lilah shook her head. "He's friendly to everyone, but there's no one who I'd consider his buddy or anything. I mean, Grams and family were all he needed."

Lora drew a short breath, trying to brainstorm. After a few more dizzying passes around the same plaza, she agreed it was time to return to Larimar.

"Should we report him missing?" Lilah asked, looking to Lora with uncertainty. "Or should we wait? I know Pops would hate everyone making a fuss if it turns out he was just fine and visiting with someone we don't know. But on the other hand, if he's hurt or lost...I don't know. What do you think?"

Lora bit her lip in consternation. Lilah made good points. Indecision caused her to hesitate. She wanted Heath's opinion. "Let's head back to the resort and double-check that Heath hasn't found him," she suggested, taking great care to ensure her voice remained calm and sensible. Lilah was teetering on the edge of panic and someone had to stay focused. Lilah nodded and turned the Jeep around to head out of town toward Larimar.

Within minutes they were parking the Jeep and walking inside the resort. Luckily, it was the off-season and there weren't many guests so at least they didn't have to field questions by curious tourists as the Bell family went through their personal crisis. Lora and Lilah walked into Pops's office and found Heath on the phone, his expression grim.

"Thank you. I appreciate your help," he said, ending his conversation as the women walked in. Lora's stomach pitched when she saw Heath's expression. Whatever Heath had discovered didn't bode well for Pops. "The ferryman remembered seeing Pops on the midday ferry to St. Thomas." Lora stared in horror and Lilah gasped audibly. Pops in St. Thomas? Alone?

"Oh, God…" she breathed, fear tickling the back of her throat. "Heath…"

"I know." He acknowledged her apprehension with the same fear in his eyes. "We need to make the call."

HEATH MADE THE CALL to the St. Thomas police to report Pops missing but he didn't receive much satisfaction. Until Pops was missing for twenty-four hours, they weren't going to actively search for him.

"Did you tell him he has early-onset dementia?" Lora asked, dissatisfied with the attitude of the police. "This is ridiculous. He's an old man who doesn't know where he is or how to get home. Doesn't that warrant a little attention?"

"They have to follow procedure," Heath said, feeling much the same way but he knew he had to get Lora to cool down before she hijacked a boat and started combing St. Thomas street by street. "We'll call back first thing in the morning and maybe he'll call between now and then. You know, Pops isn't always disoriented. Sometimes he's lucid and almost normal. Maybe we're getting all worried for nothing."

"But he's been worse lately," Lilah reminded Heath as she bit her fingernails until the cuticles bled. "He thinks Grams is still alive and out shopping somewhere. I have a bad feeling about this. St. Thomas is a dangerous place for an old man without money or a way to call home. How are we supposed to find him?"

Heath didn't know but he wasn't about to admit that to the girls. Lilah looked ready to shatter and Lora, in her own way, looked equally fragile. "One thing at a time," he said. "We can't do anything right now. Let's try to be positive. Pops has lived here a long time. He'll know where he's going, even if he doesn't remember how he got there. It'll be okay."

Lora nodded, accepting that logic, but Lilah

was stuck in panic mode. "He doesn't have any money with him. How will he get back on the ferry, assuming he knows to do that tomorrow. For all we know he could be sleeping on a park bench or on the beach somewhere. *In St. Thomas!* They don't call it St. Trauma for nothing!"

"Heath's right," Lora said quietly, sharing a look with Heath that said she shared all the same fears as Lilah but knew that freaking out wasn't going to help anyone, least of all Pops. "We need to take a wait-and-see attitude before we let emotion and fear cause us to do something rash and unnecessary. Why don't you go lie down for a little while? You look exhausted."

Lilah swallowed, her eyes brimming but she ground out the tears with a rough movement as if irritated by her own weakness. "I'll stay," she said stubbornly. "I want to be here if and when you find out anything."

"It's better if you get some sleep," Heath said. "That way we can man the phones in shifts. If he calls, then someone will be able to answer. We'll take the first shift and you can take the second. Okay?"

That seemed to make a modicum of sense to Lilah and she reluctantly agreed. He knew she was trying to appear as strong as Lora but Lilah wasn't hardwired that way and she just looked ready to break. "You promise you'll come wake me up if you find out something sooner?"

"Of course," Lora answered with a nod. "I promise."

Lilah dragged her feet but finally turned and left the lobby, heading to her room.

Once alone, Lora looked to Heath, her expression somber. "This is bad." It was a statement, not a question and he didn't pretend otherwise.

"Well, it's true that without a phone or money, he'll have a difficult time finding his way back home but he's not an invalid. He knows how to take care of himself, even if he doesn't remember things so well. I think it'll be okay."

"You don't have to sugarcoat it for me. I'm not as fragile as Lilah," Lora said stiffly, though the convulsive motion of her throat as she swallowed told another story. She was scared. And he didn't blame her. He was scared, too. But he wished she'd stop trying to be so stoic.

"No one would think less of you if you showed a little emotion," he said.

"I hardly think sobbing into my hands is going to help the situation. A cool, clear head is what's needed right now."

"True, but you know, sometimes letting people know you're human with the same fears and insecurities goes a long way toward building bridges with the people you've pushed aside."

"Are you talking about me and my sisters?" she asked, the clip in her tone hard to miss. "Let's stay on topic, please. My relationship with my sisters isn't the main focus." But even as she said the words, Heath sensed something eating at Lora, jabbing with sharp points of judgment and disillusionment. In a way, he felt bad for Lora. She'd been so busy trying to build her career that she'd completely lost touch with the ones who had loved her the most. He didn't know if the relationship with her sisters would ever be mended but he did know in order for that to happen, Lora would have to learn how to bend—and that wasn't a skill Lora had ever possessed.

"I shouldn't have gone out with you," Lora murmured, rubbing her temples, blaming herself. "I knew I should've stayed to watch over Pops."

"Hold on," he said, not willing to let Lora

beat herself up over this, especially not when he couldn't bring himself to regret what had happened between them, even though he knew he should. "No one here keeps Pops in a cage. He putters around as he pleases. He's never hopped the ferry by himself before, but it isn't like he hasn't ever done this in his life. The old memories are fine in his head—it's the new stuff that he has trouble with. Chances are, he's just fine and we'll find him a little hungry but none the worse for wear. Okay?"

"I don't know how you can be so calm about this," she said. "My grandfather is lost. The bottom line is, you don't know what is happening to him right now and I don't know if he's safe. Perhaps my sisters and I should explore the option of a home for him."

Heath glowered. "No way."

"Excuse me?"

"He's not going into a home. If you don't know how miscrable that would make your grandfather, then you don't know him at all."

"I think I'm in a better position to decide what's best for my grandfather than you."

"Like hell you are."

"I'm not going to discuss this further with you. It doesn't concern you—end of story."

"Good luck trying to convince Lilah to agree."

"I don't need Lilah to agree. I have power of attorney for the estate."

"True. But let me tell you how that story will end, since you seem to be ignorant of how your family really thinks and feels. Lilah and Lindy would never understand why you'd do something like that and Pops would never be the same. Part of his joy comes from being in this resort. All his happy memories are right here between these walls. Not in some apartment complex surrounded by strangers. And the twins would never forgive you for that."

Lora glared, but he knew he'd struck a nerve. "I think the twins are adult enough to realize what would be decided for Pops's best interests. Lilah and Lindy will agree."

"I will agree to what?" Heath and Lora both turned to see Lindy standing there looking travel-worn but fabulous pulling a small carry-on of rolling luggage.

"Lindy!" he exclaimed with pure joy, so happy to see the other Bell twin. Lindy had always been a kick in the pants. She was like one of the guys but hot as hell. He didn't envy the man snared in her crosshairs because it would be a brutal life being attached to this hellion. She attracted men like bees to honey and enjoyed a sampling of everything that came her way. Being the other half of Lindy Bell was likely excruciating. Of course, he didn't have to worry about it, because to him, she was simply like his sister and that was the only way he saw her.

"Heath Bar!" Lindy dropped her luggage and ran squealing to hop into Heath's arms as she used to when she was a teenager. He could feel Lora's stare burning through him, but he didn't care. He placed Lindy back on the ground and she reluctantly acknowledged Lora.

"So…how's it going, sis?" she asked, though Heath knew Lilah had probably ratted out their older sister already. "What's so bad that you've got Lilah putting out the SOS?"

"Lilah didn't tell me you were coming," Lora said stiffly.

"Well, I came earlier than I'd planned. Good thing, too. From what I've been hearing you've been bullying Li."

"Bully? I've never bullied Lilah!"

"Believe what you want—you always do— but I call them as I see them," Lindy said, her tone flip, but the stone in her stare was anything but light.

Heath tried to interject, saying, "Okay, girls. We're all on the same team, right? What's important is that you're home and we can use all the hands to help find Pops."

Lindy aimed a forgiving smile Heath's way. "Oh, Heath, when are you going to stop sticking up for her?"

"Be nice," Heath said, forcing a chuckle. Maybe it wouldn't be so great after all having all three Bell girls home again. He'd missed Lindy, but he could sense an underlying coat of anger directed at Lora and that was the last thing Lora needed right now.

Lindy smiled angelically at Heath and said, "For you, anything." But within a heartbeat she returned to her sister, her expression sobering. "So what's the deal with Pops?"

Lora, looking as if she'd been pinched in the butt, neither smiled nor greeted her sister with anything more than a swift and curt explanation. "In addition to the resort owing a horrific amount of back taxes, Pops went into business with *Heath Bar,* sinking all the reserve into his glass-fusing business so that we don't have enough for the taxes or repairs. Oh, and Pops is losing his mind. He thinks Grams is still alive and this afternoon he took the ferry to St. Thomas. Hence he's lost and we can't file a missing-person's report until he's been gone twenty-four hours." She looked to Heath with a narrowed, wintry stare. "Does that about sum it up?"

"Da-yum," Lindy breathed at the finish, her mouth dropping open in a shocked gape. "That sucks."

"That's all you have to say?" Lora exclaimed, fresh irritation on her face. "'That sucks'?"

"Well…yeah…it does, right?" Lindy said with a shrug as if Lora was being intentionally obtuse. Heath would've laughed but he sensed Lora was ready to lose her cool and that wasn't going to benefit anyone, particularly when they all needed to work together. The irony was that he was the only one not related by blood to Pops and the girls, but he was the one trying to keep the peace between them all. Lindy yawned and twisted to the right to crack her back. "Argh. My back is killing me. I hate that long-ass flight from California. Not worse than flying to Japan, but definitely not great for the bod. I could feel my butt getting flabby just sitting there.

Anyway, I'm starved. Sailor's still open? I would kill for a hamburger."

"Did you not hear a word I said?" Lora asked, angry.

"I heard every snippy word," Lindy retorted, matching Lora's stare. Heath could feel the electricity jump between the two women and he almost felt compelled to leave the room and let them hash it out, but Lora had been through enough for the day and even though she probably deserved whatever Lindy was willing to dish out, he stopped her.

"I could use a bite. I'll drive." He looked to Lora. "You want anything?"

"I'm not hungry."

"Your loss," Lindy quipped, linking her arm through Heath's. "Lead on, my brother from another mother. I can practically taste that burger already. All I've had to eat were those dinky peanut packages on the plane and a Vitaminwater. I know I live in L.A., but even L.A. girls can't exist on that diet!"

Heath hesitated, glancing at Lora, but by her stony expression he knew she wasn't going to change her mind. A part of him wanted to cajole her into coming with them because she was probably hungry by now. But she and Lindy were like two angelfish in an aquarium two sizes too small, worse than Lora and Lilah because Lindy had never hesitated to speak her mind, whereas Lilah would simply roll over and withdraw, ceding victory to Lora. He shook his head. Let the fireworks begin....

CHAPTER NINETEEN

LORA WATCHED LINDY AND HEATH walk away, arms linked together, and that squeeze of something indefinable returned to squeeze even harder. Lindy had always been an irrepressible flirt—that was nothing new—but watching her so easily charm Heath made Lora want to snarl.

The primal and visceral reaction was unnerving. *Get a grip,* she admonished herself, hating how bothered she was over Heath's easy comfort around her sisters. First Lilah and now Lindy, she wanted to huff, turning away and striding to her room.

Her stomach growled as if to remind her that she'd made a foolish decision to turn down an opportunity to grab a bite but she ignored the hunger pangs to shower and change. Everything had happened so quickly when they returned that her original plans had been scrapped and she could still smell Heath on her skin. The scent alternately warmed and embarrassed her. The fact of the matter was, she liked it.

In the privacy of her own bathroom, she inhaled deeply the masculine scent clinging to her skin and with great reluctance started the water. Why did he have to smell so good? So sexy? Why did she have to care that Lindy had hopped into Heath's arms like some hypersexed Hollywood centerfold looking for her next good time? And for that matter, why did Lindy have to act all giddy and happy to see Heath yet had picked a fight the moment she laid eyes on Lora?

I don't care. It doesn't matter. She deliberately stepped under the spray and closed her eyes. What mattered was finding Pops and saving Larimar. End of story. Heath could bunk up with Lindy for all she cared and ride off into the sunset together. More power to them.

Oh, criminy, she'd never been a fan of self-delusions but right about now, she was marinating in them. She cared, damn it. She cared! And she certainly didn't like the idea of Heath going from her bed straight into Lindy's arms like nothing of importance had happened between them only a few hours prior. She had half a mind to tell Lindy exactly what Heath had been doing a few hours ago—*her*.

A small unattractive guffawlike snort popped out at the inappropriate thought and Lora wished for just a second, she could see Lindy's face when she discovered that her older sister—the one she thought for sure was a workaholic prude with dust and cobwebs in her vagina—had actually thrown caution to the wind and did something reckless and bold. She smiled as the memory washed over her, but even as she closed her eyes to relive the sensation of Heath's body moving over hers, she popped them open with a sigh. Now was not the time to be nostalgic. Pops was out there somewhere, alone. She could only hope he was safe.

She tied her hair up in a towel and changed into something more comfortable, then stopped by Lilah's room to announce that Lindy was home but she should've known that Lilah already knew.

Lora paused, lingering in the doorway. "So, Lindy seemed pretty happy to see Heath," she remarked with what she hoped sounded like a casual observance. "I didn't realize they were so close."

"Lindy adores Heath. Everyone does," Lilah added pointedly.

"I like him well enough…for a man who attached himself to our family," she amended, though immediately wondered why she had to tack that part on. Somehow she just couldn't be nice. *Damn*… What was her problem? Was she permanently frigid inside? She hoped not. The insight wasn't flattering. "Lilah…I don't blame you for what happened with Pops."

"Yes, you do."

The blunt retort stung a bit but Lilah wasn't stupid and Lora had been foolish to try and smooth over the obvious with a badly constructed lie. She drew a deep breath then lifted her hands in a helpless gesture. "Okay, so maybe I blamed you a little at first but I don't blame you now and I'm trying to apologize. Can't you meet me halfway? You said you wanted me to act more sisterly, well, here it is. And right now, little sister, you're acting like a spoiled, petulant brat when I really need you to be a grown-up."

Lilah looked away, shaking her head as if Lora was hopeless and not the other way around and Lora gave up. "Fine. Whatever. I'm going to go sit by the phone just in case Pops finds a way to call home."

"Lora…"

The sound of her sister's voice at her back caused her to pause and wait. "Yeah?" She turned slowly. "What is it?"

"Thanks for being here."

She held a brief smile, a pang of guilt hitting her. She should be here. The fact that she'd dragged her feet to try and save her career seemed laughable at best and pathetic at worst. Heath had been right in one respect: her family had needed her and she'd relegated them and their problems to the back of her mind—and this was her consequence. She nodded, saying, "We'll get it figured out," and ducked out before the tears filling her eyes had the chance to spill.

LINDY TOOK A MONSTER BITE from her burger and groaned in pure pleasure. There wasn't a place on this planet that made burgers like Sailor's. "So tell me," she said, in between chews, swallows and bites, "what's really going on? Seems like all hell is breaking loose."

"Lora put it in a nutshell."

Lindy's mouth lifted. "So hell really is breaking loose?" At Heath's somber expression, she swigged her beer and tried to ignore the flutter of anxiety that followed. She wasn't an alarmist and she refused to start being one just because her sisters were losing it. If she knew her Pops, he was just fine... somewhere. "Okay, so what are we going to do about Pops? Are you sure he hopped a ferry to St. Thomas?"

"Fairly positive. And you know the ferry stops running at nine o'clock, so we're stuck waiting until tomorrow morning. Honestly, I wouldn't even know where to start looking," he said, shaking his head.

Lindy felt his pain as clearly as she saw it in his face. She wiped her mouth with a napkin, then rubbed his hand in a show of support. "Pops is a wily one. Chances are he's enjoying a mini campout on the beach. I'm not worried."

"Lindy...I hate to be the bearer of bad news, but Pops is in no shape to be traipsing around strange places. He loses time, forgets where he's at and gets easily confused. He has a better chance of getting robbed than he does of finding a way home. I didn't want to worry Lora or Lilah, but this is a pretty serious situation."

Lindy ignored that and focused on sucking a piece of burger free from her teeth before exhaling with a sated belly. "God, I've missed Sailor's," she murmured with nostalgia, choosing to focus on her food rather than the niggling voice that was scaring her with all the worst-case scenarios that could happen to Pops. "L.A. with all its fancy restaurants and world-renowned chefs ain't got nothing on a burger from that old, rusted-out grill right here."

"You don't have to pretend for me, Lindy," Heath said, causing her to look up. "I can tell you're worried."

"I'm not going to worry until there's reason to worry," she retorted stubbornly, then drew a deep breath to quell the sudden trembling in her hands. She shook them loose with a short laugh. "Waited too long to eat. Low blood sugar attack, I think."

Heath gave her an indulgent look as if to say, *Call it what you like—I know the score,* but refrained from further comment, which she appreciated. She finished her beer and signaled for another, ready to change the subject before tears betrayed her. "So what's up with that big-shot sister of mine? She looks more uptight than usual, which seems like an impossibility, but Lora is an overachiever," she quipped, laughing at her own joke until she noticed that Heath didn't share her jocularity. "What's up? Did Pops take your sense of humor along with him?"

"Listen, Lora's been under a lot of stress lately. Go easy on her."

"Heath, why do you defend her?" Lindy queried sharply.

"She's not impervious to pain and, trust me, there's a lot going on under that still surface."

Lindy snorted. "If I didn't know better I'd say that you were hot for my sister. But since I know you're not certifiably crazy or a masochist, I might have to check your temperature. What gives?"

Heath hesitated and a horrible suspicion, one she hated to even consider, nagged at the edge of her brain. "Oh, no. Please say you didn't go and fall in love with her again? Obviously I've been gone too long and you've been inhaling paint fumes or something, because Lora isn't the lovable, romantic type like you. You're oil and water in a combustible engine. Sand and a wedgie jammed up a wet crack. Two things that just don't mix well without causing major damage or chafing. Please tell me you're smarter than you were when you were a teenager." When Heath neither confirmed nor denied, Lindy wanted to hit him upside the head with her empty beer mug. Empty… She craned her head to signal the waitress again, then returned to give Heath her best "what the hell are you thinking?" look.

"Somehow we got off topic," he said, shifting in obvious discomfort. "How long can you stay?"

"Long enough to help you pull your head out of your ass," she teased.

"Very funny."

"Yeah, well, I live by my wit alone."

"Sure you do," he returned wryly. "And I'm sure it doesn't hurt to have that smoking-hot body or model-hot looks, right?"

She flashed him a deliberately coy look. "Well, my, my, Heath…are you flirting with me? I do think I could clear my dancing card for you."

He gave her a sardonic look saying that he knew she was kidding and thank God, because they both considered each other like family. Kissing Heath would be like kissing her…brother. If she had one, that is. She sighed, flashing a smile at the waitress, who had finally remembered to bring her refill. "Okay, so down to business. I can stay for a few weeks. I just found out I didn't get this part I auditioned for...I'm real bummed. It could've been a real moneymaker, but some little brunette slut who I know gave the casting director a blow job got it instead. And frankly, I refuse to stoop to that level."

Heath laughed in spite of her indignation at the remembered proposal the casting director had given her, as well. "Glad to know you have a smidge of personal integrity left in you in spite of spending way too much time with all those fake people in L.A."

"Yeah, well, integrity comes at a high cost," she grumbled. "I could've been the next It girl, you know."

"What was the gig?"

"Tampon commercial."

He sputtered and looked at her with something akin to relief and confusion as to why she'd be disappointed. "Gross."

"Oh, grow up, you big kid. Girls have periods. What's really gross is when you're on a date with this incredibly hot guy and forget that it's your time of the month and you're stuck without any supplies. Talk about a terrible way to end an otherwise promising date. And yes, I am speaking from experience." Lindy's peal of laughter at Heath's sudden green tinge caused a few people to turn and stare. She slapped him playfully on the shoulder. "You're such a sweet thing and still so easy to embarrass."

"You did that on purpose," he accused, and she shrugged.

"Guilty."

"Of that and more, I'm sure," he said.

She blew out a slow breath and rubbed her full belly before throwing some cash on the table. "Let's get out of here. I want to go for a swim. I feel like I have airport grime on me and I can't stand it."

He grinned. "Trunk Bay?"

She linked her arm through his and returned his grin. "You know me so well." It was so good to be around people who were simply who they appeared and not who they thought you wanted them to be.

The artifice of Hollywood had begun to wear on her nerves, anyway.

"Why didn't anyone call me and tell me Pops was losing it?" she asked quietly as they walked to the car.

Heath sighed, the sound heavy as if he'd struggled with the same question. "It was my call. Lilah wanted to tell you, but I convinced her not to. I didn't want you to rush home when there was nothing that could be done. Besides, it was mild. Most times he was the same old Pops. And you were out in California, getting famous. How could we ask you to come home when your career was just getting off the ground?"

Lindy forced a smile, but it almost hurt to make the effort. Famous? Hardly. More like getting used for very little gain. "Family is more important than anything happening in Los Angeles," she said. "I would've come."

"I know you would've."

"How'd you get Lora to come?"

"A certified letter."

At that they both burst into laughter and it felt good to let loose. She grinned, feeling hopeful again. "Lord, I've missed you, Heath. You sure there's no way I could convince you to return with me to L.A.?"

He grimaced. "God, no. Not my scene. Besides, I can't act to save my life."

"Neither can half of L.A. You'll fit right in," she said, smiling and closing her eyes. The worry remained, but for now she pushed it away so she could simply enjoy the moment of being home.

CHAPTER TWENTY

BY THE TIME HE AND LINDY returned, it was far later than he realized and, judging by the stormy look on Lora's face when she took in their dripping hair and obviously wet clothes, she disapproved of their impromptu swim. "Any news?" Lindy asked, towel drying her hair before winding it on top of her head.

"No."

"All right, then, I guess we didn't miss anything," Lindy quipped airily, moving past Lora to head to her room. "I'm exhausted. Call me if anything of interest happens. I'm beat."

Lora waited for Lindy to disappear into the private section of the resort and then she turned full force on him, her eyes blazing. He should've known this was coming. "Did you enjoy your little swim?" she asked, her voice tight with barely restrained anger. She didn't wait for his answer. "How nice of you and Lindy to play catch-up while the rest of us are worried out of our minds about Pops."

He opened his mouth to explain, but she didn't seem interested in hearing his side. She was winding up for something big, so he decided he ought to wait her out and see what happened.

"I was *this* close to believing that you cared about Pops and that maybe you truly hadn't been aware of Pops's mental decline when you struck that deal, but seeing how quickly you got chummy with my sister mere hours after we'd...we'd—" She stumbled, her cheeks flaring in the most attractive shade of embarrassed pink. She recovered with a stiff "You know what we did. There's no need to spell it out," before continuing. "And after seeing you and Lindy I feel sick to my stomach. It isn't often someone can boast that they'd played me, but congratulations, Heath Cannon. You played me well and good. I feel like an idiot for letting you come near me."

"Calm down," he said, refusing to let her spitting fury incite a riot inside him. He was tired, emotionally exhausted and ready to go to bed. "Throwing a temper tantrum isn't going to help anyone."

"I've never thrown a temper tantrum in

my entire life," she said icily, looking down her nose at him with her most haughty expression. He probably shouldn't tell her it just made her look ridiculous. And sort of Victorian. Likely not the look she was going for. Damn, he must be nearing delirious. He needed sleep.

"Did you sleep with my sister?" she asked, practically stamping her foot with fury.

The question, delivered with the most accusatory tone he'd ever heard, also smacked of raw pain and disappointment. She cared. Hot damn. She cared. He smothered the inappropriate grin and instead walked slowly toward her. She balked and took a step away. "What are you doing? Answer the question," she demanded, splaying her palm against his chest when he continued to advance. Suddenly his fatigue had fled. "Heath?" She licked her lips, trying to hide her nervousness. "What are you doing?"

He dipped his head to capture her lips before she could say another inflammatory word. She stiffened against the onslaught of his mouth but softened within a heartbeat, matching him stroke for stroke. "That's better," he murmured against her mouth. "The only Bell sister I've ever slept with is you. The only Bell sister I want to sleep with is you. Now hush up and listen. Here's what we're going to do. We're going to go to bed. We're both tired and it makes sense for me to stay here instead of go home, given the situation with Pops. Then bright and early we're going to search for Pops. Sound like a plan?"

She jerked a short nod, her eyes wide and unsure, as if she wasn't entirely sure how they'd gone from spitting at each other to devouring one another. He grasped her hand, not willing to give her a chance to question her actions. "Bed," he instructed, giving her hand a tug.

And she followed without another word.

SHE OUGHT TO YANK HER HAND free and slap him with it, but she was caught in a strange lethargy that propelled her toward an uncertain outcome. The stark truth of it was she wanted to go with him, to curl up beside him and forget for just a few hours that their lives were incompatible and that her Pops was missing. Was it selfish? Likely. But even knowing that, she didn't pull away; she simply allowed him to go into her room and close the door behind them.

It felt odd to have Heath in her childhood bedroom.

She let out a discreet breath, wondering what to do next. "Well, this is…" But before she could finish, he'd pulled off his shirt and tossed it to the armchair, quickly followed by his shorts. The spit, along with any words that she might've been poised to say, dried up and disappeared. Breathing became frightfully difficult and her heart rate thundered in her chest. "You should sleep with your clothes on."

He stared in confusion. "That's not exactly the reaction I was hoping for… You want me to keep my clothes…on?"

"Yes." *No. I want to spend the night doing shameful and wicked things to you.* She licked her lips.

"Why?"

"Because I need to get some sleep and right now sleep is the last thing on my mind." He chuckled and by the way the sound danced up her spine and caused her knees to turn to jelly, she knew he felt the same way. She spoke quickly so as not to lose sight of her sound reasoning. "And I don't want to miss

Pops's call in the morning because I slept in. Okay?"

"You're serious, aren't you?"

"As a heart attack."

"How about a compromise? My shorts are wet and unless you have a spare pair of boxers lying around…"

She reached into her dresser drawer and pulled a pair free, much to Heath's surprise. "I like to sleep in them. They're comfy," she said by way of explanation. He took the cotton boxers and slid them on. She breathed a sigh of relief mixed with disappointment. Heath naked was a glorious sight. She could safely say that she could gladly and happily awake to that view every day.

Heath sighed and crawled into bed, settling in as if he'd always been there. Dare she say, he appeared quite natural in her bed? Odd, she thought to herself. She'd never been one to invite sleepovers with her lovers. She preferred her privacy and she wasn't exactly a cuddler—in fact, a man who looked to excessively snuggle annoyed the crap out of her—so she didn't have a lot of experience in this department. Was there a protocol? Etiquette? "Do you snore?" she blurted out as the questions whirred through her head. "Because I'm a really light sleeper. If you snore, this isn't going to work."

"Everyone snores at some point in their sleep pattern. Even you, sugar bird," he said on a yawn. Before she could refute that statement, he tucked her against him, fitting snugly against her backside as if he were made to fit there.

"I don't like to snuggle," she said, fighting a yawn herself. "Snuggling is so…personal and clingy," she added, her eyelids feeling weighted by cement. Heath's body felt so good pressed against hers. It was as if she'd never truly known how wonderful the feel of another human being could be.

"Me, neither," Heath mumbled, clearly almost dropping off into Slumber Land. "Stop talking. The morning comes early." And then, right when she was almost asleep herself, she heard him say, "You smell so good…like fresh pineapple and coconut cookies."

And for some reason, she found herself burrowing deeper into Heath's embrace, blissfully content.

Maybe just this once, they could snuggle. It wasn't as if they were going to make a habit of it. And since she was only allowing just this once, she could admit, it felt…really…good.

HEATH AWOKE BEFORE LORA, the sun barely cresting the horizon. He'd always been an early riser and that habit had stuck into adulthood. Propped on his elbow, he watched Lora sleep, taking in every subtle difference in her skin, every mole, every freckle. He never thought in a million years he'd be lucky enough to be lying next to Lora one day.

He knew it was too early to tell her how he truly felt, how he'd always felt about her. She'd run away so fast, the sparks from her tennis shoes striking the pavement might start a fire. Honestly, he didn't know if she'd ever be ready to hear that from him. Lora had some truly messed up philosophies when it came to love. He knew her views stemmed from her father's abandonment and her mother's subsequent death, but if anyone was going to be messed up in that department, he ought to be, because he hadn't been given a single good lesson in how to be a loving partner.

"This is why I don't like sleepovers," she murmured sleepily, reluctantly opening her eyes to glance blearily at Heath. "Please stop staring. It's weird."

"You're so damn gorgeous," he said, his tone implying he wasn't pleased with the fact, which in part was true. Perhaps if she'd been less stunning, he wouldn't have been hooked so early. But age had only matured her beauty into something unnaturally perfect—at least in his eyes. If only he could tell her that. "And I hate to break it to you but you snore. Quite loudly, in fact."

At that she lifted her head to give him a hard stare. "I do not."

"Do so. I have the evidence of it on my cell phone."

She frowned. "You're lying."

"Maybe. But it made you wonder, which means you know that you do, in fact, snore."

She rolled her eyes and turned away. "It's too early for this. Wake me up when there's coffee."

He grinned. He knew of a better wake-up call. He nuzzled the back of her neck, nipping at the soft, sweet skin. She sighed, giving him better access, a silent invitation for more. And he was more than willing to oblige.

AFTERWARD, AGAINST HER better judgment, Heath convinced Lora to shower with him— to save time, of course—and while he was taking an inordinate amount of time to soap her breasts, she laughed and swatted him away with her washcloth. "I think they're clean," she said, shaking her head. "What is it with men and boobs?"

"They're patently awesome," he answered as if that ought to be obvious. "If I had breasts, I'd touch them all day." He pretended to cup two sizable imaginary breasts on his chest and affected a blissful expression as he squeezed. "Oh, yeah. I'd never get anything done. It would just be me and my boobs. That's why men don't have them. God knew it would be disastrous."

Lora couldn't help herself and laughed out loud. "You know you're a nut, right?"

"I've heard rumors, but I don't believe everything I hear. The grapevine is notoriously unreliable when it comes to acquiring accurate intel."

"Oh, is that so?" she murmured, glancing up at him with a smile. "And what else have you heard that's untrue?"

He pretended to search his memory then said, "Well, there was this rumor that you were difficult to get along with but I've found " he drew her closer to nip at her neck softly, eliciting shivers on the sensitive skin "—that all one needs to loosen up the formidable Lora Bell is the right touch."

"Such as?"

"This." His hands slid around her backside to firmly cup her ass. "And this," he said huskily, as he nuzzled her neck at the junction of her collarbone. He ground himself against her until she gasped and her knees felt weak. "And definitely this."

She smiled, letting her head fall back. Something sweet blossomed inside her as she allowed the sheer pleasure of being in Heath's arms override the niggling sense that told her they shouldn't be doing this. There were plenty of good, sensible reasons why carrying on with Heath was ill-advised but she greedily enjoyed what felt like a stolen moment amidst a backdrop of chaos while she still could.

As Heath pressed her against the shower wall, pleasure cascaded down her body as he did wondrously wicked things to her. She threaded her fingers through his thick head of hair and closed her eyes, wishing they could shut out everything else that got in the way of this sweet feeling. Had she ever felt so able to let go of it all, to allow someone else to get close enough to see her truly vulnerable? The easy answer was no. She didn't want anyone that close to her but somehow Heath had managed to breach that wall and she felt somewhat lost as she clung to him.

She shuddered her release and sagged against Heath, almost sobbing as wave after wave of toe-curling pleasure rolled through her. She couldn't do this. It was more than she could handle, more than she could assimilate into her life. Heath was not the kind of man who would defer to her like the other men she'd been with. He wouldn't quietly stand in the background. Where did Heath fit in her life? Unhappily, she realized, she didn't know.

After a long minute, Heath sensed something had changed and he peered at her. "What's wrong?" he asked, worried.

How did she put into words an emotion she didn't understand? She shook her head and Heath assumed her worry was for Pops. "It's going to be okay. We have to stay positive."

She nodded, preferring to allow Heath believe Pops had been her focal point of worry. Of course, she was worried about Pops so it wasn't entirely a lie. "I don't know what I'll do if anything happens to him," she murmured.

"That's why we're going to think positively," he reminded her, kissing her forehead lightly.

Lora flashed a brief smile and then turned to finish washing up. The day had already progressed further than she'd realized while lost in Heath's embrace and it was time to face reality.

LILAH TIPTOED INTO LINDY'S room and crawled into bed with her twin. She wrapped her arms around her, her heart filling with joy to have Lindy home again, even if the circumstances weren't optimal.

It was true what they said about twins and how they often felt like one half of the same person. Even though they were fraternal, Lilah felt a physical ache each time Lindy left home, and since she'd relocated to Los Angeles, Lilah had seen less and less of her. It was almost more than she could bear, but she didn't want Lindy to feel obligated to stay on her account. She ought to be able to handle a little separation, but sometimes Lilah wondered if there was something wrong with her.

Lilah knew she wasn't unattractive, but stacked against her sisters she felt like a pale, wilting wallflower, ready for the compost heap. A counselor had once told her she suffered from low self-esteem but that hadn't really resonated with Lilah. Perhaps a little, but not enough to hang her hat on the reason why she seemed the shyest of the Bell sisters, preferring the quiet solitude of a lonely beach to the crowds of the marketplace. Of course, that was another reason why Lilah knew Los Angeles would eat her alive if she tried to follow her wild and crazy twin into the world of acting. Oh, the very idea. Ludicrous, really.

But she really wished she'd stumble upon her niche, her place in life. Lora was the go-getter, the overachiever workaholic; Lindy was the drop-dead gorgeous, charismatic artist; and then there was Lilah, who was borderline socially phobic, a bit uncoordinated, with a singing voice only a mother could tolerate, and of course negligible talent in any other field or discipline.

"You're such a ridiculously early riser," Lindy mumbled as if irritated, but she broke into a sleepy grin to hug Lilah.

"I tried not to wake you up," Lilah said, settling beside her sister. "But it is almost seven o'clock and I figured you'd want to shower and get ready before we hit the ferry to St. Thomas."

Lindy yawned. "My own little travel manager. You're so sweet. Did you happen to bring a little coffeepot with you?"

"Sorry," Lilah said. "But if you get your butt out of bed, we can get a fresh smoothie down in the plaza."

Lindy sighed and rolled over, her arm flung over her eyes to block the sun. "Sis, a smoothie is so *not* the same as a cup of coffee, but because I love you, I'll forgive you this time." Lindy pulled herself out of the bed and slid on some loose linen pants and a pull-over, then jammed a baseball cap on her head. "Ready."

Lilah grinned and they headed for the Jeep. "So tell me about your glamorous life in Hollywood," she said as they drove the short distance, her gaze scanning for an available parking spot. Parking was sparse and you had to get creative. Fender benders were common and most times if you happened to accidentally rub someone else's fender with your own, it was no big deal.

Lindy shrugged, yawning again, still not quite awake. "Nothing to tell. Same as anything else. It's not like I rub elbows with Steven Spielberg. The pace is faster, there are more people everywhere and the game is played best by those who have fast and flexible morals and ethics."

"And where do you fall on that barometer?"

Lilah asked, a little apprehensive. She didn't like to think of her sister selling her soul just to get famous.

Lindy rolled her head to stare at Lilah. "Where do you think? I'm not exactly famous yet, am I? Besides, I already told you, I lost out on a national commercial because I wouldn't suck off the casting director. The man was a pig and besides, who wants to be known as 'that tampon girl'?"

Lilah nodded, but she knew Lindy was still smarting over losing that gig. She may not have wanted to be known as the tampon girl but she sure would like to be known as something. A hunger burned inside Lindy that Lilah had never understood. "You know what Grams used to say when something didn't work out our way. The universe was just making room for what was coming next. Maybe you didn't get that gig because you're not meant to be a commercial actress, but rather a movie actress."

Lindy smiled. "I love you. You always know what to say to make me feel better, even if it's total crap." Her smile faded. "But what if I'm not meant to be anything? Maybe I suffer from delusions of grandeur and everyone but me can see that I'm simply a mildly pretty girl with mediocre talent."

"You and I both know you are the one who got all the talent. If anyone has something to cry about in that department, it's me. I haven't quite figured out what I'm good at other than screwing up."

Lindy's expression softened in concern, not liking Lilah's admission at all. Lilah wished she hadn't said anything. She didn't want Lindy's pity. "Why would you think that?" Lindy asked.

"Because it's true."

"No, it's not. Did Lora put that into your head?"

"I didn't need Lora to put anything in my head. I realized it myself. But it's okay. I'm not losing sleep over it. It is what it is. Let's talk about something else. We got all serious all of a sudden and I have had enough of serious for the time being. Okay?"

Lindy plainly wanted to dispute Lilah's claim some more but she acquiesced for the moment, returning to their previous conversation. "Oh, I met one of those reality television guys…you know the ones who do nothing but talk about doing laundry, banging girls and tanning."

Lilah gave her a blank look. She never watched television. "Sorry. Not well versed in pop culture. Was he nice, whoever this man was?"

"I guess. He was more interested in sleeping with me than getting to know me and I didn't care enough to sleep with him."

Lilah wrinkled her nose in distaste. "What happened to that guy you were seeing…that film director?"

"*Independent* film director," Lindy corrected with a snort of disgust. "Which I discovered roughly translates to no budget, gorilla shooting and, not that I'm a snob or anything, but having money helps smooth out the rough spots if you know what I mean."

Lilah didn't but she nodded anyway. "So what happened to him?"

Lindy waved away her question. "Nothing. He's likely right where I left him—with his pants down around his ankles, begging me not to leave."

"You caught him cheating on you?" Lilah couldn't imagine anyone being so stupid as to be unfaithful to Lindy, but Hollywood was a different world, one she plainly didn't understand. "That must've been awful."

"To be honest, I was relieved. I was ready

to move on and he was so damn clingy. He fancied himself an artist and as he'd told me so many times artists need to express themselves. So I guess he felt the need to express himself in the bed of the actress in his latest B horror flick, *Zombie Love,* so more power to him."

"How can you be so blasé about it? I'd be devastated."

Lindy graced Lilah with a genuine smile. "And that's why I love you, Li. You're so pure of heart. I'm not as much. Frankly, I bore easily. And seeing as there are so many men to choose from in Los Angeles, I never feel the need to get too attached. So, don't worry. I wasn't hurt at all. If anything I was a bit irritated because he'd had the gall to screw her in the sheets I purchased. But whatever. I left them with him. That's the beauty of Target. Plenty more sheets where they came from."

Lilah felt a pang of something sad for her sister. Maybe Lilah gave of herself too deeply but Lindy didn't give anything of herself to the men in her bed. Lindy's personal motto was Always Looking for the BBD—Bigger, Better Deal, and thus far she hadn't deviated from that creed.

Lindy and Lilah finished their smoothies

and started to head back to Larimar when Lindy asked, "So, how long have Heath and Lora been sleeping together?"

And Lilah nearly drove off the road.

CHAPTER TWENTY-ONE

"HOLY SHIT, LI, WHAT the hell are you doing?" Lindy exclaimed, gripping the handrail as Lilah swerved and nearly sent them tumbling down the steep cliff below. "I didn't come home to die, you know."

"I'm sorry," Lilah said immediately, her face flushed as she righted the vehicle. "What are you talking about? Heath and Lora aren't sleeping with each other. They can barely stand to be in the same room together."

"Li, they're totally sleeping with each other. Angry sex can be some of the best there is."

Lilah stared at her sister, wondering if Lindy had fallen and jarred her brain. She shook her head. The idea was ridiculous. "No. You haven't seen them around each other. Lora accused Heath of swindling Pops and putting Larimar in this position. I hardly consider that pillow talk."

Lindy laughed. "Okay, I could be wrong, but my sixth sense is going off like crazy.

He's so damn protective of her and we both know that Lora doesn't need a champion. That woman chews nails for a midday snack. Why else would Heath be so quick to defend her unless he was getting something on the side for it?"

"Heath's not like that." Lilah glowered at her sister, annoyed that she would even suggest something so ungentleman-like in terms of Heath. "I think being around all those Holly*weird* people has you seeing the worst in people even when it's not there."

"Calm down, Li. I'm not attacking Heath or casting aspersions on his character but you're blind if you can't see the tension between those two. Besides, didn't Heath have a thing for Lora back in the day? Crazy as it seemed."

"Yes, well, maybe," Lilah amended. "I was never really sure, but I think he did. But that was a long time ago. And she was never really nice to him."

"God no, she was a royal witch to the poor guy. I always wondered why she was so damn mean, but I stopped trying to figure out Lora a long time ago. I have a hard enough time trying to figure out my own actions much less those of someone else."

"Are you still seeing that counselor?" Lilah ventured cautiously. It was a sensitive subject with Lindy, one that she didn't share with many.

"No, she was a kook…an expensive one at that," Lindy said. "To paraphrase, she said I have daddy issues. Can you believe that? Do you see me hanging out with Hugh Hefner? I could, you know. I was invited to the Playboy mansion but declined. Now, wouldn't you say that if I had 'daddy issues'—" she bracketed the phrase with air quotes "—that I'd have jumped at the chance to hang out with that multimillion-dollar fossil?"

Lilah's head was spinning. "What is a daddy issue?"

Lindy sighed. "She said that I was trying to resolve the issues created in the past by our father's abandonment by acting out in the present. What a crock. Just because I don't like to be tied down for any length of time and that I'm *mildly* attracted to *slightly* older men doesn't mean I'm trying to rectify the actions of our deadbeat dad."

"You're afraid of commitment?"

"So she says."

Actually, that made a lot of sense, but Lilah wisely kept that opinion to herself and besides, they were at Larimar and it was just about time to pick up Lora and Heath to hit the ferry.

They walked into the lobby and saw Pops, looking none the worse for wear, standing by a police officer. Lilah squealed in total relief and ran to her grandfather, so happy to see him. She didn't even notice Lora and Heath talking to a separate officer off to the side.

"Pops! Where have you been? We've been so worried!" Lilah framed his weathered face with her hands, so relieved he was safe. "What happened?"

"Oh, not you, too," he grumbled, shocking Lilah with his irritation. "Lora's all up and arms. Treating me like a child who can't walk without help. I just went to get supplies and forgot my damn cell phone here. Larimar was near out of toilet paper, you know. Cheaper in St. Thomas to get it in bulk."

"But, Pops, you were gone all night..." Lilah said, her voice trailing in open confusion.

"Well, I must've lost track of time and then when I realized I needed to get back, the last ferry had already left for the night." He scratched his head, his eyes cranky as he tried to recall the exact details of his adventure. "Anyway, I don't know what happened but the next thing I knew I was being harassed by a couple of thugs. They took my TP and ran off with it."

Lilah looked to the officer, horrified. "My grandfather was robbed?"

The officer looked as if he were struggling not to laugh, but Lilah didn't see the humor at all. She glared at the officer and then fussed over Pops. "Are you okay? Are you hurt?"

"I'm fine, sugar bird," he said, but his expression was one of embarrassment. He hadn't even realized Lindy was standing there yet. Lilah's heart ached for him. She looked to Lora, who was speaking quietly with the other officer. She knew Lora was handling the details, so she moved to distract Pops by taking his arm and pointing at Lindy. "Look who's home?"

He followed her movement and his face crinkled in a raw smile of joy that totally eclipsed his earlier expression. "Lindy girl! When'd you get here?" Lindy bounced over to Pops and embraced him tightly. "All my sugar birds are home! Wait until your Grams finds out. She's going to wet herself with happiness!"

"Goodness gracious, I hope not." Lindy

laughed, seemingly unfazed by Pops's mention of Grams as if she were alive. Lilah wished she had her strength. Sometimes when Pops talked about Grams it was like a slice to her heart. "What are you doing worrying everyone like that? Lilah made me hop a plane right away and come home because you were being all crazy. Is that true?"

"I've always been a little left to center, part of my charm you know," he added in a conspiratorial whisper. "But let's get some breakfast. I'm starved. I can't remember when I ate last, but it feels like forever. You up for some scrambled eggs and bacon?"

"Of course. You know I have the appetite of a growing boy," she said, smiling. And just like that they left the lobby as if nothing of consequence had happened, as if Pops had not spent an entire night in St. Thomas alone, robbed and brought home by two uniformed officers.

Lilah rubbed her eyes and felt the overwhelming urge to just go back to bed.

LORA FINISHED WITH THE POLICE officers and felt drained. She looked to Heath and he seemed to understand. Lindy, damn her, had flitted off with Pops as if everything was fine, barely blinking an eye when he'd mentioned Grams as if she were in the other room, and Lora was still trying to wrap her head around what the hell was happening between her and Heath. What colossal bad timing, she thought grumpily. Now was not the time to start a complicated and potentially damaging love affair.

Needing to put some space between herself and everyone else, Lora murmured something about needing to go for a run, and quickly departed the room. Of course Heath was hot on her heels, understandably so. She was acting bipolar. One minute she was snuggled up tight to him and the next she was trying to get away.

"I need some time alone," she said sharply, irritated that he'd followed.

"What's going on? You're running away. That doesn't seem like you."

She turned to face him. "I'm not running away," she denied hotly, secretly hating that he'd zeroed in on her intent. "I'm not used to going so long without the gym. I need some exercise. It helps clear my head."

"And what do you need help clearing? Let me help you. I'm a good listener."

"Stop it. I don't want you in that role. I

want *space*. I'm not interested in becoming bunk buddies, or more than superficial lovers. I don't appreciate you following me as if you have the right to intrude on my business, and I definitely don't like you acting like we're all cozy in front of my family."

Heath stared, his expression going from concerned to pissed off in about the same amount of time it had taken Lora to tear down all the great moments they'd just shared together. She'd gone too far, but her head was jammed full of details that were all clamoring for attention—she definitely didn't have time to sort out the inconvenient thread that represented her sexual relationship with Heath.

"I'm sorry—"

"You said your piece. I heard you loud and clear." And then he turned and strode from her room, slamming the door on his way out.

"Real mature," she muttered, but she felt the urge to stomp her foot in the same show of immaturity. She was truly too old for this. There was a reason she'd avoided these types of relationship traps in high school, and she had no desire to give it a try now.

Her life was so much simpler when she was focused on her career. This emotional stuff with her family and now Heath…it was far more complicated than anything she'd ever negotiated in the corporate world.

IT WAS OFFICIAL: he was nuts.

Temporary insanity was the only plea he could offer when he thought of his decision to take a chance on Lora Bell.

He was fairly certain she'd lost her soul to the devil in exchange for her physical attributes. Lord knew, he'd been taken down by the promise in her eyes and seductive sway of her hips.

And he, of all people, should have known better. Had she not plainly told him that she was interested only in no-strings-attached sex? She'd made him feel like some hormonal girl when he'd been stung by her rejection. And now he was sure she'd ripped his balls from his scrotum and held them in her dainty hand.

His first instinct was to leave and get some air, maybe go for a swim, but in spite of Lora's piss-poor attitude, he needed to hang around a while longer and check on Pops. Lora could kiss his ass. Pops was his family, too.

He found Lindy, Lilah and Pops at the big table, chowing on an expansive breakfast of scrambled eggs, sausage, toast and fresh orange juice. Lilah was pretty good in the kitchen and Pops loved to cook anyway so between the two of them, they'd managed to whip up a pretty decent meal on short notice.

"Just in time," Pops announced, wiping his mouth. "Grab a chair. There's plenty. I want to talk about the gift shop."

A groan from Lilah surprised him. "Business at the breakfast table? What would Grams say about that? She says breakfast is for family time, right? So let's just enjoy our food, okay?" Heath caught the faint strain in Lilah's tone but Pops seemed oblivious, for which Heath was grateful. Actually, he was glad for Lilah's intervention.

Heath knew he had no reason to feel nervous, but his own guilt caused him to jump at shadows even when they weren't there. A part of him worried that Pops would suddenly realize he'd mortgaged Larimar's future on Heath's talent, and maybe that hadn't been the wisest of decisions.

Pops nodded, as if remembering Grams's admonition, and selected another forkful of bacon. "You're right, Lil," he said. "Business can always wait but family is a different story."

Heath smiled, secretly relieved. The gift shop was a needed conversation, but with everything that had happened in the past twenty-four hours, he'd rather not jump into that heavy a discussion just yet.

"Come on, Heath. You know you can never turn down the prospect of a meal, especially when it's right here in front of you," Lindy teased, taking great pleasure in sticking her nose by the mound of bacon on her plate and inhaling the scent.

"You got that right," he agreed easily, taking his place and proceeding to fill his plate. "Food is my weakness."

"I'd say Lora is your weakness," Lindy teased under her breath, earning a sharp look from him. She grinned and blew a kiss without apology. He shook his head and returned to his food, grateful Pops hadn't heard that little comment.

"Ahh…home cooking. You know, in the circles I hang around," Lindy continued, "especially the women, bacon is a four-letter word. So much fat, so cruel, yadda yadda. Bottom line—bacon is good and I like to eat it."

Lilah grinned and poured some juice. "You're going to die of hardened arteries if you keep eating like that," she warned with mock seriousness.

The camaraderie around the table was much like it used to be, evoking warm memories of the past when he'd been made to feel as though he was part of this family at all times.

"Where's Lora?" Pops asked.

Heath shrugged, not wanting to talk about that woman. He couldn't trust his mouth right at that moment so he stuffed it with food. But trust Lindy to stir things up when he just wanted to enjoy breakfast without having to think about how Lora alternately infuriated and aroused him—sometimes in the same instance.

She popped a grape into her mouth and then said, "So loverboy, when did you and my older sister start shacking up?"

Heath was caught off guard by the blunt question and nearly choked on his bacon. Lindy grinned like the wiseass she was, showcasing perfectly white, straight teeth, and clearly enjoying his discomfort of being put on the spot. She shrugged when he glared. "I'm just stating the obvious. Of course, I say do what you want. You're consenting adults. We're not kids any longer. There's nothing wrong with you two hooking up, but I have to wonder what you see in her. I mean, aside from the physical. We all know Lora is pretty with a decent bod."

Pretty. It seemed a silly, weightless word when applied to Lora. She was beyond pretty. She was heavenly. *Hello? Remember, that heavenly creature was the same one who just kicked you out of her room, accusing you of acting like a clingy girl.*

"We're not seeing each other," he answered with a short glance aimed at shutting her up. But Lindy was having fun and continued to poke.

"Oh, come on, Heath, we all know you've had it bad for Lora since we were all kids. Actually, I'm glad you've finally admitted it. How about you, Pops? What are your feelings about a Lora-and-Heath union?"

Pops grinned in answer. "Sounds good to me. The girl needs someone to remind her how to smile. My sugar bird works too hard. I was just telling Grams the other day that Lora looked tired. She needs a little island time. I don't know what they've got in Chicago that they don't have right here."

"Well, for one, snow," Lindy quipped.

"Don't be a smarty-pants," Pops said.

"What I mean is, what's so special about that cold place that she'll pick there over her home?"

Heath cursed himself for being ten kinds of stupid but he said in Lora's defense, "That's where her job is. She's a top marketing executive. There aren't too many openings in her field on the island."

"Well, I don't think it's good for her. It's eating her up inside. My sugar bird likes to act all hard-boiled but inside she's softer than the lot of you."

"That's no act," Heath muttered before he could stop himself, earning a sharp look from Pops. "Sorry…I'm on edge this morning. I think I'll just grab this to go, if no one minds."

Lindy said, "Swim later?"

Heath thought of how tweaked Lora became whenever he hung out with her sisters and he hesitated. But then, he realized with a wash of anger, he couldn't allow Lora to dictate his actions. She didn't care, so why should he? "Sure. I have some work to do this morning. How about this afternoon."

"Sure."

Pops jumped in, asking with interest, "What are you working on today?"

"Inspecting for roof damage from the storm. Before checking out, one of the guests reported a leak in their room. I want to make sure it's not coming in from a hole."

Lilah looked fretful. She was afraid of heights. "Be careful, Heath. Can't we hire someone to do that? It's so dangerous."

Heath grinned and pressed a kiss to her forehead for caring. "Thanks, Li, but I'm the handyman around here. That's what Pops pays *me* for."

"Heath will be fine," Pops said, patting Lilah's hand. "He's done this a million times. I've trained him well. He knows what he's doing." He gestured to the food. "Take what you need. And let me know what you find up there. There's a bigger storm front rolling in, gonna be a windy one."

Heath nodded and grabbed a handful of bacon and eggs to go and wrapped everything in a large piece of toast. He hefted it in salute then exited the room before Lindy could ask him any more questions he couldn't answer and before he said something he ought to keep to himself.

CHAPTER TWENTY-TWO

LORA FOUND POPS A WHILE LATER after she'd taken a quick shower and dressed. She'd berated herself for letting Heath muddle her thinking and made a stern promise to herself to stay focused on the true and important issues at hand instead of allowing herself to get sidetracked by her libido.

"There you are," she remarked mildly, finding him chatting up Oscar the mailman. She smiled in a perfunctory manner and then said to Pops, "Would you mind talking with me for a minute? It's important."

"Of course, sugar bird," he said, finishing up his conversation with Oscar with an introduction. "This here is my oldest granddaughter—the go-getter as her Grams like to call her. There's no obstacle too tough for her to scale. Straight-A student all through high school and then an honors graduate in college."

"You must be so proud," admired Oscar,

smiling at Lora, who was fighting the instinct to brush off the compliments. She'd never felt comfortable with so much praise but she'd learned to accept it with a modicum of grace, particularly when her grandfather loved to gush about his sugar birds to whoever would listen. "You have a lovely place here. The name Larimar, it's the same as the stone right?"

"Larimar is the *legendary* stone of the Caribbean," Pops answered with total seriousness, and Lora wanted to groan. Her grandfather loved to tell stories, especially about legends and tall tales. This one was his favorite. She'd be lucky to tear the man away at all now. "It's only found in one place in the world—in the Dominican Republic, not too far from here, of course—and the legend is that once you take a larimar stone away from the island, you're bound to return someday. Do you have a minute? Let me show you a few pieces we have in the gift shop."

"Sure," Oscar said, breaking into a smile. "You know I just got this route and I'm still learning the ins and outs. I love local history, though."

Lora watched with warm exasperation as

her Pops led Oscar to the gift shop window where a larimar pendant was displayed.

"My girlfriend back in the States would love this," he said, admiring the stone. "Do you ship?"

"We sure do," Pops said, and Lora smiled. Her Pops was a natural salesman. Whether he was losing his marbles or not, he could sell ice to an Eskimo.

"I might have to come back when I'm off work and pick one up. Her birthday is coming up," Oscar said, returning with renewed interest to a larimar pendant necklace hanging behind the glass case. "How fascinating…so it begs the question, is the legend true?"

Pops looked Oscar straight in the eye and said, "I was serving in the navy, stationed in the Caribbean when I was about twenty years old. I bought a larimar pendant from a street vendor to give to my girl back in the States. Two years later I brought my girl here and married her. I'd say it works. At least it did for me."

"I'm trying to get my girl to move here, too," the man said, smiling, looking to Lora. "That's a pretty cool story to have in your family."

Lora nodded.

"So when you ask if Larimar means something—to the Bell family, it means everything."

Lora blinked away the sudden wash of moisture pricking her eyes. She didn't think she'd ever find anyone who would love her the way her Pops loved Grams.

"And each of my sugar birds has their very own larimar pendant, given to them on their tenth birthdays."

Lora thought of her pendant sitting in her jewelry box in her apartment in Chicago, forgotten, and she flushed with guilt. Lilah and Lindy always wore theirs, no matter what. In fact, they often had the chains switched out just so they didn't accidentally lose the pendant by a broken clasp. Lora hadn't looked at hers in years. She rubbed her nose when it tingled in warning. Tears weren't far behind. "Damn," she murmured, excusing herself quickly before she made a spectacle in front of the mailman.

Lilah was walking down the hall and caught her as she was wiping her eyes. She stopped with an expression of wary concern. She couldn't blame her little sister for being cautious around her—it wasn't often that she was easy to approach. "Are you okay?" Lilah asked.

"I'm fine. Just a little hormonal, I think. Do you know where Heath is?"

"He's repairing a leak on the roof," Lilah answered.

"The roof? Isn't that dangerous?" Lora asked, uncomfortable with the idea of Heath up there without the proper safety equipment. "I don't think that's wise. Larimar certainly doesn't need a lawsuit if he hurts himself."

And just like that Lilah's tentative concern withered. "Why can't you just be concerned for him because you care for him as a person, not as a potential liability?"

Lora stared, privately wincing at her sister's apt accusation. She certainly appeared to be the raging bitch at most times and she hadn't done anything to change that opinion as of late. And it bothered her, but she couldn't seem to censor her mouth when she should. "Of course I'm concerned about his safety," she amended quickly. "I'm just so accustomed to thinking in terms of dollars and cents that sometimes it bleeds over into my personal perspective."

Only moderately mollified, Lilah said, "Well, I don't like him up there, either. That storm is coming in faster than we anticipated and the wind is already kicking up. It's not safe for him. Maybe you could persuade him to come down and fix the roof after the storm has passed."

Celly entered the room, a ferocious frown on her face. "Dat boy is going to fall! Not safe! Dis storm coming with a vengeance and bringing wit it a misery."

Lora fought the urge to send a scowl Celly's way, but Lilah nodded in sage agreement. "Lora's going to try and get him to come down."

"You have bettah luck dan her." Celly sniffed, not even trying to sugarcoat her opinion of Lora. She and the front-desk woman had been circling one another since the first day Lora had returned home, but Lora had yet to find a way to either make her go away or find a common ground.

"Watch it," Lora warned under her breath, but Celly simply sent Lora a hard stare and then turned on her heel, saying over her shoulder, "Bad tings blow on de wind."

"I'm going to fire her as soon as I can find a way," Lora vowed darkly, but Lilah waved away her promise with a fretful motion.

"Focus, Lora! Celly isn't the issue. We need

to get Heath down from the roof. I have a bad feeling about this. My stomach is in knots!"

"Likely because that voodoo woman just filled your head with nonsense," Lora said, still glaring in the direction Celly had left.

"Voodoo? C'mon, Celly is not into voodoo. But I agree with her. Something doesn't feel right. Maybe I'm overreacting, but better safe than sorry, right?" Lilah implored Lora. "Please…get him down before he gets hurt."

"I doubt he'd listen to a word I have to say," Lora admitted, a bit apprehensive. If she were him, she wouldn't listen, either. She'd been pretty harsh.

"Oh…I thought you two had become… close?"

Oh, misery. Lora wanted to sink into the floorboards. Her sister knew? That meant Lindy knew, too. Trying to keep a secret in this house was like trying to herd kittens: nerve-racking and pointless. How to explain when she didn't quite understand herself? Yes, *misery* was the word. "It's complicated," she said lamely, hating herself for even uttering the ridiculous phrase. Most times when people made that statement it meant they were in dysfunctional relationships that they clearly didn't have the good sense to get free from.

Ugh. Was she one of those incessantly annoying people?

"He's a good man. Don't break his heart."

Lora stared. Did her little sister just champion Heath? Where was the love for her? "What about me? What if he broke my heart? He's no saint, you know."

At that Lilah smiled. "Lora, I'm not dumb. If anyone is in danger of losing themselves, it's Heath. Not you. And I care for Heath, so please don't play with his heart. That's all I'm asking."

Lora struggled for a comeback, but hadn't she already acted in a way that was emotionally confusing? Because the answer was yes, she choked back the hot words in her defense, knowing she was fighting her own hypocrisy. "I'll go see if I can persuade him to come off the roof," Lora finally managed to say, earning a nod of relief from Lilah.

Switching tracks, Lilah handed her a certified letter. "This came yesterday. In the confusion and turmoil of Pops's disappearance I forgot about it. It's a certified letter from the IRS."

Damn. She accepted the mail. "Thanks. Did Pops see it?"

"No."

"Good. I don't want this to upset him. I'll handle it."

Lilah's smile widened with true relief. She didn't even try to disguise that she was glad it wasn't her facing whatever nasty news was in that letter. Lora squared her shoulders and, tucking the mail under her arm, went to find Heath.

She found him on the south side, replacing a broken tile, frightfully high off the ground. A warning bell jangled in her head and she hollered up at him. The wind blew her hair in her face and into her mouth. She pushed it away and tried again. This time, the banging paused and Heath's head popped over the side, a quizzical expression on his face.

"Come down," she yelled up to him. She pointed to the storm clouds. "Come down. It's not safe."

"I'm just about done. Two more tiles that need replacing. Otherwise the leak will cause water damage. More expensive to fix," he yelled back, returning to his repair.

She looked toward the dark gray clouds roiling in the distance and saw the rain coming. "Heath, please come down!" Those tiles would get slippery as soon as the water hit them. She had a horrible vision of Heath slipping and tumbling to his death. *Stop being such a worrywart,* she told herself when her heart rate started to thunder. But she tried again as the first raindrop pelted her in the face. "Heath, the rain is coming. It's not safe! Come down, now."

"Stop being so damn bossy," he shouted. "I'm not coming down until this is fixed. I don't need you trying to blame me for the water damage or something. It's going to be fixed or I'm not coming down!"

She bit her lip. He was still angry. "Stop being stupid. You're going to get yourself killed just to spite me. And that's just recklessly stupid!"

"Well, that's me! Stupid as all get-out! The proof is in the pudding, right? I fell in love with you!"

Lora sucked in a tight breath, stunned. *Did he just...* She could only stare. Heath realized his mistake and swore loudly before disappearing again. Now he'd never come down. What did she say to that kind of admission? Love? Where did that come from? They couldn't even get along for ten minutes without one or the other storming off in a huff. That was the very definition of *dysfunctional*.

The rain started to pour, plastering her hair

to her head. This was just fabulous. Was she supposed to profess her love to him? Love she didn't feel? This was an awkward moment, one she'd endeavored to avoid her entire adult life.

Anger percolated through her worry, blotting out the latter. What the hell was he thinking falling in love with her? She'd never promised him anything of the sort in return. And now she'd likely get blamed because of this whole mess. How would she explain to Lilah that she hadn't meant to allow Heath to fall in love with her, therefore, she wasn't at fault for his subsequent broken heart.

"Damn you, Heath!" she yelled just as a peal of thunder shook the air. She jumped at the sound, then glared at the roofline where she could hear Heath pounding away, trying to beat the storm. "I never said it was okay to fall in love with me."

"Get inside before you drown, you idiot." He peered over the side, his hair dripping.

"I never asked you to fall in love with me," she shot back, another warning tingle dancing up her spine. She could feel the static electricity zipping in the air. "Now, will you please get off that stupid roof before you kill yourself?"

"I don't quit when things get difficult," he retorted with a snort of disgust.

Was he calling her a quitter? If she was anything she was obsessively competitive. "What are you talking about? I'm not a quitter, either."

"No, you're right, you're not a quitter—you're a coward," Heath said. "The minute you started to feel something for me, you backed off like a scared little jackrabbit."

Her squeal of outrage was timed perfectly with the next clash of thunder and streak of lightning. Another gust of wind rocked her on her feet, whipping her hair in her face. The truth stung a bit. But now was certainly not the time to start going all introspective. She gestured at the storm that was barreling down on them. "In case you haven't noticed, there's a hurricane coming this way, you jackass! Can we table this discussion until after the crisis?" A small collapsible lawn chair toppled over on the patio with a clatter causing her to jump again. Running over to the patio furniture, she dragged each piece into the shed and locked the doors. Lilah ran out, gesturing wildly at Lora.

"Come on! The weather station said we're going to have fifty-mph winds! We have to board up the windows before someone gets hurt. Where's Heath?" Lora pointed to the roof and Lilah made a sound of distress. "I thought you were going to get him to come down?"

"I tried," she said, freshly aggravated. "He chose this moment to throw the *L* word into the situation and clearly, it's not the best time!"

"Do you guys ever get along?" Lilah asked, exasperated. "There are bigger issues here!" She stomped past Lora and called out to Heath. "Heath, please come down! It's me, Li! Please, it's getting bad and it's going to get worse real fast!"

Heath popped over the side, grinning. "All done! Be down in a flash."

Relieved, Lilah cast Lora a disapproving look as if it was her fault that Heath was acting like a stubborn child, then ran inside, already soaked from the rain.

Lora opened her mouth to say something snide to Heath about his attitude when she saw Heath jerk and flail, pitching forward and, suddenly, instead of words, there was nothing but a scream.

Heath had fallen.

CHAPTER TWENTY-THREE

LORA SCREAMED TO HER SISTERS, the words an endless stream of high-pitched panic as she ran to Heath, splashing through growing puddles on the flagstone patio. Heath was lying unresponsive on the patio, a pool of blood gathering beneath his head in an ominously bad sign. She dropped to his side, skinning her knees in the process but she didn't feel the pain. She didn't know if she should touch him, but she wanted to pull him to her and hold him tight, to demand that he stop scaring her and wake up.

"Help!" she screamed again, crying. "Someone call the ambulance!"

The twins burst from the door and skidded to a halt when they saw Lora rocking on her knees, crying, afraid to touch Heath but desperate to know that he was still alive.

"Oh, God," Lindy whispered, her face pale. Lilah cried and ran to Heath's other side, her hands fluttering gently to his neck, searching for a pulse.

"Lindy call the ambulance," Lilah said, her tears mingling with the rain. "He's still alive."

Lora looked with gratitude to Lilah for knowing what to do, shocked that she hadn't thought to check his artery for a pulse. Lindy spun on her heel to call for help. Pops appeared and Lora rose on shaky feet to keep him from running to Heath, too. The shock of seeing Heath, crumpled and still, was enough to stop Pops's heart and they didn't need two tragedies at once. "He slipped, Pops," she said, explaining. "He was just getting down when a wind gust knocked him off balance and he slipped on the wet tile. He's going to be all right," she said, almost desperately. Maybe if she said it enough, it would be true. "He's going to be fine."

Pops's mouth trembled and she thought that he was going to lose his grip on reality but suddenly, he seemed to catch hold of lucidity again and Lora was immensely grateful. He cocked his head and then said, "Ambulance is here. I'll let them in."

She nodded, her throat constricting. Heath had to make it. He just had to. *You have to give me the chance to apologize,* she wanted to whisper but with Lilah so close, Lora didn't dare.

Maybe if she'd just been a little nicer... maybe if she hadn't picked a fight with him earlier... There were too many what-ifs and maybes...and each one cut like a knife.

"YOU WERE ALWAYS SO STUBBORN," a disembodied voice said from the fog of his thoughts. He couldn't quite turn his head to make out where the voice was coming from but he'd recognize that voice anywhere.

"Grams?" he called out, his voice scratchy and weak. Ah, crap. Was he dead?

"No, you're not dead, silly boy." Grams's chuckle floated on imaginary wind currents. "But you're hurt pretty bad."

Heath tried to remember what happened but his head ached and trying to remember only exacerbated the pain so he stopped. "What happened?"

"You fell and cracked your head open like a raw egg."

"But if I'm not dead and you are, where does that leave me?"

"In an interesting place," Grams suggested with a soft laugh. The lady had always been a bit of a cuckoo bird. A well-loved cuckoo bird, but nutty just the same. She sobered. "Go easy on Lora. She's real worried about you."

At the mention of Lora, sadness and heartache replaced the pain in his head. If he didn't remember going Humpty Dumpty, he certainly remembered her reaction to his inadvertent admission of his feelings. And it hadn't been pretty...or flattering. He closed his eyes. Maybe he'd just stay in this *interesting* place. At the moment, it was far better than waking up to a world where Lora avoided him like the plague.

"She's scared of being hurt," Grams said, as if this was a completely normal conversation happening in real time and not some damaged section of his brain, kicking out wild dreams. "She's the kind of person who loves so deeply that she's afraid of the pain of losing. She's lost so much in her life, you know. First her father, then her mother and then me. I don't think she's quite recovered."

He must know all this because otherwise, why would the Grams in his imagination know it?

"Will you stop trying to figure out the *how* and *why* of what's happening and listen? It's not as if I have a lot of time to sit around and chew the fat."

Deciding to play along with his own delusions, he said, "She misses you a lot."

"I know. I miss her, too. I miss all my sugar birds," Grams said, sighing. "But I have front-row seats and I'm not missing a thing."

If that was the case, then she was probably watching her husband lose his sense, one marble at a time.

"Yes," she said, as if listening to his internal dialogue. "But at least he hasn't lost his sense of humor. That man is a card. He could always make me laugh."

"You're not worried?"

Grams thought for a moment then said, "No. Not really. He has you and the girls to look after him and besides, he's not really to the point where he needs babysitting. He's not a danger to himself or others. And I love our afternoon chats."

That made him do a double take. "Come again?"

"Oh, yes, a benefit to losing his mind, I guess. Opens doors that otherwise would remain closed. Fascinating stuff."

The pain returned to his head and Heath gritted his teeth against the grinding agony.

Grams clucked in concern and he almost thought he felt her cool, soft hand on his cheek. She'd been the first woman in his life who'd shown him that love didn't come with a price. That a mother's kindness wasn't conditional. Sure, she wasn't his mother, or grandmother for that matter, but Grams had never made him feel like an outsider.

He closed his eyes and for a second the pain subsided. He exhaled slowly, relieved the pain had stopped. Until he felt a sharp whack on his arm.

"Nope. Can't do that," Grams announced, jerking him from his growing lethargy. The pain returned with his awareness. He groaned and twisted in misery. "That's a boy. On the other side of that pain wall, is the life you've always wanted. You just have to hold on…"

LORA STRUGGLED TO REMAIN still and calm but the words coming from the doctor's mouth washed over her in a tidal wave of worst-case scenarios.

Possibility of brain damage.

Cracked skull.

Medically induced coma.

"Because his brain is still swelling, we've removed a section of his skull cap to give the brain more room. The damage occurs when the brain is smashed against the skull. When the swelling subsides, we'll have a better opportunity to assess the damage."

Lora nodded at the appropriate moments, but she barely heard more than the initial assessment. She kept replaying that moment when Heath pitched from the roof, his shout cut short as his head smacked into the flagstone with a sickening crunch. She could still smell the blood and rain.

Suddenly, Lindy was by her side, tucking her into an embrace. She sagged against her sister. "I was so mean to him," she whispered, horrified. "I said terrible, awful things. What is wrong with me?"

Wisely, Lindy remained silent, and simply held Lora like a sister ought to when the other is heartbroken. Lora didn't deserve her sympathy or support. If Lindy knew how wretched she'd been to Heath… She shuddered. "It all happened so fast," she said, seeing the scene over and over.

"He's going to make it," assured Lindy. "He's as hardheaded as you. And then when he recovers, we're going to tease him about the bald spot they shaved on his head when they removed that square of skull."

In spite of her misery, Lora actually laughed. "You have a wicked sense of humor, sister mine."

"It's a quality that keeps me sane in Los Angeles when I'm surrounded by pervs and weirdos, and those are just the movie execs."

Lora laughed again, seeing her sister in a fresh light. How had she never known how cool her little sister was?

"Thank you," Lora murmured.

"Sure thing," Lindy said, yawning. They'd been at the hospital for hours and this was the first update they'd had on Heath. They were all exhausted. The storm had finally passed but everything was still dripping wet outside. The news reports were showing coverage of the damage. A falling tree had crushed one house. Luckily, it'd been an empty vacation rental.

"Why don't you take Pops and Lilah back to Larimar. I'll stay and call if there's anything new to report."

"Are you sure? I could stay," Lindy offered.

Lora shook her head. It didn't feel right to leave. "I'm sure. I'll call. I promise."

Lindy yawned again. "Okay. Try to get some rest, too."

Lora promised she would catch a few

winks if necessary but knew that she likely wouldn't sleep. Her mind was tormenting her with scenes and flashes of times when she'd been unaccountably rude or mean to Heath.

And then her mind would conjure the memory of how she'd reacted to the knowledge of his true feelings.

Suddenly, it became clear why her offer of no-strings sex had been so distasteful and insulting. How long had he felt this way about her and why? She'd never given him any reason to like, much less love her.

She flushed with shame. She didn't deserve someone like Heath. He was good and kind; patient and generous. In spite of being raised by two drug addicts, his moral compass was truer than her own. The things she'd done in her career—former career, that is—would appall the average person.

She'd stabbed coworkers in the back to jockey for position on a choice account; she'd lied, manipulated and stepped on anyone in her way.

She couldn't imagine Heath doing half the things she'd done in her thirst for success and yet she'd flat-out accused him of swindling her grandfather.

Lora nearly hung her head in disgrace. No

wonder Heath had looked as if he wanted to strangle her.

The doctor returned to let her know that she could see him if she wanted. Lora wanted to see Heath but a part of her was afraid.

"You're a coward."

The words hung in her mind and she swallowed her fear. She nodded and followed the doctor to the ICU. She tried to prepare herself for the sight of Heath so diminished, so broken but nothing could've prepared her for the gut punch that followed.

A giant white gauze covered the opened skull and a plastic drape surrounded him to minimize germs coming into contact with the exposed tissue. She stuffed a knuckle in her mouth to keep from crying out. *What if he died,* the fear whispered but she shoved it back. *He won't.*

"You better not die, Heath Cannon. Our story isn't finished yet," she murmured, tracing her fingers lightly against the plastic drape, wishing she could touch his skin, to let him know she was there.

Regret was always a bitter pill, but right now, she was choking on it.

CHAPTER TWENTY-FOUR

HEATH REMEMBERED THE FIRST time he'd seen Lora Bell. Her long dark hair had been tied up in a ponytail, a blue polka-dot bikini and a tiny white sarong wrapped around her little hips. She was drinking a smoothie while her mother had been buying some fresh fruit at the market stands. Even at ten she'd snagged his eye.

She'd noticed him staring and she'd stuck her tongue out at him.

He'd reciprocated.

A tiny smile had tugged at her lips made red from the flavor of her smoothie, and then she'd scampered after her mother.

After that moment, he'd always kept an eye out for the striking brunette with the pale ocean-blue eyes.

He didn't know that her mother was dying of cancer—likely she hadn't known, either. It was several months later that the diagnosis had been made, from what he remembered Pops telling him.

The next time they met, he'd been starving, probably half-dead.

She'd saved his life and she probably never knew it.

"Are you ready to wake up yet?" Grams asked him. He knew better now than to try and crane his neck to find the voice because she was simply always out of range. And she was totally in his head. But he liked the sound of her voice, even if it was an illusion.

"Not yet," he answered, troubled. "She doesn't love me. That's hard to face."

"You're a sweet boy. Always were. When I first saw you I thought, there's a kid who needs this family. I'd always wished we'd have petitioned the court for you but we weren't blood family so we likely would've lost. Not to mention your parents were local and we were still outsiders. It would've been a mess."

He nodded. "It's okay. My life was good."

"Don't be giving up just yet. You've still got a whole lot of living to do."

"Good to know," he said wryly, wincing when his brain seemed to contract with pain. He waited out the wave of agony and then when he could breathe again, he said, "I'm ready to wake up if it means this pain will stop."

"Can't promise that, but awake is definitely better," Grams agreed.

LORA SAT BEHIND POPS'S desk staring at the certified letter that'd been delivered a few days ago. Since Heath's accident everything else had taken a backseat but she couldn't ignore it any longer. Heath was recovering slowly, his brain had stopped swelling and the doctors were able to put his head back together but he was still in a coma. Lora was reluctant to leave his side but the problems facing Larimar were more dire than ever.

Lindy walked in, a somber expression on her face. She sat in the chair opposite the desk with a sigh. "So you weren't exaggerating, then? We're going to lose Larimar?"

"If we can't come up with the money in sixty days."

"How much? I have some money saved up," Lindy offered.

"Sixty thousand. Do you have that much lying around?"

Lindy's expression fell. "No."

"Me, neither." Lora also had some money

saved, about twenty thousand, but it wasn't nearly enough. Even if she cashed out her various CDs and liquidated some assets, such as her condo, she wasn't sure she'd have the money in time. "And Heath is going to be out of commission for some time so it's not like he's going to be able to pitch in as he'd planned."

Lindy looked sharply at Lora. "Don't go blaming Heath again. It wasn't his fault he fell off a roof."

"I'm not blaming him, Lindy. I'm simply stating a fact. Heath's original plan is moot. And we're screwed."

"We need a new plan," Lindy said.

"Duh. Thank you, Captain Obvious," Lora said wryly. "I've been trying to come up with Plan B since I got back home. I never thought Heath's plan was completely solid. I mean, granted the fused glass is selling—better than the other gift items—but not nearly well enough to pull Larimar out of this hole. Heath hasn't been able to make a single loan payment yet and we need money now."

"What are we going to do?"

Lora thought hard, then came to the only conclusion she could find and Lindy wasn't going to like it.

"You and I need to move back home. I will put my marketing experience to work and you will put your entertainment experience to work and together we're going to save Larimar."

LINDY FOUGHT THE URGE to instantly decline—she had a life in Los Angeles—but how could she when her family home was in danger? "What about your job in Chicago?"

Lora looked away. "I don't have one."

Lindy's eyes bugged. "Excuse me?"

"I was fired before I came out here."

Lindy didn't know what to make of her sister's admission but she knew Lora's pride was probably in tatters. Lora had never been fired in her life. She set standards for everyone else to dream of reaching. "What happened?"

"I don't really want to talk about it," she said, moving to straighten the papers in front of her. "Suffice to say my talents were no longer in line with the company's needs. I'd planned to start circulating my résumé with our competitors but I've decided I don't want to go back. So that leaves me free to stay in St. John for the time being."

"Oh," Lindy said softly, sensing there was more to the story but Lora wasn't exactly a sharer. Under normal circumstances Lindy would've pressed for details but she could tell Lora wasn't going to budge. Whatever was behind her termination was personal and painful. And frankly, even Lindy knew that Lora had enough on her plate to deal with.

"How can I help? I don't see how my acting experience is going to help Larimar."

"I'm putting you in charge of the outdoor adventures we're going to start offering at Larimar. And I want you to start inviting your Hollywood friends up here—start spreading the word about Larimar. If marketed correctly, we can make this the premier getaway for the rich and famous."

Lindy hated that idea. Part of Larimar's charm was that it was a hidden treasure and it didn't put on airs like some stuffy five-star establishment that catered to the "rich and ridiculous" as she liked to call them.

Lora continued, completely missing Lindy's expression of distaste, saying, "I will market to my corporate contacts, to suggest for corporate retreats. Lilah will run the front desk and we should be able to turn this around."

"Pops will hate this idea," Lindy said stubbornly. "And I'm not crazy about it, either.

And what do you think Heath will think of it?"

"Not to be unnecessarily blunt, but Pops and Heath put Larimar in this position, not me. We have to do what's necessary to pull out of this hole. If you have a better idea, by all means, share." Unhappily, Lindy didn't and by her silence Lora took that to mean as such. "Right. So, how much money do you have saved up?"

"About eight thousand, why?"

"I have about twenty thousand. I think if I can offer some significant cash, then I might be able to buy some more time from the IRS. It shows good faith."

Lindy nodded, swallowing the lump in her throat. Of course she'd do anything to save Larimar but she'd worked hard to put away that nest egg. And now it was gone in one fell swoop.

Lora noted Lindy's crestfallen look and tried softening the blow, saying, "Just pitch in five thousand and I'll pitch in the rest."

"No. That's not fair to you."

"That's what I have in liquid assets. I have some other assets I can tap," Lora said.

Of course she did. Lora was a financial whiz. Even as a kid she'd always managed to make her money work for her, whereas Lindy had always found money quickly left her hands the minute it touched her palms, which was why she was so proud of herself for managing to save a couple bucks from her last few gigs. She sighed and said, "All right. I'll stay. But I'm not completely on board with this new direction and if I come up with something better I'm going to suggest it."

"Fair enough," Lora said, returning to her paperwork. But Lindy wanted to talk about something else. She figured if she was staying, she ought to put in her two cents about this situation with Heath.

"So are you going to the hospital today?" Lindy asked, coming to the topic in a round-about way.

Lora avoided eye contact as she answered, "No, I don't think I have time today. Why don't you go and then give me an update?"

Lindy frowned, a spark of anger growing in her chest. "I think you should go see him," she suggested firmly. "It helps for him to be surrounded by people he loves."

Lindy thought she caught a wince on Lora's part but she couldn't be sure because Lora had moved on briskly, saying, "Exactly. And he loves you and Lilah like sisters. Heath and

I were never close so it doesn't make much sense for me to be hanging around the hospital when I have so much work to do here."

"Stop it!" Lindy shouted, startling Lora into dropping her pen. Lora recovered her pen with a glare but Lindy was not going to back down. Lora was retreating into that hard shell of hers because she was afraid of losing him. "You're so damn transparent! When are you going to admit that you have feelings for him? Didn't him falling from a roof scare some sense into that thick skull of yours?"

"Lindy...it's complicated. And I think by staying away from the hospital, he has a better chance of recovering. He doesn't need any negative energy around him. And when he fell, we were actually shouting at each other. Do you really think my face is the first one he wants to see when he wakes up? Likely not."

"You're afraid of losing him so you're putting distance between yourself and Heath but he needs you, not me and Lilah. He loves you! And if you weren't so damn hardheaded and stupid when it comes to your feelings, you'd realize that you love him, too."

"I don't," Lora said quickly, too quickly. Lindy narrowed her stare at her sister, seeing right through her. Lora squirmed and avoided her gaze. "You know how you felt when you saw Heath fall? That terror? It's because it was that moment when you realized that you could lose him and you could no longer hide behind that damn cold wall of yours, pretending that no one, especially Heath, mattered. That was real, Lora. That moment—that feeling—was real and true. Trust that, not in whatever your brain is telling you now."

Lora blinked back moisture and Lindy knew she'd hit a nerve. "Why does he love me? I've never given him a reason to," she said, almost begging for an explanation so she could understand.

Lindy shrugged, also baffled by Heath's unrequited love for her sister, but as Grams used to say, "The heart wants what the heart wants." "What does it matter? He's always had eyes for you and you ought to count your lucky stars that a man like Heath would look past your many faults to find the woman beneath."

"Many faults?" Lora said, stung. "That's a bit harsh don't you think?"

"C'mon, Lora, you're as prickly as a hedge-hog to most people, even to your own family.

So, yeah, you've got some serious flaws you ought to work on."

"Oh, should I be more like you?" Lora said, going on the offensive, which Lindy was surprised she hadn't done earlier. "You're so busy falling in love with the *idea* of falling in love that you go through boyfriends like toilet paper."

"My issues with commitment are not in question here," Lindy maintained stubbornly. "I'm not the one running away from a good man just because I'm scared."

"If you love Heath so much why don't you go after him?"

Lindy stared at her sister, then answered bluntly. "Lora, if Heath had ever once looked at me the way he looks at you, he wouldn't have had to chase me. A man like Heath comes along once in your life. You'd be stupid to walk away. And if you are foolish enough to walk away because you're too afraid of putting yourself out there, you're not the strong woman I always thought you were. The fact of the matter is, he never looked at *anyone* the way he looked at you. It was like the sun rose and set in your eyes. It was poetry and rock ballads. He defended you when you were acting like you do on most days—difficult—

and he stayed with Larimar because he loves this family. Like it or not, he's here for good so you better do a heart check and ask yourself, do you want to ruin a good man for the sake of safeguarding your heart or do you want to take a chance on something great?"

CHAPTER TWENTY-FIVE

LORA STOPPED HERSELF from yelling after her sister. Everything Lindy had said was true. Lora was terrified.

Giving your heart to someone was a risky venture. What if they had clumsy fingers and dropped it? Her heart couldn't take another bruising. When you're only invested in yourself, you only have yourself to watch out for.

But she couldn't deny that being in Heath's arms had been an awakening experience. It felt like home in ways that she'd never known. Had she truly gone through her life closed off to that warm and loving feeling?

It hadn't been sex with Heath—it'd been making love. That was the difference she hadn't been able to name. She'd felt cherished, protected, desired and loved. No one else had made her feel that way. Maybe because she'd never felt that way about anyone else.

But in a way, she'd always known her feelings were there for Heath. He'd been such a handsome boy. In spite of his hollowed cheeks and ragged clothes, she'd seen the island boy and her heart had beat faster. And when he'd smiled at her, she'd never known such joy. And when he'd disappeared for a year like a feather on the wind, it'd scared her.

When you loved someone, they went away. First her dad, then mom, then Heath and then Grams. The lesson had been pounded home.

So she'd subconsciously vowed not to love Heath.

But that hadn't stopped him from loving her.

Damn you, Heath, she thought, dropping her head into the shelter of her arms. *I love you, and I'm scared. No, terrified.* What if he doesn't make it? The thought of Heath dying froze the blood in her veins. He couldn't die without giving her the chance to make amends. She couldn't picture living without him.

Then get your ass out of that chair and go to him, a voice instructed brusquely.

And for once in her life, she actually thought the voice in her head had told her something worthwhile.

HEATH HEARD A VOICE, only this time, it wasn't Grams.

"The first time I saw you, I thought you were the most beautiful boy I'd ever seen— almost too pretty, you know? You had that long, dirty, island-boy hair that only surfers can get away with and I thought, he's the cutest boy alive."

Heath smiled, or at least he tried to smile. His mouth stubbornly refused to cooperate.

"I know I've pretended not to remember but I remember bringing you that basket of food. I was so worried about you. I worried that no one was feeding you and that no one tucked you into bed at night. I looked for you the next day but didn't see you. I looked for you for two straight weeks. You never showed. I thought you were dead. A year went by and I had to put away all the feelings I didn't know how to handle and forget about you. But then you showed up again and I was angry with you for making me think you were gone from my life. I'd missed you so much. I'd wondered where you went and why you hadn't told me. You were just gone. And I couldn't take one more person leaving me."

Heath remembered that day with the basket. It was etched in his memory. It might've even sealed her fate in his eyes. He'd followed her to Larimar, saw the beautiful place she called home, and knew he'd never be worthy of a girl like her. But when he returned home, he discovered his parents had decided to move to St. Thomas. They were packing their meager belongings into the ratty Suzuki Samurai. His stuff had been forgotten.

"What's going on?" he'd asked, his heart plummeting when he saw that they'd planned to leave him. "Where are you going?"

His mom, teeth missing from too many years doing crack, had looked nervous and twitchy. "Just going to St. Thomas for a bit to get a job, baby. There's no way to make a living here, you know?"

"But what about me?" he'd asked, his young voice faltering. His parents were probably the worst but at least he didn't come home to an empty house every night. "You can't leave me…"

"Baby, we'll be back," his mother had promised. "You're a big boy, you can handle being on your own for a few nights, right?"

But as his stare traveled to the stacked Samurai, he knew they weren't coming back. He was on his own.

And he'd been right.

It was a year of hell and he didn't want the pretty girl to see how pathetic he was. He'd actually tried to find his parents in St. Thomas but it was like trying to find a single, particular grain of sand in the ocean. Impossible.

When Pops had found him, digging through a restaurant Dumpster, he'd brought him home for a meal and made a deal with him.

"Son, are you a hard worker or are you lazy?" Pops had asked him.

"I'm a hard worker," he'd answered in earnest, hoping for a sandwich in return for mowing the lawn or picking weeds from the garden. That's how he'd stayed alive to this point.

"We'll see," Pops had said. "I'll tell you what, you can do odd jobs around Larimar but if I discover you're lazy and looking for a free ride, it's out you go. Got it? Where are your parents?"

"St. Thomas," Heath had answered in a barely audible whisper. Pops knew his parents weren't around. Everyone knew Heath's parents were addicted to crack. He was "that poor boy" but no one lifted a finger to help.

Except Pops.

He did more than that—he taught him how

to be a man with self-respect and dignity, integrity and honesty.

He owed that man his life.

And he would never repay that generosity by messing around with the man's granddaughters, even if the very sight of Lora had caused his heart to flutter like a butterfly's wings.

So he'd loved her from a distance.

But now he could hear her voice, telling him stories, sharing personal bits of herself that she never would've shared in a million years. He wondered briefly if he was dying.

"I was actually jealous of you for a time when Grams decided to homeschool you. I wanted to be homeschooled, too, but Grams said I was too smart for her and I needed the structure of the school system. I guess she was right. I would've ran circles around her. I was voracious in my need to conquer every obstacle in my path, including homework."

He wanted to laugh. The idea of Grams trying to homeschool Lora was crazy. Lora's Type A personality would've driven Grams to drink rum for breakfast. His style of learning had been more laid-back. He and Grams had gotten along well. For the first time ever, he'd started to enjoy schoolwork. Because of

Grams he'd graduated a straight-A student. If Pops had taught him to be a man, Grams had given him the gift of knowledge.

"Remember when you had that crush on Samira Jones in high school? I was turned inside out and backward with jealousy. I wanted to rip out each of her braids and smack her with them."

Samira…he chuckled. He wanted to admit to Lora—since she was in the sharing mood—that he'd never truly liked Samira that way, he'd just been trying to finally get Lora's attention. It had backfired. He'd learned quickly that Lora wasn't easily manipulated, yet another aspect of Lora that he admired.

"I was fired from my job," she said, drawing a deep breath. "When I got your certified letter, I'd been clearing out my desk. It wasn't your fault that the letter arrived with impeccable timing. I took out my frustrations on you and Larimar. I'm…sorry. For so many things, Heath. I'm so sorry. I don't even know why you ever fell in love with me. I wish I could see me through your eyes for once. Maybe then I'd learn to trust what I don't understand. Because if I were you, I'd steer clear of someone like me."

The quiet, pain-filled admission struck at

his heart. And he wanted to tell her all the reasons why she was the only one for him, why she was *ever* the only one for him, but his body felt locked and out of his control. Frustration gnawed at him and he forced himself to focus. *Open your eyes. Move your mouth. Say something!* A garbled mess of incoherent moaning escaped from his mouth and he heard Lora's sharp gasp.

"Mmmwwhhstummnn." That wasn't exactly what he'd been going for. He tried again, his throat moving in rusty movements to produce sound. "Lllora."

"Heath? Are you awake? Oh, my God, Heath! Hold on, let me get the doctor!"

Within seconds Lora had produced a doctor, likely she dragged the first man in a white lab coat she could find into Heath's room, and a light was shone into his eyes. He blinked and tried to shy away from the source but his muscles were sluggish and not fully cooperating.

"Hello, Mr. Cannon. I'm Dr. Welsh. Can you blink your eyes for me?" He worked at it and managed a slow blink. "Good. Can you wiggle your toes?" That was a bit more difficult but he managed by concentrating deeply on making it happen.

"Excellent. Your motor skills are returning. It seems your brush with death has left less of a lasting mark than we feared. You're a lucky man."

He heard Lora start peppering the doctor with questions about his recovery and he wanted to laugh. Ever the bulldog. God, he loved that woman.

With great effort, he kept his eyes open and he immediately tracked the sound of her voice to find her face. She glanced over and found him staring at her. She seemed to forget the doctor and her list of questions and simply held his stare.

He saw a wealth of emotion—fear, happiness, joy, nervousness—staring back at him.

Dr. Welsh, sensing they needed some privacy, said he'd come back a little later to run some neurological tests and then left them alone.

"You're going to be all right," she said.

He tried to nod but the motion sent excruciating pain into his brain. He winced and she was instantly by his side. "What's wrong? Should I get the doctor again?"

"No," he answered, clumsily reaching for her hand. His strength wasn't there so he couldn't pull her to him but she got the message and sat by his side. "I'm sorry I didn't listen. I shouldn't have been on the roof during that storm. It was stupid. I knew better. I was mad and wanted to punish you for being honest with me."

She shook her head vehemently, tears filling her eyes. "Don't you dare make excuses for me, Heath Cannon. I was the one who'd pushed you away because I was scared. I'd always known how you felt about me but I kept pushing you away because I knew if I gave in to the feelings, I would fall head over heels in love with you and I wasn't ready. I do love you, Heath. It sounds terrible but the minute you fell from that roof I knew. And I was terrified that you'd never wake up and I'd never get the chance to tell you how sorry I was for being...well, so awful to you for so long. It was selfish of me to think only of myself. Can you ever forgive me?"

"There's nothing to forgive. As Grams used to say, 'I love you for your flaws.'" He tried grinning, but the action exhausted him.

"Grams was a smart lady," Lora said, her voice breaking. "I wish she were still here. Maybe she might've been able to talk some sense into me sooner."

"That's what she said," he murmured, the

need to sleep stealing what energy he had left, leaving Lora to stare quizzically.

The last thing he remembered as he dropped off was the wonderful pressure of Lora's hand clutching his and he knew everything was going to be all right. Somehow.

EPILOGUE

IT'D BEEN SEVERAL WEEKS since Heath's accident and Lora was discovering she was neither a good nursemaid nor a talented glass-fusion artist.

"I don't know why you enjoy this," Lora said, dropping the misshapen mess of fused gunk into the recycle bucket to try again later. Her finished products were nothing like Heath's. "It's hot, boring and my back is killing me," she said, a hint of petulance in her voice.

He laughed and gathered her in his arms. "So I take it glass fusion is not your thing?"

"No."

"I told you it was an art form, not just some process of throwing together a bunch of broken glass to melt together. But you had to try it for yourself. Now will you let Lilah take over? She's got more of an eye for this stuff."

"Yes," Lora agreed reluctantly. "I just hate

the idea of someone else having that in common with you. It's a bonding thing, you know?"

He drew her closer and nuzzled her neck. "We have something else that bonds us. And if I recall, that's even more fun than fusing glass. And more effective."

Her cheeks heated and her breath caught when she recalled earlier that morning. Heath was still recovering so they had to be careful, which is why she insisted on doing all the work—particularly in the bedroom. She'd *bonded* with him multiple times once the doctor gave them the reluctant okay to resume their sex life.

And hearing him gasp her name was a thrill she'd never tire of hearing.

Luckily for her, Heath felt the same way.

As she snuggled up to Heath, deeply content in a way she'd never known, she marveled at the power loving the right person could have on your perspective.

Larimar was still in danger. The IRS had accepted their payment arrangement but there was still a large bill hanging over their heads with an uncertain prospect of meeting the obligation; Pops was still having imaginary conversations with his dead wife; and Lindy and Lilah were intensely displeased with Lora's decision to make the resort more accessible to certain groups but in spite of these things, she couldn't be happier.

Love…so this was what she'd been so afraid of all these years?

Seemed silly now, especially when she thought of all that wasted time.

Speaking of…she let her hand drift south. Heath's sharp intake of breath made her smile.

"How about a little afternoon delight?"

Heath groaned playfully but started to eagerly unlace his board shorts. "You're the boss…." And within moments his mouth was on hers, showing her with his actions that she was the only woman for him—and always had been.

Funny how it had taken nearly losing him to realize the same thing about him.

Well, as Grams used to say, "There is no rhyme or reason to the logic of the heart."

Amen to that.

She hoped wherever Grams was, she was happy. Her sugar bird had finally realized home was where the heart was.

And as she felt Heath's touch on her body, she knew without a doubt that she was home.

* * * * *